Behind the Scenes
Tabor Hts., Year 1, Book 8

Michelle Levigne

M† Zion Ridge Press
Books Off the Beaten Path

www.MtZionRidgePress.com

Mt Zion Ridge Press LLC
295 Gum Springs Rd, NW
Georgetown, TN 37366

https://www.mtzionridgepress.com

Published in the United States of America
Publication Date: August 15, 2025

Editor-In-Chief: Michelle Levigne
Executive Editor: Tamera Lynn Kraft

TABOR HEIGHTS

Welcome to Tabor Heights:
A friendly little town on Ohio's North Coast, where sweet romance is always in the air.

Here you'll be able to explore the lives of the members of the congregation of Tabor Christian Church in the space of two years. The stories overlap, and there's no one right place to start.

Just like any small town, you come in, you meet someone, you hear their story and get to know them, and they introduce you to their friends, tell you something about them, and you learn those stories. As you get to know these new friends, they introduce you to other people, and tell you about other interesting stories in town.

It's the same way with Tabor Heights. Start with the story that interests you the most, and then branch out.

Settle back and enjoy your visit.
Welcome!

<u>Year One</u>

THE SECOND TIME AROUND
DETOURS
COMMON GROUNDS
WHITE ROSES
THE FAMILY WAY
FORGIVEN
FIRESONG
BEHIND THE SCENES
THE MISSION
ACCIDENTAL HEARTS
A QUIET PLACE

<u>Year Two</u>

Dedication

Dedicated to the theater faculty and students at Northwestern College, Iowa, where I earned my BA in theater/English and spent all my time behind the scenes, building sets, sewing costumes, directing and writing. My years in college were some of the best times of my life. I remember building the rigging for *H.M.S. Pinafore*, and painting the set for *Taming of the Shrew* until 1 a.m., then walking through town to my dorm, in perfect safety. Orange City was a great place to go to school. Thanks to our triumvirate of teachers at that time: Boss, Mr. T and Mr. P, who (I swear!) have absolutely nothing in common with Joel Randolph, Daniel Morgan and the General, except for the love we students had for them. Orange City, Iowa, is one of several foundations for the town of Tabor Heights, and Northwestern one of several templates for Butler-Williams University.

Chapter One

Saturday, April 19

"Max Keeler anywhere around?" Heavy footsteps crunched in the gravel of the yard behind the scene shop at Homespun Theater.

"Who's asking?" Max Randolph finished putting the freshly sprayed copper plates down on the wire drying rack her stepfather had created decades ago. The chemical stink of the spray paint made her feel a little dizzy, which was why she took advantage of the nice weather to do her spray painting chores outdoors.

When she had a hard time working on a scene for her latest book or screenplay, she put in a few hours in the scene shop or the printing shop. Today, she worked on props for *The Taming of the Shrew*, Homespun's next production. She had been doing a lot of scene shop chores since her writing partner and best friend, Tony Martin, went to UCLA to do his writer-in-residence stint. If he didn't come back in mid-May as promised, her writing career just might be stalled out permanently.

"I'm Steve Coheny," the stranger said.

"Sorry, don't know the name." She stood up, careful not to wipe her paint-smeared hands on her jeans. Max turned around and nearly staggered backward into the damp plates. A jolt of adrenaline drove away the paint fumes headache that threatened to turn into nausea.

She knew that face, but fifty years older. The face that haunted her worst nightmares had similar coarse curls, but shorter, tighter, gray-frosted, not dark chocolate. Steve Coheny wore Carlo Vincente's face. Or an unreasonable facsimile, as Tony would say. He was taller than Carlo; his shoulders wider, and his complexion not quite so Mediterranean dark.

Max took a deep breath and felt some of that tension knotting her guts loosen and fade. No, he only looked a *little* like Carlo. It was more her imagination than his bone structure. She had to get her mind off that problem she had been gnawing since the mail from the Gabrielli Film Fellowship came yesterday.

I have got Carlo Vincente on the brain, she silently snarled.

It wasn't Carlo's fault that he was single-handedly shredding her latest triumph. He had no idea she even existed, and Max preferred to keep it that way. For the rest of her life, if possible.

Okay, God, I admit I was stupid choosing my mother's maiden name for my screenwriting name, but do You have to keep rubbing my nose in it?

"Buddy Sanker sent me. He said his good buddy Max had a couple openings in the tech crew," Steve said.

"Buddy is a brainless dweeb with a slippery grasp of reality," she said with a chuckle. The tension unwound more, making her feel giddy. "Technically, I don't have any openings in the tech crew because this isn't *my* theater. But if Buddy vouches for you, well..." Her impending headache gave one last throb and faded away.

"This is Homespun Theater, right? Is Max Keeler here, or was Buddy yanking my chain?" Steve took a step backward, looking around at the old firehouse connected to an old barn connected to an old shed, all turned into a community theater complex.

"Yes, this is Homespun, and Max Keeler is... me. My pen name. Max Randolph, actually." She checked her hand for paint smears before offering it to him.

Steve blinked a few times before accepting her hand to shake it. A crooked grin finally pushed away his dazed look. "Why do I get the feeling that having Buddy vouch for me isn't going to do me much good?"

"Why do you want a tech job here?" She gestured him through the open door into the scene shop.

"I've been doing some independent film work, and I figured I should see what live theater is like before I settle into one place in my career." He hesitated before stepping over the threshold ahead of her.

Max bit back a comment that he looked somewhat old for still trying to decide where to "settle." He had to be around thirty.

"Working your way from the ground up?" Joel Randolph called from the far end of the scene shop. He finished marking a measurement on a one-by, let the tape measure snap back into the case, and stepped away from the workbench. "Where are you from?"

"Pomona." Steve looked around at the array of in-process stage dressings for the upcoming Shakespearean production.

"Buddy Sanker sent him," Max said, heading for the door into the backstage area. "He's all yours, Dad. Wants a tech job."

"Dad?" Steve said.

"Joel Randolph," he said, holding out his hand. "And you are?"

"Steve Coheny." A snort escaped him. "I thought she was a he. Buddy said to ask for Max Keeler, not Randolph."

"Max uses her mother's maiden name for her pen name," Joel said. "Told you that might cause you problems," he called, as Max passed through the doorway.

"Yeah, yeah." Max's grin slipped, reliving that moment when she thought Carlo Vincente stood before her. He was the last person on the planet she ever wanted to run into.

Why did you choose a writing name sure to catch Hollywood's attention?

Not one of your brightest moments. Max sighed, anticipating another frustrating two hours at her computer, with no progress to report to Tony when they had their regular collaboration phone call this evening.

~~~~~

"I figured out why Buddy Sanker makes such weird comments on the group chats." Max's voice raised a slight echo in the phone connection.

"Yeah?" Tony Martin scooted down in the pitiful excuse for a sofa in the apartment the university had provided him as writer-in-residence. From where he lay, he could see the single framed photo he had brought with him to California. In the last few weeks, he had studied it with all the aching intensity of a boy at summer camp for the first time.

"He thinks I'm a guy." She snorted.

"Well, you never did come out and say you're a girl."

The day of the photo had been one of those bright, perfect spring days that made his heart ache for something he couldn't identify. He had joined the Randolphs on a trip to Kelley's Island last year, one of those spur-of-the-moment adventures that made people say, "Why don't we do this more often?" Joel and Emily had rented a golf cart, while Tony, Max, and her brothers Joe and Jeremy had rented bikes.

"It's not something that comes up in conversation." Max sighed.

"So what made you think of Buddy?"

When they stopped for a picnic lunch, Emily had asked another tourist to take their photo. They were all sunburned, sweaty and windblown. They had perched on the picnic table. Joel and Emily sat quietly smiling in the center; she golden-blonde and gray-eyed, her heart-shaped face and serene smile focused on her brawny, dark-haired, gray-bearded husband. Joe and Jeremy, sixteen and fourteen, were raw-cut images of their mother. They clowned for the camera, standing on the bench on the other side of the table, trying to push each other off. Max, twenty-five, dark of hair and eye like Joel, sat on the ground at Emily's feet. She smiled up at her parents, but Tony could make himself believe she smiled at him, standing at Joel's side.

"Dad hired a new guy for the tech crew. Oh, and Dad decided to let him rent your apartment until he finds his own place."

"Great. I appreciate it."

The Randolphs had made Tony a member of their family ever since his own parents had been killed in a plane crash. He supposed he had Joel's wide shoulders, and Emily's gray eyes, but where he got his thick mop of black curls—liberally sprinkled with silver at thirty-two—Tony would be hard-pressed to say.

He wanted to belong to the Randolphs as more than just Max's writing partner, good friend and a backstage helper at Homespun Theater. He wanted Max to love him as more than just her best friend.
~~~~~

"Yeah, but... there's something creepy about him. Not dangerous — Dad would never let somebody dangerous get in the door — but just weird. Mom kept looking at him like she knew him, but she couldn't remember where she met him. Anyway, Buddy recommended him."

"What's his name?" Tony asked, a shiver up his spine. The thought of danger infiltrating Homespun made him want to cancel his writer-in-residence stint right now.

It was bad enough that arrogant diva — divo, for a guy? — Jake Holt was still hanging around Homespun, waiting for his undeserved shot at fame and fortune. The guy was an overgrown playground bully. He showed respect for Joel as the owner and director, and Emily because of her former career. Jake's attitude clearly said that everyone else at Homespun Theater existed only to help him climb to stardom. Any woman who didn't respond to his charm was mentally challenged. Max had disliked Jake from the start. The unfairly talented and handsome young actor returned her dislike with constant criticism badly camouflaged under 'friendly interest in her career.'

"Steve Coheny."

"Doesn't sound familiar. Did Buddy ever mention him?"

That settled it. Tony needed to be back in Tabor, where he could watch over his adopted family. It had taken this enforced separation from Max to make him wake up. He had finally figured out what that aching, hungry feeling from that day on the island meant.

Problem: How did he find out if Max could ever feel the same without scaring her away or destroying what they already had? He couldn't exactly email and tell Max he was in love with her. He certainly wasn't going to unload this revelation on her now, over the phone.

"There was an email from him when I got online to ask. I really wish I never mentioned to him that Will was going to England and leaving a big hole in the tech crew." She sighed again.

Tony grinned, having a clear image of Max lying upside down on the old puke green couch in the center of the Green Room at Homespun Theater, with her feet hanging over the back and her head hanging halfway off the edge of the seat cushion.

"Your dad wouldn't have hired him unless he got good vibes," he offered.

"Yeah, but Dad said he's going to call his other references again, just to double-check. On Monday." Max groaned, and Tony knew she was trying to roll over without falling off the couch. "Maybe I'm just paranoid. I mean, he could have made the calls this afternoon before they went out."

"Date night tonight?" Tony choked. Now was the perfect opening — although, how cheesy would Max consider it if he said something like, *By the way, how about you and me trying a date night when I get home?*

"They drove to that Amish restaurant halfway to Columbus. They better bring me a cherry fry pie, that's all I can say, leaving me to hold the fort all by myself."

"Yeah, poor pitiful abused Max." He shifted around, trying to find a comfortable spot. Well, that was one opening he had missed.

Maybe he had lost his timing, unsettled by the realization that he felt cut in half without Max. Ironic, because it took missing Max to the point of physical discomfort to realize he didn't want to be anything more than Max-and-Tony.

"Dad's been communicating with his sister. He said something about her visiting."

"That's good, isn't it?"

"I guess. But I can't help feeling like she's taking her life in her hands, if her father finds out she's been talking to Dad." Max snorted again. "She's not really my aunt... but I guess I care because Dad's worried. He said his father's been sick."

"Is he talking about going to Boston to visit him?"

"Dad's too smart for that. That nasty old man isn't anywhere near dying. I am so glad I don't have to call him Grandpa, y'know?" Another long sigh. "I can just bet, if Dad did go, he'd insist on Dad giving up theater and becoming a lawyer to take over his practice, like the last thirty years of silence never happened. Y'know?"

"Uh huh." Tony was glad to know that even all the distance between Ohio and California couldn't diminish his ability to read Max. This non-issue was letting her warm up to telling him something that had been gnawing on her. "What's really bothering you? Don't make me leave the university and come home and beat a confession out of you." He envisioned cornering Max and making her listen to quite a few things, while he was at it. Maybe throw her over his shoulder? Would the caveman routine convince her that he was serious?

Problem: Max hated the caveman routine and the never-talk-unless-we-argue routine in various romance books they had read for research. She would either get angry when he confessed his changed love for her, or think he was joking around.

"You and whose army?" Max retorted.

"Dare me?" He grinned as a half-groan, half-chuckle escaped her. "Fess up, Maximilian. Something's eating at you. Let old Uncle Tony fix your problem."

"Nobody can." A short sigh. "Okay, here's the scoop. I just got news on the Gabrielli Fellowship."

"You're not a finalist after all?"

"No." Max laughed. Tony wasn't sure if that was a good sign, or bad. "They've been doing some reorganizing. Carlo Vincente is the head of the board of directors now. He came on board just after the judging closed."

"And?" he prompted, when Max fell silent. "What about him?"

"I'm just... okay, this is probably stupid. But what if people accuse him of rigging the contest in my favor?"

"Huh?" Tony sat up and shook his head. "What are you talking about? Your mom hasn't had contact with him in years."

"Oh. Yeah."

"Max? What are you keeping from your best buddy in the whole wide world?" Now was one of those times when Tony really missed not being able to see her face—or shake her.

"It never came up. Why would it need to come up?" she muttered.

"Max?"

"Mom and Carlo... lived together for a while. Until he went to France and she left Hollywood for good."

Tony almost blurted that Max was teasing him. Carlo Vincente was a moral figurehead in Hollywood, the face of a growing movement demanding higher standards from the film industry. Even if he didn't have that reputation, Tony couldn't believe such a thing of Max's mother.

"Miss Emily and Carlo... wow."

"Yeah. I get that oogy feeling whenever I think about it. They both went through a rebellious phase, and he fought with his wife's relatives after she died. There was some custody battle over his son. Mom thought he wasn't too hot on being a father, which is part of what they were arguing about when he left her."

Tony clutched the arm of the sofa, but he couldn't drive away the sensation that the floor had dropped out from underneath him as an earth-shaking idea filled his brain.

"Max... is Carlo Vincente your father?"

"Joel Randolph is my father," she nearly growled.

"You know what I mean."

"Yeah, I do. And yeah, he is, but only in the biological sense."

"That's not..." Tony sensed Max's fear and the pressure of secrets. And there was a thin thread of anger that she hadn't shared that deep dark secret with him. Weren't they best friends? "Does he know?"

"Are you crazy? I have the best dad in the whole world. What do I need that—" A growling sigh punctuated by the creak of the couch indicated she again shifted her position.

"So what are you afraid of?"

"Fellowship rules prohibit relatives or spouses of staff and board members from participating. Period."

"Ah. Right." Tony bit back laughter. Leave it to Max to focus on the threat to her screenwriting career, silently denying the fear of meeting her natural father. "If anyone finds out, they'll boot you from the fellowship."

Tony just couldn't envision Emily deliberately keeping Carlo away from his daughter. There was something more going on behind the scenes than he could grasp right now.

"Which is why I'm definitely not going to the seminar and awards ceremony." The couch groaned more. "That's what I have an agent for. Chuck can just show up at the ceremony in my place. Uh oh."

"What?"

"There's a police car in front of the house with the flashers going." Max laughed, her voice cracking a little. "I'll bet you anything, the youth group got caught TPing Pastor Wally's house again. Last time, Chief Cooper threatened he'd haul them home in handcuffs."

The doorbell ring came clear through the phone.

"Be right back," Max said, followed by a rustling sound as she put the phone down.

Tony heard the thud of her feet hitting the hardwood floor of the former firehouse, then a few moments later the creak of the big front door. He heard a male voice... but not Max's laughter or the sounds of her brothers good-naturedly arguing with the escort officer. A shiver ran up his spine again. What was happening?

"Tony? Mom and Dad—I have to go to the hospital," Max gasped, her voice cracking.

Then the connection broke.

Tony lowered his cell phone from his ear. The display said the call had ended. He stared at it, willing it to open up, and for Max to say he had misheard. But the phone didn't light again.

"Please, Lord, whatever happened..." Tony listened to his heart thudding in his ears for a few moments. Then he got up and walked over to his desk. Where did he file those papers with all the information he would need for his stay? He hoped the Dean of the Humanities Department had given him his home phone number, and the man was in a good mood right now. This writer-in-residence was going home to the people who needed him.

Sunday, April 20

Nine a.m. Max knew she should call Tony. At the oddest times during the long, stressful night of waiting at the hospital, she thought of Tony anxiously waiting for news. She couldn't. Telling Tony her parents' condition would be admitting how bad it was. The three-hour difference between California and Ohio would only be a valid excuse a little longer.

The hospital had set aside an entire waiting room, just for their family and friends. At least twenty people waited with her and her brothers at any one time. The noise alone had to be a problem.

Pastor Glenn and Rita had been there from around 11:00 until 3a.m., then they had to go home to get a little rest and prepare for the worship services. Jeannette Marshall had come around 8:00, with breakfast and fresh clothes for her and the boys. Dr. Morgan had keys to the theater. He let her in, then followed her to the hospital. From the moment Morgan walked in the door, he had been a rock of support and common sense. Not ten minutes ago, he ran interference with the first newspaper reporter who tried to slip into the waiting room. Max hadn't even realized what was happening until Morgan was at the door, throwing the full weight of professorial disapproval on the stranger with the digital camera. Then a hospital security guard showed up and led the reporter away before any damage was done.

Max supposed the moment the name Emily Keeler appeared in the accident report, a flag program somewhere on the Internet passed the news on to a thousand sites. The concept of "viral" took on a whole new meaning.

Worrying about the paparazzi was low on her list. She had a book deadline to meet. *Taming of the Shrew* was supposed to open up next Tuesday. The set wasn't finished yet. The costumes weren't finished. Joel was playing Petruchio—who was she going to get to replace him with eight days to learn the lines and the blocking? Maybe she should cancel the production. She had a long list of things to do when she went home from the hospital. If she ever went home. How could she go home and leave her parents here? Why wasn't Tony here to hold her hand and help her think straight? She was cut in half without Tony. Why did he have to pick now to leave her all alone?

"Max." Morgan sat down next to her and caught hold of her hands. "One thing at a time. You're not alone in this."

"Considering it's standing-room-only?" Her face ached with the effort to dredge up a smile. A vaguely familiar face appeared in the doorway and looked around. She thought the woman was a doctor, maybe with some news.

"Lynette?" Morgan stood, still holding onto her hand, and his eyes widened with surprise when the pretty, auburn-haired woman hurried through the crowd of friends. "Max, this is Lynette Teague. She's—"

"I've met your parents, Max. I'm so sorry to hear about their accident. If I can help with anything, please, tell me." Lynette wrapped her arms around Max, hugging her quickly.

Max's brain skidded to a halt when Morgan put an arm around Lynette's shoulders, and she blushed. Then everything shifted, and Max remembered something Joel had said a week ago, snickering about Morgan finally having a love life. So this was the lady?

"Max?" Jeannette hustled over. "Is there anyone you'd like me to call, to let them know what's happened?" She looked around the room and her smile went crooked. "Not that you need more people in here, but don't you have a production coming up? Shouldn't the cast and crew know?" Leave it to one of her closest friends to remember that.

"I can make calls," Lynette said, pulling out her cell phone.

Minutes later, Max and her brothers sat down to throw together a long list of people—BWU staff, cast and crew of Homespun, customers, and friends who wouldn't have heard about the accident. She had never really appreciated how many people were part of their lives until she had to think of appointments to reschedule, deliveries to change. How had her parents handled all these details, day in and day out?

Afternoon came, along with a flood of her father's students and fellow professors from the university. Morgan and the General were more than able to take care of Joel's classes for the remaining few weeks of the school year. Bekka Sanderson, Dani Paul, and Nikki James teamed up to bring in lunch, and then dinner, and took turns sitting vigil at the theater office to take care of the flood of phone calls. The entire country now knew that Emily Keeler had suddenly reappeared after twenty-six years.

And, of course, someone had to be there to receive the flood of food from the church family and the neighbors. Max reported that predictable detail when she was allowed ten minutes to visit Joel that evening. He was finally awake, after being sedated while they worked on his shattered leg.

"On the bright side, we're not going to have to cook for the next week," she told her stepfather. "On the negative side, I think Mrs. Spinelli dropped off a double order of her mushroom casserole."

"It's not that bad," Joel whispered, his eyelids fluttering as he fought to keep them open. "How's your mother?"

"She's..." Max gripped the bed rail hard enough she thought she would dent it. "She's not awake yet, Dad. They let me see her. She looks fine," she lied, still nauseous from the sight of Emily with her hair shorn on one side and blood seeping through the thick bandages, "but... she just won't wake up."

Max wished she hadn't eavesdropped on Dr. Holland and the neurologist conferring in the hallway outside Emily's room, worrying about brain damage.

"How long?" Joel said.

"How long what?"

"How long have we been in here?"

"It's only about 9:00. Not even a whole day yet."

"Got me so doped up... feels like forever." Joel licked his lips and tipped his head to the side to look around the room. "The production—"

"We're going to cancel." Max found the cup of water with the straw in it and held it for him so he could drink.

"No." He tried to sit up, but his arm slipped out from under him.

"Lie still, Dad."

"Show must go on." He managed a shaky grin and gave up the battle to keep his eyes open. "Stupid cliché, but it's true. Everything's set. You'll do fine. Everybody's ready."

"Kind of hard to do *Shrew* without Petruchio."

"Oh. Yeah." The chagrin in his voice brought a weary giggle from her. "We'll find a replacement."

"Who?"

"Gimme time to think." He flinched when someone outside rapped sharply on the door.

"Tomorrow. That's my cue to get out and let you sleep." Max squeezed his hand and leaned over the rail to press a kiss against his eyebrow, about the only spot on his face that wasn't bruised or scraped.

"You'll be fine. Don't really need me." He squeezed her hand but didn't open his eyes.

"I'll always need you, Dad." Max thought his lips twisted in an answering smile. She suspected he was asleep before she shut the door.

What she really needed was to talk to Tony. Out of all the people who had surrounded her with support and offers of help and shoulders to cry on, the one she needed to see most was the one who couldn't be there.

She suspected God was trying to tell her something, but she was too tired, her head too full of details to be handled, to figure it out.

Chapter Two

"Hey, Max?" Steve Coheny called her when she turned the corner and braced herself to face whoever remained in the waiting room. He broke away from a hospital security guard who blocked him from coming down the hall. "Tell Godzilla here I'm with you, okay?"

For half a second, she was tempted to tell the guard, another church friend, that she didn't know him. Max's head throbbed.

"Andy, he's new on the tech crew."

"Thanks." Steve hurried over, holding out a hand, and for just a second she thought he would wrap his arm around her. His expression said he was upset over something more than being stopped by security.

Why would he care so much?

"I just heard a little while ago. I was busy moving my stuff from the hotel and... how are your folks? How's Miss Emily? What can I do?"

"Miss Emily?" Max's tired brain tripped over that label. Yes, a good number of people called her mother that, but Steve hadn't even been in Tabor two whole days. Who could he have picked it up from?

"Ah... I talked with some people who knew your mom when she was doing college theater, setting up programs. I started thinking of her that way." Steve caught hold of her arm and guided her to the waiting room. Joe and Jeremy were there, but not alone.

"Excuse me," she said. Fury triggered one last burst of energy when she saw the town's know-it-all busybody had cornered her brothers. "Guys? Visiting hours are over. Dad said for us to go home."

Jeremy smirked as they hurried away from diminutive, wrinkled, prune-mouthed Mrs. Pluch. What was she doing there? The woman had been a vocal critic of the residents of Homespun for years, so no one could say she was a friend of the Randolph family and had come here out of concern for them. There was a reason why the boys referred to her as "Mrs. Puke." Actually, a multitude of reasons.

"Maureen." Mrs. Pluch folded her hands at her waist, and her mouth folded into pleased lines as she looked Max over, head-to-foot. "You look awful. It must be so stressful, holding things together. Your parents have such disorganized lives."

"You know, there's a word for people who make *untrue* statements about things they know *nothing* about, but I'm too dang tired to think of it right now." Max stalked past the woman, whose mouth dropped open in shock. Did Mrs. Pluch realize Max implied she didn't know what she was talking about? Or did she hear a worse word when Max said "dang"?

Max snatched up her backpack and her computer case, noting that one of her brothers had packed up everything for her while she had been visiting their father. She turned around and nearly ran into Steve, who gathered up the boxes and bags of leftover food and various gifts left by the many visitors throughout the day. Max thought for a moment about leaving all the bakery behind for the hospital staff, but she had to feed her brothers while taking care of the theater and the print shop and working on her book and going to work at the newspaper.

"I'll forgive you this time, because it's obvious you're under a lot of stress," Mrs. Pluch said, and sniffled, as if she fought tears.

"Fair warning, Mrs. Pu — Mrs. Pluch," Max said, as she led the other three out of the waiting room. "I'm going to be under a lot of stress for a long time to come. Spare your tender feelings and stay away."

"Yeah, far away," Jeremy muttered, as they escaped into the hallway. "Like the other side of the galaxy."

Max held her breath and waited for Mrs. Pluch to follow them down the hall, ranting about their rudeness and how she had always known the Randolph family would destroy Tabor Heights. Her usual litany.

"Maureen?" Steve said, when they reached the elevator in safety and the doors closed behind them.

"Mrs. Puke says Mom didn't know what she was doing when she named Max Maxine," Joe explained. "She insists her name is Maureen. Even got in a fight with Mr. Coffelt at the paper about it, when they were running staff bios during the Sandstone Festival last year."

"She uses every excuse she can to fight with the *Picayune*," Max said. She closed her eyes and leaned back against the elevator wall.

"Why?" Steve's voice was rich with laughter.

Max decided she might like him, despite the uneasy first impression.

"Back about four years ago, when the reporter for the *Dateline: Tabor* column left, Mrs. Pluch decided she was the most knowledgeable resident of Tabor, so she should take over. She *waited* for the owners to offer it to her. When they ran a contest to see who could write the best article, to choose Barbie's replacement, her column didn't get a single vote. She claimed it was rigged."

"Gee, if nobody votes for your column, you think maybe people don't like you, or you can't write?" Jeremy said with a chortle.

"So, she basically hates anybody who is loyal to the paper and the Coffelts." Max opened her eyes as the elevator doors opened on the ground floor. "Every once in a while, she tries to guilt-trip Dad into letting her start a rival paper out of our print shop." They stepped out and hurried across the lobby to the doors to the parking lot.

"For free," Joe added.

"Wow," Steve said with a grin, shaking his head. "I don't suppose you'd ever put her in a book or one of your scripts?"

"Max has a couple times already." Jeremy snickered.

"Max gets back at a lot of people by putting them in her books and plays and then blowing them to pieces," Joe added.

"They never recognize themselves," Max said.

Steve burst out laughing. They were all laughing, softly from exhaustion, by the time they got to her car and the four parted ways.

When Max and the boys got home, Bekka was still on duty. She handed over half a dozen sheets of scribbled notes from phone calls she had answered on the kitchen phone. That was the unlisted number, known only to friends, the church staff, and Max's co-workers. After showing Max where she had stowed all the casseroles and cakes and salads, in the upstairs refrigerator and the auxiliary refrigerator and freezer downstairs in the theater, Bekka was ready to go.

"You're going to love this. Hope you don't mind if I use it in a book someday," she said as she headed for the back door through the kitchen.

"Must be good, with that smirk."

"Did you know you have a sister named Maureen?" Bekka paused in the doorway.

"What?"

"We've had six—count 'em, six—reporters or camera crews show up in the last four hours. Somebody in town told them Emily Keeler's children are Joseph, Jeremy, and Maureen."

"Mrs. Puke." Max sagged down into the nearest kitchen chair. "I actually wondered why she took so long getting to the hospital. She must have had a field day, intercepting everyone and telling them our life stories. And she has insisted for years that I don't know my own name."

"Actually, it kind of helps with things, if you think about it." Bekka shrugged and took a step outside. "It's like when telemarketers call and slaughter our names. You can honestly say there's no such person living here. When those reporters ask about Maureen Randolph, tell them the same thing. It's a secret identity."

"Yeah, that's what I need right about now."

For the first time in nearly a day, Max thought about the Gabrielli Fellowship, and the major tactical error of entering under the name of Max Keeler. She should have contacted them as soon as she learned Carlo Vincente was now head of the board and declared herself disqualified. Still, she reasoned, if Carlo never knew he was her father, why hold an accident of biology against her?

Chuck Winters, her agent had probably expected her to do the right thing and ask him to handle the PR fallout from that little revelation. *If* he guessed Carlo was her father. Emily had never told him, but Winters had been a close friend since before Max was born. He had to have guessed, so he had to know what the announcement of Carlo's new position on the board would do to her standing in the fellowship. Right now, Max and Winters were both too busy handling the media storm that swirled around her family. Hospital security had kept away the paparazzi today. How soon would those nosy reporters resume invading tomorrow? And the day after? And the day after that?

The world had discovered that Emily Keeler was still alive. Tabor Heights was likely on the evening news. How long could the comfortable, safe life her parents had built for their family last against the invasion that was already gathering speed and force?

"Hi, I'm looking for Maureen Randolph. Seen her around?" she asked, adopting a slightly British accent and holding out her hand to Bekka.

"Whatever you need, you know I'm here. Anything at all," Bekka said, stepping back into the kitchen to wrap Max in a hug.

When the door had closed behind her, Max rested her head in her hands and braced for another deluge of tears. For the first time in nearly twenty-four hours, she was entirely alone. It was time for the frantic, furious storm of tears to hit.

But it didn't.

Monday, April 21

"Hey, Max?" Jeremy skidded around the corner and grabbed onto the doorframe as he flung himself at full speed into the scene shop, where Max finished up the last of the props. That was at least one thing she could control. "Mr. Winters is on the phone." He wiped his sweaty forehead on the sleeve of his T-shirt and started back outside.

"Thanks." She pried herself from her knees and stumbled a few steps until she reached the door. "Hey — what are you doing home from school?"

"I forgot my homework. Mr. Carpelli let me come home since I have study hall right now. You know, I can just stay home and work on the set," her brother offered as he fell into step with her. He tilted his head back and squinted at her as they walked along the flagstone path around the back of the theater, to the back door of their home.

"No such luck. Dad wants us to go on with life as usual. That means school for you, and work for me."

She slid an arm around his shoulders. Jeremy was at just the right height for companionable arm wrapping. She wondered how soon his tousled, sandy head would start shooting up past hers.

With the hospitalization of their parents, Chuck Winters functioned as public relations man and buffer between the three siblings and the media. The sudden reappearance of Emily Keeler was big news. People who had turned their backs on her years ago when she abruptly left Hollywood were flooding the media with fond reminiscences. Max despised them all. Whatever Chuck Winters wanted, he would get. Including a speedy pick-up of his phone call. It wasn't quite 9a.m. in Hollywood. What was he doing at work so early?

"Hi, Chuck." She settled into the sagging corner of a couch in the cavernous living room, which also served as the costume shop and Green Room for the Homespun Theater.

"How are you three holding up? How's Joel? What do the doctors say about Emily?" His sympathetic smile came through the phone.

"Dad's more alert. Dr. Holland is threatening to take the phone out of his room if he doesn't stop trying to run things from flat on his back." Max congratulated herself on keeping her voice steady. "We're doing okay. Rehearsal tonight. You're coming for opening night, aren't you?"

"Haven't missed it in seventeen years. Certainly won't miss it now." He sighed.

Max heard a multitude of unspoken messages in that sigh. Chuck Winters had been friend, critic and supporter to her parents when they first established Homespun Theater. He had given away the bride when Joel and Emily married. He had spirited away talented new actors Joel and Emily had nurtured, to careers on both coasts. When Max began writing, he had hounded and harassed her until she improved it enough to be saleable. She blamed him for her current misery, caught in a book she no longer wanted to write. She would be lost without him.

"Got some good news today," he said. "Pelican wants an option on your Gabrielli script. You'll get just over 8,000 after my fee, but it's a start. They want a bio piece before they make a final decision."

"They heard about Mom and made the connection, didn't they?" Max wondered how she could feel so elated, and then two sentences later feel like a lead weight had settled into her stomach. "They don't want a family comedy script. They want something written by Emily Keeler's daughter."

"Son." Winters chuckled. "For some reason, they think you're a boy."

"Let them."

"Max—"

"We're getting hounded here, people asking about Mom. If everybody thinks Max is a boy, that'll be some protection for us, won't it?"

"And when you have to go to L.A. for meetings? If they're expecting a man, and a woman shows up..."

"For now, could we leave them in their ignorance?" Max sighed and pushed her problems aside. This was no time to feel sorry for herself. Future problems would just have to be handled in the future. She had her brothers and parents and the theater to worry about.

"All right." Winters sighed too. Max wondered what kind of rotten day he had had yesterday. "I'll send a safe, unisex biography. I hope you won't be too proud to accept the option check, even if all they do want is something from Emily's kid."

"I'll take all the money I can get right now. Insurance doesn't cover everything." Max leaned back over the swayed arm of the sofa and stared at the ceiling.

The spider web of crack marks across it had four new arms. Someone would have to climb up and spread tarpaper and sealer on the roof before it rained again. With the hospital bills that weren't covered by insurance, and no real hope of getting restitution from the drunk truck driver who hit her parents, how could she find the money for this new expense? It was all resting on her. It seemed to Max that every hour brought some new responsibility and pressure. For the last two days, her prayers had mainly consisted of "Help!"

Maybe Steve was an answer to those prayers?

"At least we got a new guy in the tech crew. I'm still figuring out how to shuffle roles, but I don't have to worry about the crew. Dad seems to think Steve knows his stuff."

"Where'd he come from? What's his name?"

"Steve Coheny. Buddy Sanker recommended him."

"Coheny, did you say?" Winters asked, his voice strained.

"Yeah. Steve Coheny." She went on to describe him, and barely stopped herself from saying, "A young Carlo Vincente." Not smart. "Dad didn't get any bad vibes from him, but Mom... I swear she recognized him." Max fought down a shiver.

"You don't have to keep him around if he makes you uncomfortable, Max. Even with all the help you need right now. Just give me the word, I'll contact some tech guys here who owe me, to come fill in until your folks are back on their feet."

"No, that's okay. Dad hired him. I'd rather keep an eye on him, if he's going to cause trouble."

"No, I don't think he will." The slight hesitation in his voice told Max there was an unspoken 'I hope' added to that sentence.

~~~~~

"Mr. Winters?" Gloria, his secretary, stuck her head into his office and gave him a trembling smile, her brown eyes bright. Her shaggy mane of platinum hair seemed to fly around her face with excitement.

"Something going on?" Winters looked at his blunt hand, dusted with coarse white hairs, still resting on the phone from hanging up. All the muscles in his arm tensed under the tan. He forced himself to sit back in his chair, straighten his new polo shirt and run a hand through his graying
~~~~~

chestnut hair. There was nothing he could do for Max or her brothers that he couldn't do from his desk chair. That hurt.

"Carlo Vincente just called." She scurried across the carpeting and deposited the phone message slip on his desk with all the reverence of an acolyte at the altar. "I mean, it was him, personally, not a secretary or assistant or anybody."

Winters sighed and bit his lip against a smile. If he could have been as vital and attractive at sixty-plus as Carlo, he wouldn't have minded getting older. But then, he reflected, he hadn't started out as a leading man or even comic romantic interest. He had always been a supporting actor until he realized his forte was behind the scenes.

Maybe he was losing his grip. What was Steve—using his mother's maiden name, for some unfathomable reason—doing in Tabor Heights? Why had he gone to Homespun? Did his family know where he had gone? Had he gone as an advance scout? Or had he and his father had a fight, like they hadn't had in a dozen years, and he was off on his own quest? If Steve knew about Emily and Max, maybe his father had seen the Gabrielli paperwork and made the connection between Max Keeler and Emily Keeler.

Winters closed his eyes and let out a cleansing breath, then sat back in his well-padded chair and looked at the note in his hand. One problem at a time. That was all he could handle. Or maybe not.

"What does old Carlo want?" he muttered. He did grin when Gloria gave him a dismayed look, just before she retreated from his office and shut the door.

The grin died.

He should have been expecting this, he knew. With all the fuss the media made at discovering Emily Keeler's whereabouts and solving the 'mystery' of her disappearance from Hollywood, it was expecting a miracle to hope Carlo Vincente wouldn't be curious. Especially since all press releases were coming from Winters Representation Services. Winters had been a mutual friend of Carlo and Emily. He had been relieved when, after Carlo finally returned from France and Emily was nowhere to be found, Carlo hadn't asked him anything about her.

Winters didn't like lying to his friends, even when another friend begged him to do so.

When Emily fled Hollywood twenty-six years before, she did an efficient, complete job of vanishing. She had depended on her few industry contacts to protect her privacy. Winters had kept his silence. It had been easy because no one asked him about Emily.

But now, the message said Carlo wanted to talk to him. The message didn't say what about, but he could guess. Had Carlo learned Winters represented Max Keeler, Emily's daughter, born six months after Carlo left for France? Winters was positive Emily had never told anyone but Joel and Max who Max's father was. He suspected they were heading for just the type of questions he couldn't and didn't want to answer.

Did Max know Carlo Vincente was on the Gabrielli Fellowship board of directors? Winters had received the information packet just three days ago. He would have warned Max if this crisis hadn't struck. When could he warn her? Should he warn her? What would this do to Max, amid all the other crises she faced now? Technically, she was disqualified from the fellowship program, from the moment Carlo Vincente accepted the invitation from the embattled board to join them, become their leader, and clean house.

Winters studied the message slip for a few seconds, letting the thoughts and questions and years-old speculations swirl through his mind. Then he crumpled the paper and threw it in the wastebasket.

Chapter Three

Max threw another pile of laundry into the washing machine in the theater basement, took Jeremy back to school, delivered a printing job for a regular customer, and drove to the hospital to spend the afternoon with her parents. Emily didn't seem to have moved since Max visited her the evening before. The nurses were busy with other patients and Max knew better than to bother them with questions about her mother. She went to her stepfather's room, two floors down. Joel was asleep, worn out from the strain of eating his lunch. She curled up in the chair by his bed and watched him sleep.

Please, God. I know I should just be glad they're alive. But it isn't enough. Why did You have to let that drunk hit them and nearly kill Mom? Why does all this have to happen now? Why does everybody keep saying we'll grow and learn something from all this? I don't want to grow or learn anything! I want life back the way it was...

Joel and Emily had been coming back from dinner when a drunk driver thundered down on them at nearly eighty miles an hour in a twenty-five mile zone, in a construction truck he shouldn't have been driving in the first place. The driver, who got out of the accident with little more than bruises, blamed Joel and Emily for the accident.

Her mother always said God let bad things happen to make His people stronger, to teach them, to test them, and prove to them they were capable and able. Sometimes, Max wondered if her mother really knew what she was talking about.

She spent the afternoon wandering between her parents' rooms and the little lounge where she had enough quiet to handle paperwork for the theater. She had to keep moving because what felt like a tag team of reporters and photographers kept sneaking through the vigilance of the hospital staff, to penetrate ICU or try to interview hospital staff. She clued in the nurses on the name mix-up, and managed not to laugh aloud when she heard Sylvia, a friend from church, tell three different strangers on three occasions that no, she hadn't seen Maureen Randolph and didn't know when she'd be in. It was intensely satisfying to watch the hospital security guards come in and herd the intruders away.

When Joel was awake, she discussed the cast changes and theater business with him and got his approval. Neither of them mentioned Emily more than once every third sentence. She entertained him with the ongoing drama of warding off the invasion of the paparazzi, and relayed text messages between him and Chuck Winters.

Around 3p.m., she managed to choke down some too-salty chicken soup from a vending machine, and checked with Doug and Steve, who were finishing the balcony for the set. Soon she would have to give up and go home. She had to face decisions about the set, about costumes, and find something among several dozen casseroles to feed her brothers before rehearsal started.

"Max?" Nikki James startled her, appearing from nowhere when Max went outside to make a phone call to Tony without disturbing Joel, who had fallen asleep. It was about time she let Tony know what was going on.

"Hey, Nikki." Max looked around for Gray, Nikki's bodyguard dog, a massive Akita. "Where's the bear?"

A muffled growling snort came from behind Max, stopping her when she would have stepped backwards. She looked over her shoulder and into the almost human eyes of the big dog.

"She claims that means he likes you," a woman said, sauntering around the corner of the building. "Personally, I don't buy it."

"Max, this is Jenni Doran. She's a reporter for *America's Voice*. She's here to help," Nikki hurried to say, when Max opened her mouth to yell— she wasn't sure what, only that she needed to yell.

"The only way to defeat the Evil Empire is to steal their thunder," Jenni said, with a diffident shrug. She tucked a long strand of her straight, platinum hair behind her ear. "Nikki told her sister how the media is coming in like sharks in a feeding frenzy. Joan asked me to come and play spin doctor. You know how royally pissed some of those gossip rags will be, if you're giving exclusive stories to a goody-two-shoes publication like mine?" She offered a wide, cheesy grin. Then for good measure, dug her index finger into her cheek and managed a curtsey worthy of Shirley Temple at her most sugary adorable.

Max thought for two seconds. The image of all those intrusive paparazzi burning up in fury was more persuasive than knowing that Joan and Nikki obviously trusted this woman.

"You're hired."

~~~~

Joe and Jeremy came to the hospital straight from school, with a load of cards and candy and flowers and stuffed toys given by friends in town and at church. Joel stayed awake during their entire visit, which was a vast improvement from the day before. The boys showed real reluctance to leave this time. Seeing their father flat on his back the day before, pale and bruised, with a shattered voice, dozing off without warning, had been an unsettling experience for all. Joel was the one who could do anything, win any game, stick with any project or chore longer than anyone. They hadn't liked seeing him in the hospital bed. They didn't want to leave him now.
~~~~

When the three got home, Max stumbled upstairs to her room to change her clothes, harboring a dream that her brothers would find their own dinners for a change. But what were the chances? The refrigerator and freezer threatened to burst from all the food friends from town, from the newspaper, from church, had brought by. That didn't mean her brothers could figure out what to eat on their own.

Max wished she could stay in her room until after rehearsal. She sensed a storm brewing between her brothers. They had been on their best behavior too many days in a row. She didn't want to get caught in the fight due to erupt at any second.

She locked the door, put on a soundtrack CD—loud—and stretched out on her bed.

Movie posters stared down from the ceiling at her, a conglomeration of swashbuckler, adventure, fantasy and science fiction. Max stared until Errol Flynn's *Robin Hood* merged with *Indiana Jones*, then she rolled over. Bookshelves lined every inch of available wall space in her room. Nothing interested her, and she needed desperately to get her mind off the present moment. Where was Tony when she really needed to be distracted?

"On the West Coast, of course," she muttered. It didn't alleviate her sense of abandonment to remember that she hadn't made that phone call yet. Of course, it went two ways, didn't it? Tony should be calling her to find out what was up.

A yelp of indignation came through the closed door—it sounded like Jeremy, meaning Joe had made the first strike.

Max felt better. Loud thuds echoed through the heating ducts. It sounded like the boys had settled into a fight downstairs in the living room. Their favorite way to spar used cushions from the mismatched sofas as weapons. She hoped they wouldn't knock over the makeup tables.

"Should get writing again," she mumbled.

Another depressing thought.

"Dad," she whispered, "what am I going to do? How am I going to run the theater and take care of the boys and keep up my writing?"

Max knew she needed to cry, she wanted to cry, but she couldn't. She was just too tired.

"God, I know I'm supposed to pray at times like these," Max said, hearing her voice thicken, feeling the ache in her throat. "Lately, I don't think You listen anymore. Who really cares about the Randolph family and Homespun Theater?"

"Max?" The door creaked open, nearly masking Jeremy's voice. "You okay, Max?" Her little brother sounded five years younger. "Joe's calling Dante's Delivery for pizza."

"What about Mrs. Spinelli's mushroom casserole?" She grinned when her brother made gagging noises.

"We haven't had pizza in weeks. Besides, I'm paying."

"In that case, go for it." Max forced laughter into her voice. Her brother—mathematics wizard, theater accountant, and notorious skinflint—only paid for something when he wanted something in return, or when he felt especially bad.

Cheering everyone was *her* responsibility, now.

She hit the power button for the CD player and stumbled to the door. Jeremy waited in the hall, hair mussed, shirt half-unbuttoned, in stocking feet, with a lopsided grin on his face.

"Hey, brat-fink," she whispered. Jeremy let her put an arm around his shoulders as they walked down the hall.

~~~~~

The outpouring of volunteers from the university overwhelmed Max. Some didn't surprise her, students who were also friends from church and town, such as Bekka. Max immediately made the other girl her assistant. Bekka knew the routine, both at Homespun and behind the scenes in theaters in general, and it made the first rehearsal after the accident far smoother than Max had anticipated.

After everyone went home, she settled down at her computer and found she couldn't make any sense of the words on the screen. She had written that scene Saturday night before she made her regular call to Tony, amazed and relieved at how the dreaded book was flowing. Right now, the words were gibberish.

She knew she would be better off going to bed. She needed the sleep more than she needed to force herself to write. But with everything on her mind—especially the fact that when she called him, Tony didn't answer his phone or respond to the message she left—sleep would be a long time coming, if at all.

"Yeah, there she is, slave to her muse," drawled a low, female voice.

Max smiled as she turned to see the woman standing in the door that led to backstage. Her jumpsuit of neon green with pink slashes glowed in the shadows. The electric blue beads in her dozens of tiny braids clicked as she moved over to the office alcove where Max wrote and Joel kept the theater books, tucked between the deep storage shelves full of props.

"How come you aren't home in bed yet?" Max asked as Brenda Nyota slid into the swivel chair in front of Joel's desk.

"I know you. You'll sit up all night working yourself into a shadow, trying to figure out how to handle everything until your folks get out of the hospital." She shrugged and slouched a little further in the chair. "I figured I'd keep you company tonight."

There were times Max dreaded seeing Brenda stroll through the theater door. Her friend carried so much hurt and resentment for the world in general, and fought back with a sharply bitter humor that had
~~~~~

already won notice in several magazines. But in the last two days, Max had seen a new side to Brenda. The woman who had known the pain of loss and deprivation and confusion knew how others felt in similar situations. The same bitter humor could make people laugh through their tears. Max needed that. Especially since Tony was so far away.

Besides, Brenda gave her an excuse to shut down her computer.

They claimed their usual couches and covered a coffee table with ice cream, nachos and grapes. Brenda and Max curled up among pillows and blankets, nibbling and talking and letting the long day drift away.

"When's that wretch, Tony, coming home?" Brenda asked, after a lull only broken by the creaking of old wooden beams in the ceiling and the crunching of nacho chips.

"Might be August."

"I thought he was only supposed to teach spring semester. What happened?" She propped herself up on one elbow and studied Max from under lowered eyebrows.

"He got an offer to stay for the summer term about... four days ago." Max had to think back to organize the last few days into a semblance of order. "He's considering another term. They really like him there."

"Yeah, Tony gets all the breaks." She snorted and retreated back to her cocoon of blankets. "Wish I was independently wealthy and could take time off from my writing."

"Tony wishes he had sent you to California to do all that guest lecturing, instead of him."

"He should have taken you with him."

"Don't be ridicu—"

"But no, Max wouldn't go. She's a good little girl who goes to church every week and she wouldn't think of kissing on the first date," Brenda drawled.

"Tony and I never dated."

"That's the problem with you two. You have got the most gorgeous guy in Ohio as your writing partner. You see him almost every day. You're writing steamy love scenes, and neither of you get any ideas."

"They're *not* steamy," Max protested.

"I *know* you act out all sorts of scenes in your other books. Why don't the two of you have the guts to act out the bedroom ones?"

"That's too stupid a question to even answer," she growled between clenched teeth.

Max kicked herself for letting the conversation get this far. She usually never got into discussions about romance writing with Brenda unless Tony was around, because her friend at least had the tact not to say such things when a man was present.

To make matters worse, Max had let herself daydream about what it would be like if Tony looked at her like the heroes in their stories looked at the heroines. There were times she wondered if Tony Martin even realized she was a girl. Then she would resolve yet again not to wish for what couldn't be. Max knew what happened when people tried to take what didn't belong to them.

What if her parents had waited to get married? She might not have been born — but her mother might be married to her natural father.

If Tony wanted more than best pals, he would say something. Wouldn't he? She had seen too many friends ruin great relationships with guys by taking the plunge and saying they wanted the whole enchilada — diamond ring, white picket fence, kids and a dog. Nothing in the world would convince her to risk losing her other half. Did it really matter if they didn't kiss, if they weren't going to wake up next to each other for the rest of their lives?

"I'll tell you why," Brenda rolled on. "Because you're both great dreamers, but you're wimps. You don't have the guts to break through stupid social customs that aren't valid anymore."

"God says no sex outside marriage, so that settles it. God doesn't change, so His rules don't change." Max felt stupid — and childish — as soon as the words left her lips. She hated the way Brenda could back her into corners with a few words.

"Yeah, yeah. Convenient excuse. Did you ever think that Tony might just be interested, but you're giving him the vibes to stay away?"

"If Tony loved me, he'd be here." That statement hurt. Especially since she had been avoiding the idea, the image that accompanied it, ever since she hung up on him Saturday night.

"Well, that's a point." Brenda nodded, lips pursed in a thoughtful expression. "But you gotta admit, the logistics are kind of hard."

"What's so hard about jumping on a plane?"

"Hello? He drove to California." She pulled her cell phone out of her thigh pocket and tapped through the directory. "What's he going to do about his car?"

"What are you doing?"

"Calling Tony. Asking why he doesn't have his lazy butt on a plane right now, coming to your rescue."

"Don't!" Max lunged out of her nest of pillows and blankets, and immediately hit the floor, tangled up too much to move.

By the time she got untangled, Brenda had her phone to her ear. She stuck her tongue out and scooted over the back of the couch, putting it between her and Max.

Giving up, Max sank back down on her couch and rested her chin in her hands, her elbows on her knees. She felt almost justified, even as a heavy weight landed in her stomach when Brenda scowled at her phone and closed it.

"No response, leave a message?"

"That wretch. Tell you what you need to do." Brenda dropped down on her couch again. "Go put the moves on that new guy, Steve. He sure looked interested in you. Nudge, nudge. Wink, wink." She snickered. "If that doesn't make Tony jealous, nothing will."

"No thanks." Max lay back down and hoped her friend didn't see the shiver that ran through her. Every time she looked around tonight, Steve had been watching her. Brenda and the other girls in the cast and crew might enjoy that kind of attention, but it made her feel exposed.

Please, God, where's Tony? Why isn't he answering his phone? He ought to at least be worried about Mom and Dad. Even if he doesn't care about me beyond writing partners.

Max reached for the plate of nachos but stopped and sank back into her blankets. She definitely wasn't hungry anymore.

Tuesday, April 22

Seven a.m. found Max at her computer in the little office alcove. She stared at the screen. Since dreams drove her out of bed two hours ago, she had rewritten the same five paragraphs four times. She had kept count. Fortunately, Brenda had gone home around midnight on a blast of inspiration for her current work-in-progress.

"Stupid contract," Max muttered, and leaned back. She regretted that half a second later, when all her stiff back muscles sent messages of rebellion to her aching head.

The office phone rang. Max groaned and got up to answer it. She brushed her tangled hair out of her face, wondered if it was time for a cut, and picked up the phone. Then she remembered the answering machine was still turned on. Too late now.

"Homespun Theater," she said. The man on the other end wanted box office information. Max stifled her wish to scream and ask why he called at *7a.m.* "Opening night is next Tuesday. The box office is open for advance ticket sales all day Saturday, and from 5 to 9 weeknights, or you can use the order form on our web site."

He hung up without thanking her. She suspected he was yet another reporter, checking to make sure someone was home. If she went outside to get the paper, would someone ambush her? Doug had guarded the backstage door to let cast and crew in for rehearsal, and had kept six intruders away. At least the avalanche of phone calls had slowed down. It only took three days of refusing to return calls or answer the phone to get the message through. Too bad she couldn't sue the media in general for harassment, entertainment magazines and TV shows in particular.

Hopefully, Joan and Nikki's theory was correct, and once the news hounds learned that *America's Voice* and Jenni Doran had an exclusive on all news having to do with the Keeler-Randolph family and Homespun Theater, they would go away.

Max returned to her seat and stared at the screen. Nothing had changed. She was tired enough to wish elves would magically appear and write something for her. She deleted four words and typed in two more sentences. It looked like her hero and his sister were heading into a fight. Now might be a good time to write fights.

The phone rang. She stared at the screen and tried to ignore the rattling along her weary nerves. Should she try to go back to bed for another hour before heading in for work at the newspaper? She only had to put in a half day today. Maybe she could sleep when she got home.

The answering machine kicked in and the message played. Max stared at her screen, stymied again.

Upstairs, Jeremy stumbled down the hall from his room to the balcony railing. He slid through the gap and grabbed the firemen's pole, left in during remodeling because it supported the roof, and slid down to land on the cushions on the floor at the bottom.

"Thank you for calling Homespun Theater," the answering machine said with Max's voice, slightly touched with the English accent that had sent their mother into giggles when she recorded it. "Performances resume with *Taming of the Shrew* on Tuesday, April 29. Please join us for this timeless classic."

Max managed three more sentences before her inspiration dried again. Jeremy tiptoed up behind her and read over her shoulder until her fingers stilled on the keys. He frowned, his gaze returning to the top of the screen, and re-read the page.

"That's the same place you were after dinner," he said.

"Congratulations." Max knew she was tired if she didn't elbow him for startling her. "School isn't a waste of time after all."

"Wanna bet?" he returned with an impudent grin. "What's for breakfast?" He headed for the swinging kitchen door before she answered.

"Oatmeal." Max leaned over the keyboard, another flash of inspiration giving her two more sentences.

"In April?" He vanished into the kitchen.

"We're completely out of bread and cereal. Let's save the cake and gooey stuff for dress rehearsal, okay? I'm going shopping this afternoon," she added, raising her voice. The thud of the refrigerator closing answered her.

Jeremy came out eating a slice of cold pizza. He tucked his green plaid shirt into his jeans with his free hand. Max thought about cooking oatmeal. Pizza sounded better.

She heaved herself out of her chair and stepped over to the winding stairs. "Joe!" She waited, listening for running water. "Joe, you're going to be late!"

"Get your rear in gear and get it down here!" Jeremy added.

Max headed for the kitchen. She hoped there were at least two slices of pizza left—one for her and one for Joe.

Jeremy took three steps up the stairs and called, "Joe, Karen Peterson is on the phone."

He stepped out of the way as a loud bang announced Joe's running exit from the bathroom. Their brother thudded down the hall and nearly missed five steps as he spun down the stairs. His sweatshirt was on backward, his blond hair rumpled and wet, and he zipped his jeans as he ran over to the office phone. He skidded to a stunned stop when he found it still sitting on the hook. Jeremy burst out laughing.

"You little—" Joe flung down his shoes and lunged at his brother. Jeremy darted out of the way, and they both nearly collided with Max as she came out of the kitchen.

"Thought I heard your elephant feet. Here." She handed him the cold pizza.

"For breakfast?" Joe stopped short.

"That, or oatmeal." Max sighed and grinned when Joe grabbed the pizza and crammed it into his mouth.

"This is more like it," he said through a mouthful. He bent over and caught up one shoe to slide onto his foot.

"Don't get used to it." She headed back to the computer to shut it down before she got ready for work. "I'll get groceries this afternoon."

"No more mushrooms or chicken surprise?" He slapped a hand over his heart and staggered backward, eyes wide in shock.

~~~~~

The sign on the ski-slope roof of the building read *Tabor Picayune* in three-foot-tall emerald letters on a white background. Max looked at the sign, pausing on the sidewalk, and smiled. She actually looked forward to coming to work. It made her feel like things were getting back to normal. She missed the more park-like setting of the old office, which had backed up to the river, but she didn't miss the litter and other hazards that came from having a bar in the lower level of the building.

Through the glass double doors, she saw everybody settling into their Tuesday morning routine. From the bobbing of the switchboard operator's head, just visible over the divider half-wall, the phones were going crazy with last-minute advertisements or people trying to get news into the community calendar section. Max smiled, even knowing the complaints she would hear, the shrieking from rude people who thought
~~~~~

deadlines and rules never applied to them, and the occasional yelps from the back room as the art department and the advertising department collided, mentally and physically, as they assembled business ads.

It would be good to settle into her shadowy corner between the circulation desks and the reception area, put in her ear buds and get to work editing the reams of copy waiting in her computer's queue. It was good to escape the house, crammed full of hurting shadows, and settle into the usual scurry of the newspaper office. What intruding reporter and gossip rag investigator would think to look for Emily Keeler's daughter at a newspaper office? Here, at least, no one would watch her and study everything she said and ask her to make important decisions. If any decisions had to be made, she could take them to Andrew Coffelt, the owner. Important decisions went to his daughter, Angela, the editor.

A white head of hair bobbed down the dim hallway that led back to the editorial workroom, as Max stepped through the front doors. She barely had time to register that Craig, a literature major from Butler-Williams, was on duty on the switchboard that morning. Then Andrew Coffelt descended on her, his olive green spring cardigan still smelling of mothballs.

"Max, what are you doing here?" He wrapped an arm around her shoulders.

"It's Tuesday?" She met Craig's sympathetic brown eyes and tried to endure without bursting out laughing. "I have a lot of stories to edit, and headlines to write before lunch."

"Are you sure you want to come to work already?" Andrew shook his head, his tangled, blinding white hair flying like a dust mop. "Two measly days aren't enough to get all those pesky details taken care of. Your folks are in the hospital and you have that theater to run... don't know why you're even out of bed. I'd be sleeping in, if I were you."

"Don't remind me." Max forced herself to smile, when she had a sudden urge to yawn. She glanced down the hall where various reporters appeared in the shadows, drawn by the sound of Andrew's foghorn voice.

Chapter Four

"Dad, if Max wants to get back to work, we shouldn't argue with her," Angela said, emerging from the back room. Her long ebony hair was pulled back in a french braid, emphasizing the doll-like perfection of her face. She smiled at Max, her eyes conveying sympathy and apology and a bit of humor for her father's vagaries.

"I'd really rather work," Max said.

When Andrew Coffelt made a decision at the *Tabor Picayune*, people could usually argue or ignore him without retribution. When Angela Coffelt made a call, arguing was a waste of time. Even her father knew that. Fortunately, Angela was on Max's side.

Her mind darted back to the hours of frustration she had endured that morning. The only bright spot had been when she put the announcement on the web site that anyone wanting information on Joel and Emily's condition should contact either Chuck Winters' agency, or Jenni Doran from *America's Voice*. Showering and jumping into her clothes to head to work had been a welcome reprieve. The thought of facing her home computer screen again made her stomach clench tight.

Max took a deep breath as she headed over to her desk. Despite the Coffelts' assurances that they could cover her workload without any problem, she sensed there would be stacks of work waiting in her computer queue for her to read and edit and match with new headlines.

She was right. The stack of memos on her desk, taped to the keyboard and stuck to the corkboard framing her monitor, all referred to work waiting in the file server. Max sighed and grinned as she settled into her desk chair. Life was definitely back to normal.

"She's back. Thank You, God. Thank You, God," a gravelly voice whispered, approaching from behind her.

Max turned around. Ed Barkley, the police and school board reporter plunked a can of ginger ale down on her desk with one hand, an unopened package of fig bars with the other, then wrapped both arms around her shoulders in a quick hug.

"You have no idea how much you were missed around here, Max," he said as he stepped back, grinning, three days' growth of silver beard making him a scruffy, skinny Santa Claus.

"You had to answer phones, didn't you?" She put a sweet smile on her face, but it was hard to keep the gloating out of her voice.

Ed hated the telephone almost as much as Max did. They both firmly averred that the phones could be silent all day long, but the one time the phone did ring and they answered, the caller was always a lunatic threatening to blow up the paper if he didn't get what he wanted, printed the way he wanted it, within the next four hours. Such demands were hard to fulfill, since the *Tabor Picayune* only hit the streets twice a week.

"That comment doesn't deserve an answer." Ed slapped her shoulder. "Better get to work. There's a piece in there you're going to love. Headline practically writes itself."

"Hold on, let me see." She logged into her computer, fingers flying. Max was quietly surprised she even remembered the password and other commands after everything that had happened. "Log number?"

Ed gave her the number and she called it onto her screen. It was a police blotter piece, about a car full of teens trying to get into the drive-in theater that sat on the border of Tabor Heights and Stoughton, with two boys hiding in the trunk.

"Wish we could print names," Ed grumbled practically in her ear. "One kid's last name is Dillon, and the other one is Marshall."

"Marshall Dillon? And they were caught riding in the trunk of a Dodge." Max groaned. Dutifully, she typed in the typesetting commands and put in the headline she knew Ed wanted to see. "*Stowaways told to get out of Dodge*. That's really disgusting, Ed."

"Think it'll win a prize at the next press competition?" he called over his shoulder, as he headed back down the hall to his desk.

"I hope not!" Max grinned and punched in the commands to check spelling. Life was definitely returning to normal.

For most of the morning, she was able to work in peace. Her co-workers left her alone, except to ask how her parents were doing and how the next play was coming along. Curt Mehdlang, assistant editor, was apologetic when he asked for the official update to put in the paper. Max half-listened to the college students who manned the phone in shifts, and said a silent prayer of thanks that those days were long behind her.

The runner from Rick's Bakery came in every morning at noon sharp with a tray of assorted sandwiches, donuts, bagels and cookies for the staff to choose from. Max saw Eddie Santera, the stringer who covered council meetings, following on the girl's heels. She finished her headline and stood, typing in the commands to send the story over to Angela's queue. She logged out. The chair cushion barely cooled before Eddie slid into it, giving Max a crooked grin and a wave good-bye.

She forgot to pick up groceries on the way home, but Max didn't care. The last half hour of work had been a struggle because she knew how to fix the scene she had been battling this morning. She had to get home to write it while the images and sequence were still clear.

~~~~~

"And I say, if they start making movies, that means the series is dead," Pete said, directly across the lunch table from Jeremy. It was first lunch period in the Tabor Heights High School cafeteria and the din hadn't risen to the usual chop-and-liquefy volume yet. That made semi-reasonable conversations almost possible.

"So you aren't going to see it when it comes out in June?" Jeremy grinned, scooped up a mound of whipped cream mixed with strawberries from his shortcake, and slid the whole mess into his mouth. He loved it when he could buy lunch at school. He went ala carte, bought only dessert, and saved the rest of his lunch money.

"Ain't no way!" his friend yodeled, his voice still suffering from puberty, the sound breaking through the usual lunchtime din.

Heads turned. Frowns and curious stares turned into resignation and disgust. Jeremy wondered what everybody was so upset about. They *were* getting kind of loud, but who could tell in the cafeteria with everybody talking and the rattle and roar of the decrepit air conditioning?

"You guys finished?" Jeremy asked, looking around the table. The other members of the *Starship Defiance* fan club nodded and crumpled lunch bags and wrappers or stacked serving trays on top of each other.

"Look at the clones," someone called, ending in a snicker. Jeremy refused to turn to look and give them the satisfaction.

At least that was all anybody said. Jeremy had heard worse since the club had started meeting in the lunchroom instead of in the library on weekends. And it was partially true; everyone was blond and skinny, and the girls wore button-down shirts with the tails hanging down the back, just like the guys. Today, Pete and Jeremy could have been twins with the same green plaid shirts, their hair slicked with sweat from gym class, their noses red with a burn from scrubbing too hard to fight off pimples. Eleven young bodies trooped out through the cafeteria doors, down the side steps, and out onto the thin strip of grass between the parking lot and the soccer field.

"Look at the space case," someone shouted from overhead.

Jeremy turned on his heel, searching, before he remembered his resolution to ignore the usual detractors. He found two shadowy shapes up in the trees next to the school door.

"Let's get out of here," he said, gesturing toward the trees at the far end of the soccer field. "Smells kind of bad around here."

"Yeah, run away, ya babies!" one of the shapes in the tree shouted. They laughed.

"Burnouts," Jeremy muttered. His friends followed across the dying grass to the quiet shade at the far end of the field. Behind him, he heard the rustling of tree branches. The two bullies in the tree were climbing
~~~~~

down. It wouldn't come to a fight, two against all of them. Besides, he had heard everything jerks like them could say against *Starship Defiance*.

~~~~~

In half an hour of frantic typing, Max produced three pages. Now she was stuck. Again. And the block felt worse than before. She was afraid to look back and see the scene she had just typed was actually atrocious. She silently vowed, as she had many times before, she would never write another romance novel again. She would strangle Tony. He had made her write romances in the first place. Why couldn't they stick to science fiction and fantasy, anyway?

The phone rang. Max stuck her tongue out at the machine and stumbled to the kitchen to find some lunch.

Her purse sat on the counter where she had dropped it when she came home from work. She considered a moment, then nodded. She was just too tired to struggle any longer. She dug out her cell phone and punched in the number for Winters' office. For good measure, she crossed her fingers, hoping he would be out.

Gloria answered.

"Gloria? This is Max Randolph. Can I leave a message for Chuck?"

"Have to—he's on the conference phone again." Gloria sounded cheerful. Maybe that meant the media assault was finally tapering off.

"Fine with me. Just tell him I'm having trouble with *Snowfire*. Any way he can push the deadline back with the publisher?"

"He thought of that," she said, her voice softer. "He said if you called, he talked with Monica, and you can have all the time you want."

"Thanks... How much real time does that translate to?" Max closed her eyes, crossed her fingers and held her breath.

"Another month, maybe."

"Thanks. I really appreciate it. I'll call as soon as I've made some progress. Promise." She closed the phone and collapsed against the counter. "Dumb title for a book, anyway."

Max did feel a little better. Maybe with that problem out of the way, the rest of the book would flow like melting snow. She pushed the kitchen door open and headed for the stereo to put on her *Ladyhawke* soundtrack before she returned to the computer. It suited the mood of this section of the book perfectly.

Hidden by the clatter of keys and the stereo turned up to chop-and-liquefy, the door from backstage creaked open. A tiny woman with salt-and-pepper hair and dark, staring eyes stepped into the living room. Dressed in a maroon wool suit wrinkled from travel, she slowly turned to look around as she pocketed a heavy, old-fashioned brass key.

Max frowned, staring at the screen. The fight scene just didn't feel right. She slid out of her chair and grabbed a prop sword from a rack just
~~~~~

outside the office alcove. Eyes closed, she concentrated on each move, stepping backward, then lunging as she swung down, dropping to one knee and twisting her arms to bring the blade up. She froze two seconds, eyes still closed, then laughed.

"Perfect." She dropped the sword—the clatter made the little woman jerk—and went back to the computer. Her fingers flew over the keys.

While Max put out a page of action, the woman stepped further into the room and slowly took in the normal chaos of the Randolph household.

Cloth curtains across one wall hung crooked, revealing shelves crammed with props. Elizabethan costumes lay in a haphazard mess across couches, in various stages of being ironed, mended, or altered. A packing crate of boots and hosiery sat between the TV set and the wall. The woman looked around. A slow smile touched her lips. A sparkle in her eyes wiped away a little weariness.

The slowing of Max's fingers clattering on the keyboard caught her attention.

The stranger gently cleared her throat. "Excuse me?"

Max twisted in her chair, nearly knocking it off its casters. For two seconds, they stared at each other. "Box office is closed," she said, getting up. She tried to look nonchalant as she stooped for the sword. The intruder looked like a tired old woman, but appearances were deceiving.

"I'm not here to see the play." She smiled, as if the idea amused her.

"How'd you get in?" Max took a few steps toward her, clutching the sword.

"Joel sent me a key, in case—"

"Why would Dad send you a key? Who are you? What are you doing in our house?"

"I've come to help out. Your father told me Emily would need help with the house, since she'll be directing the summer interns while he teaches that seminar next month, and then I heard about the accident..." She shrugged, fading a little. "I'm his sister, Rose."

"Okay, I know Dad has been talking to you, but... you expect me to believe you just agreed to come and play housekeeper?"

"Yes, I do," Rose half-whispered.

Max did see a resemblance between her stepfather and his sister, despite her bird-like stature and his strong build. Joel would be disappointed if she didn't welcome his sister, no matter how many years of silence had endured between him and his family.

"Hey, are you okay?" Max asked, concern forced through her when the woman swayed a little, as if she might faint.

Rose Weinberg nodded, eyes wide in her pale face. Her lips twitched close to a smile. "Could I have some water, please? It's been something of a long trip." She sank down on one of the less cluttered couches and wrapped her arms around herself.

Max scurried into the kitchen and ran the tap a few seconds. She couldn't find a single clean glass in any of the cupboards, gave up, and tried the dishwasher. By some miracle, it was full of clean dishes. She could have sworn Joe said the dishwasher was full of dirty dishes this morning.

She filled the glass, paused to consider ice, then shook her head and hurried back to the living room. Rose murmured her thanks as she took the glass and sipped. Max sat on the couch facing her and picked up the sword.

The quiet left her nothing to do but think and watch the woman. What was she doing there? Besides the stated reason?

Max played with the sword, turning it over and over in her hands. The soft smacking of wood against flesh broke through Rose's daze. She watched Max for a few seconds.

"Do you have to play with that thing?"

"It's only wood." Max gave the sword a deft twist, making it pinwheel up in the air and come down to slap flat into her hand. "It's like a security blanket."

"A rather dangerous kind of security blanket." Rose set the glass down on the hardwood floor between the rag rug and the front of the couch.

"The best kind."

"Of course." She closed her eyes and rubbed them. She looked more tired. "Joel and Emily, how are they?"

"Dad's conscious, at least." Max shrugged and tried to keep the gravel from her voice.

There was nothing that could persuade her to welcome this woman — or any member of her stepfather's family. They had disowned him. He had changed his name from Rubenstein to Randolph, and worked hard to make a name in the theater so they would regret what they had done. The long years of silence had felt like buffers between their cozy little family and Joel's bitter past. Until now.

"I'd like to see him." Rose looked around the cavernous room, taking in the shelves of props and makeup, partially hidden by curtains Emily had made years ago, the racks of costumes, filing cabinets full of scripts, the makeup tables, and jumble of mismatched sofas and chairs.

Max wondered how she saw it. Knowing so little about her stepfather's family, besides phrases like "old-world traditions" and "richer than Midas and twice as stingy," she had little clue of how this interloper viewed the comfortable mess of the living room. Probably, Rose was appalled. Her two choices were to turn her back on her brother's chaotic life and flee to Boston or try to settle in and change things. Max hoped she was offended and would run away immediately, if not sooner.

"Sure. Visiting hours started at 10:00, so you can see Dad and catch a plane out, get home in time for dinner. No trouble."

"No trouble." Rose shook her head again, managing a more real smile. "You don't like me much, do you?"

"Considering I never even met you until today?" Max shrugged.

"Yes, there is that." She raised her head and looked around the room. "Joel told me about this place, but never in my wildest dreams did I imagine..." She got up and moved to the costume rack. She examined the puffed sleeve of a dress encrusted with gold sequins.

"You don't know much about theater, do you?" She followed her, putting the dress back into place when the woman moved on.

"I know more than you think. Joel never talked about me much, did he?" Rose wandered over to the makeup table and picked up bottles and brushes, examining them as she talked.

"Enough to know your name and his family threw him out."

"Joel ran away from home to follow his dreams. When he came back home a success, the stubborn old man wouldn't let him in the house. What did he tell you about it?"

"About that much." Max paused as the backstage door opened.

No one was supposed to come through there during off hours, and now it seemed everyone used it for entering the house. Now, Jeremy crept through. Where Max and Rose stood, partially hidden by the tall mirrors of the makeup tables, he couldn't see them.

He had a bloody nose and cut lip and from the dark swelling, he would soon have a beauty of a black eye. His shirt had streaks of blood, grass stains and mud. Despite his state, he looked pleased with himself. Max hoped whoever he fought looked as bad.

Jeremy didn't see them, even after he paused in the doorway and looked around the room. A grin brightened his filthy face. He nodded, then started up the winding stairs situated between the kitchen door and the backstage door.

"Jeremiah Andrew Randolph," Max said, trying not to yell. "What happened to you?"

Jeremy stopped with one foot in the air. He slowly lowered the foot, then turned. His mouth opened in wordless query and he stared at Rose. He tilted his head toward her, giving Max a questioning look. She shook her head, hoping he would wait for answers.

"Hey, Max," he said. He crossed the room and handed her a note clutched in his hand. It only took her a few seconds to read it. Somehow, she was not surprised.

"Get upstairs and change your clothes. I'll bring some ice and we'll talk about this."

"But—" He gestured at Rose, who watched with a bemused expression and didn't offer a word of comment.

"This guest can wait." Max pointed at the stairs. As he started for the stairs, she muttered, "If there's any ice left in the house." She waited until Jeremy reached the top of the stairs, then turned back to Rose. "Well, Mrs. Weinberg, you can see we're pretty busy here."

"Fighting in school?" Her voice sounded a touch amused. "Is this how my brother brings up his sons?"

"No." Max kept her voice sweet despite the knots growing inside. "Dad doesn't bring *us* up like that at all. If Jeremy was fighting, there was a good reason." She silently added, *Jeremy, there had better be a good reason.* She almost tossed the note onto the makeup table, then glanced at Rose and jammed it into her pocket. "Make yourself comfortable. This might take a while."

Max trudged up the stairs. She would prolong the talk and hope the silence would intimidate the woman downstairs so she would give up and leave. She wished she could close her eyes, count to ten, and open them to find this had all been a bad dream.

She stopped in the bathroom on the way to Jeremy's room and ran the water cold before soaking a washcloth in it, because she had forgotten the ice. Jeremy and Joe shared the largest bedroom, though Joe often begged to be given the guest room. Since they needed a place to board guest stars, their parents had deemed it best to leave the room open. Max wished now the house had one less bedroom. The lack of a guest room might send the visitor away when her cold reception hadn't.

That was neither here nor there, Max conceded, as she stepped into the room lined with musician and car posters, a single tall, narrow bookshelf, two desks and dressers, and the bunk bed. She had to tend to Jeremy's battle scars and the reason for them.

Chapter Five

Jeremy sat on the bottom bunk, touching the swelling around his eye. He flinched as Max came in and shut the door. He gestured downstairs, through the floor. "Who's that?"

"She says she's Dad's sister."

"Aunt Rose?" Jeremy's voice squeaked, making Max flinch. "What's she doing here?"

"She claims Dad asked her to come help out. Can you believe that?"

"Yeah." He grinned when her mouth dropped open. "Dad never blamed her. I guess if she's here, she doesn't blame him, either."

"I hate it when you're logical," Max growled. She dug the note out of her pocket. "According to Mr. Jenkins, the other boys started it." She tossed the note into the wastebasket and handed him the cloth. "At least it's cold. I forgot the ice."

"I couldn't just stand there, Max. They were making fun of Mom." He closed both eyes and spread the cool cloth over his entire face.

"Mom?" She fought a sense of nausea. On top of everything else, now what were people saying about her mother? And would those slime dog reporters hear about the fight at school between Emily Keeler's son and the town morons?

"They said she couldn't have been such a good actress like the guys on TV say. They said she came here to hide because she was so bad. That's why she teaches and directs instead of acting—but Mom acts all the time!" His voice came muffled through the cloth.

"I know. They just don't want to remember." Max tried to smile, simply to fight the aching. This was worse than she had imagined. "I dare you to find me any ninth-grader who can be a decent drama critic. Besides you," she added, when Jeremy squawked and lowered the cloth.

"But Max—"

"Jeremy, I'm the reason Mom left Hollywood." She waited, holding his gaze until his eyes lost their fire. "Mom taught acting because it gave her better hours for raising a baby all by herself—and better, steadier pay, too. She did a lot of commercials. So did I, before I grew out of my cute stage." She waited, but Jeremy was still upset enough not to take advantage of the opening for a barbed comment. "She could have gone back to Hollywood any time she wanted, but she chose to set up the theater here with Dad and raise us and make some good theater where ordinary people could enjoy it. Her *choice*, not because she was stuck doing it, understand?"

"Yeah," he grumbled, looking a little ashamed under all the wet dirt and abrasions.

Max tousled his hair. "Come on downstairs and we'll get that ice."

They arrived downstairs to see Rose return with two tapestry suitcases the size of small steamer trunks. She stood a moment, meeting their gazes, face blank. It reminded Max of times she disobeyed and her stepfather just stood there, no clue as to how he would react, giving her a chance to either patch up the problem or dig herself deeper into trouble. She hated how this woman reminded her of him.

"I left my things in the lobby when I got here," Rose finally said. She set the suitcases down and straightened her hair a little. "Hello, Jeremy. I'm your Aunt Rose. Your father asked me to come out here and help with the house this summer." She met Max's eyes again. "I talked to Joel on Saturday. I guess he never got a chance to tell you."

"Lousy timing," Max said. She led Jeremy to the kitchen to get ice.

Rose followed. All three were silent as Max dug the last few ice cubes from the tray in the freezer side of the stainless steel refrigerator and wrapped them in a towel for Jeremy.

"He said Emily would need help around the house," Rose went on. "I'm a good cook and I like to clean, and I can at least make things easier on you."

"This isn't a job interview."

"Joel mentioned you had a deadline to meet and a book that was giving you some trouble, and he didn't want to put extra burdens on you."

"He must have talked to her, Max," Jeremy broke in with a chuckle. "Nobody else knows about that stupid book." He grinned and ducked when Max slapped his shoulder. "Come on, we have rehearsal tonight and you have that book to finish and it's either you cooking or me, once we run out of casseroles. We don't want to die of food poisoning, do we?" He leaned back against her, making his face into what their mother called his "sorrowful puppy look."

Despite herself, Max grinned. She felt too tired to argue and wondered if it would be smart to even try. Her stepfather probably had asked his sister to come help. Her reluctance was most likely from anger that Joel hadn't told *her* about his arrangements.

She looked at Jeremy, then at Rose. Both watched her with quiet, hopeful expressions, waiting. She thought of cleaning and cooking and feeding people at rehearsals, her book, and more time to write if she didn't have to cook or clean or make sure the boys didn't beat up on each other when her back was turned. Max envisioned Rose giving up after a week of struggling with the boys, admitting defeat and running back to Boston.

"Why not?" Max said, shrugging. "Mrs. Weinberg—"

"Can't you call me Aunt Rose?" the woman asked, smiling with a touch of pained hope.

"The boys can—they already do—whenever Dad talks about you. But Dad's only my stepfather."

"I know. Well." She looked around the kitchen in a mix of eagerness and fatigue. "It'll be a trial run, all right? For all of us. What do you want me to do first?"

"Supper?" Jeremy suggested, prompting a chuckle from Rose and a sigh from Max.

"Let me do the shopping, will you?" Max rubbed at her eyes while she thought. "I'll take care of that in a couple hours. Jeremy, you help her settle in. Show her around, explain what happens during rehearsal so she doesn't get run over tonight. And change your clothes."

"Yes, ma'am!" He stood up stiff and straight and sketched a salute. Before either one could react, he scurried out into the living room and snatched up the larger of Rose's suitcases. "We live upstairs, Aunt Rose," he called, above the banging of the swinging door. Max and Rose followed him out.

"As soon as you're ready, we can go visit Dad."

"Yeah?" Jeremy hurried up the stairs, his eyes bright with anticipation.

Rose even looked eager. Max wondered what it was like for her, to be separated from her brother all these years.

But they weren't really that separated, were they, if he could call and ask her to help out?

Max considered a family division that would keep her from her brothers for so many years. She shuddered as she sank down into the couch to wait.

Rose followed Jeremy up the stairs at a much slower pace, visibly not trusting the curving, wrought iron contraption. The boy waited at the top.

"Aunt Rose," he said as she reached the landing, "can you make those cookies with the nuts and honey inside?"

~~~~~

Joel was sitting up when they reached his hospital room. He didn't have a roommate yet, and Max was grateful. She didn't want anyone to overhear their family's personal business, to repeat to the newspapers. He was reading a newspaper and raking a hand through his iron-gray mop of hair in irritation. He looked almost normal, except for the bruises and cuts, the puffiness marring his square-cut features and the dark circles ringing his eyes. And the cast from his toes to his hip.

That, and the absence of her mother sitting beside him, comforting and teasing him back to health.
~~~~~

Emily was upstairs in ICU, but Max refused to take Rose to see her until she was sure how the woman would fit into their family. If she would fit at all.

"Up for some visitors?" Max asked, voice cracking a bit.

"Hey, my favorite people." A grin brightened Joel's face. He slapped the newspaper down onto the blankets covering his lap and the cast. "Jeremiah, is that a black eye?" He affected a gruff tone, but he didn't have the strength for acting. His arms opened wide.

Jeremy ran to his father, hugged him hard, then skittered backward a little, panic on his face. Joel just laughed and held out his arms for Max. Then the laugh broke when he caught sight of Rose, hovering in the doorway.

The hunger on the woman's face made Max regret her suspicions. If she wasn't looking at love and sorrow and years of hurting, she knew she would never recognize them again.

"Rosy?" Joel pushed against the mattress to sit up straight. "He let you come?"

"Not exactly..." Rose shook her head and let out a wobbly little laugh. "You look good, considering."

"Yeah, considering." He managed to keep smiling, but Max saw the struggle.

Her stepfather had so much to overcome, emotionally and physically. Joel wasn't the kind of man who dwelled on losses and pain, but Max knew the accident would haunt him. Anything that helped him recover, she would welcome.

"Aunt Rose said she came to help us out," Jeremy offered, when the silence stretched a few seconds too long.

"That's great." Joel cleared his throat and rubbed at one eye. "Well, do I get a hug from my big sister, or don't I?"

He met Max's eyes over Rose's shoulder. His look held pleading and implicit trust in her, mixed with his pain. Max nodded. Yes, she would make sure everything was handled as he wished. She promised to accept Rose—for his sake.

They talked about the theater and rehearsals. Joel approved the newest decisions Max had made and the list of needed supplies she had brought for him to look over. He was smug when Max reported that Daniel Morgan had agreed to take the part of Petruchio, despite some misgivings. He didn't mention Jeremy's black eye again, and Max was grateful. She didn't want him to know Jeremy had fought because of cruel things said about Emily.

When Joel started wilting, Max urged everyone out of the room, and he didn't protest.

"Joe said he'd come by after school," she said, after brushing a kiss across his forehead. "You think of anything you need, tell him then."

"Got it." Joel squeezed her hand and let her go. "It's going to be okay, Max."

"I know, Dad. You just get out of that bed, okay?"

~~~~~

"I'll go shopping later," Max said, as she parked her car behind the theater. "Why don't you take your aunt on a tour, show her what things are like behind the scenes, okay? I have a few things I need to get done before I go out."

"Yeah, sure." Jeremy nodded and fought a sigh. He couldn't understand why his sister wouldn't call her Aunt Rose.

Rose seemed not to notice, but Jeremy suspected she was just as good an actor as his father. He decided to give Max a lecture later, when she was in a better mood and wouldn't get sarcastic. For now, he waited until Rose got out of the car, then pointed at the back door for the scene shop.

"You want to start the tour over there?"

"That sounds fine." Rose watched Max vanish through the kitchen door, then she turned around and gave Jeremy a bright smile. "Let's see — I had a map your father sent me — that's where you build the sets, right?"

As they walked through the scene shop into the backstage area, up the aisle to the sound and lighting booth and the upstairs storage areas, Jeremy gave Rose the expanded version of the tour he usually gave sightseers. The Homespun Theater was actually four buildings, joined to make room for acting, set construction, and living space for the Randolph family. Another building on the side held Homespun Printing.

The auditorium portion of the theater was a massive old barn, still on its original raw stone foundations but vastly upgraded and renovated. The downstairs portion that once held equipment and a collection area for animal droppings now held the laundry and costume shop and storage. The scene shop was an old stable, moved over on skids from an estate four miles down the road. Another, smaller barn had been added to the east side to create the lobby and box office. The main body of the Randolph home was an old firehouse that once stood in the historic section of Tabor Heights. Joel had bought it just days short of being condemned and had it brought over and attached to the barn. He, Emily and Max lived two years in the downstairs rooms of the old barn until the renovated firehouse was livable. They moved upstairs only four weeks before Joe was born.

The Green Room had been established in the living room, along with makeup and the costume shop. Emily worked as a seamstress on the side. She altered clothes and designed originals for people in town for special occasions. She always made a tidy bundle during homecoming and prom, either renting out the fancy dresses and tuxedoes in the theater's costume shop or designing new ones.
~~~~~

The old pole for the firemen remained in the house as a support for the roof and an easy exit from upstairs for the adventurous. A long gallery had been added around the ceiling of the living room, to provide more storage space—and a practice balcony for romantic scenes. It was also convenient for hanging *pinatas* or drying laundry.

"Dad's just about the greatest carpenter in the whole world," Jeremy said, pointing out the ornamental arches in the ceiling of the barn/theater. They kept the much-repaired roof from crashing down on the patrons and added to the ambiance.

"Yes, he was very good. Our father constantly wavered between demanding Joel go into law with him or letting him become a woodworker. He was very proud of your father's skill. Fine cabinetry is a respectable way to make a living in our old neighborhood." Rose sighed, looking out over the empty seats below, the nearly complete set for *Taming of the Shrew,* and the shadows filling most of the theater.

"I think Dad likes making things even better than directing."

"When are the summer interns arriving?"

"You know a lot about this place." He leaned back against the wall of the balcony and grinned up at her.

"Your father writes very long, detailed letters."

Various colleges across the country sent promising students to have hands-on experience during the summer. Homespun Theater had a reputation for quality performances and good instruction from professional actors and technicians. Joel had access to quality technicians and actors at minimum wages; the students had training they could proudly put on their resumes; and the various boarding houses and shops in Tabor Heights welcomed the extra income from the steady flow of students and tourists.

"He told you a lot about us, didn't he?"

"Enough that I don't feel like a total stranger here." Rose gestured toward the stairs. "I never dreamed I'd ever get to see this place," she said as they started down.

"Aunt Rose, are you going to get into trouble for coming to stay with us?" They reached the bottom of the stairs and headed up the aisle to the stage.

"Trouble? What makes you think that?"

"Because Dad got kicked out for becoming an actor. Dad said as far as our grandfather's concerned, he doesn't have a son." He frowned as more questions came to him.

"Well, your grandfather is from the old school, but I think family is more important than tradition and rules."

"What kind of tradition?" he asked, as they headed back behind stage.

"Hmm?" Rose turned on her heel, tilting her head back to study the half-lowered grid and the lights hanging from it in stages of preparation and repair.

"It was some stupid tradition that made our grandfather kick Dad out of the family, wasn't it? Won't you get kicked out for helping us?"

"Old World tradition gave fathers power to disinherit any child who rebelled. Joel was considered dead long ago." She chuckled, managing to sound only a little forced. "How could I get in trouble for helping someone who doesn't exist?" Rose shrugged. "Besides, after twelve years as a widow, it's time I got out of my father's house and did something worthwhile with my life. I'm tired of sewing circles and gossip."

"Tradition sounds stupid." Jeremy swallowed against the thick feeling like tears in his throat. He had got into that fight to avoid the feeling.

"No, not entirely." Rose rubbed at her eyes. In the dim work lights, a few tears glistened before she wiped them away. "I know there are a great many traditions here I certainly wouldn't change. One tradition is plenty of goodies for munching during rehearsals. The other is the opening night feast. How long do I have to produce that miracle?" she asked with a wobbly grin.

"Next Tuesday."

"That's a little time, at least."

"But we don't have anything to eat. I mean, we do. Everybody in town has been bringing food, but you get really sick of casseroles and other junk like that. It's bad. Max is going shopping, but shopping always makes her grumpy. Especially if she's fighting writer's block."

"My surprise entrance didn't help matters any," Rose murmured, nodding. "Tell you what—I need a tour of the neighborhood, and I have my rental car until the end of the week. Why don't we go shopping?"

When they went back into the house, Max was hard at work, the cursor dancing across the screen at a pace closer to normal than in many long days. Jeremy pressed a finger to his lips to signal Rose to be quiet. She nodded and tiptoed up the stairs to get her purse. They crept out of the house without making Max pause once in her labors.

~~~~~

An hour-and-a-half later, their arms full of groceries, they came through the kitchen door. The swinging door into the living room was propped open for ventilation. Jeremy heard Max tapping on the keyboard, slower now. He turned to grin at Rose as she followed him inside and ran into the corner of the kitchen table. The bag caught and tore. Six economy-sized cans of vegetables clattered to the floor.

A yelp exploded from Max and she darted into the kitchen, eyes wide, shoulders shaking, her wooden sword in her hands. Max stared at Rose and Jeremy while the cans rolled across the uneven floor until they
~~~~~

fetched up against the kickboard under the sink.

"I said I would get the groceries." Max's eyes held anger, betrayal and shame.

"You were so busy. I thought I should get to know the neighborhood, and Jeremy said he would show me around." Rose rested a hand on Jeremy's shoulder, giving him a companionable squeeze. "We had a good time doing the shopping, didn't we?"

"Yeah." He grinned at Max, hoping she would take the hint. "There's stuff in the grocery store I never knew was there."

"That's real nice." Max bent over and picked up a few cans. "Just how long were you planning on staying, Mrs. Weinberg?"

"Come on, Max!" Jeremy bent over to help. What was wrong with her?

"As long as I'm needed," Rose said in a voice too soft to reveal feelings. She took the cans from Jeremy and set them on the counter.

Max looked at her back, closed her eyes a moment, then turned and left the kitchen. Jeremy followed her. She sat at the computer again and stared at the screen.

"I like her, Max," Jeremy whispered, clenching his fists to keep from hitting her. "She's a lot like Dad."

"I noticed. But, Jeremy... Forget it. You wouldn't understand."

"I don't think you do, either. Aunt Rose is great."

"She's *your* aunt." Max turned and met his gaze, glare for glare. "Why don't you go help her take over the kitchen, okay? I have to get ready for rehearsal."

"Sure." Jeremy wandered back to the kitchen, his mind racing with questions. What was wrong with Max? Something had to scare her, because she usually didn't get mad unless she was scared.

What was frightening about Aunt Rose?

~~~~

On the Iowa-Nebraska border, Tony got off at the first exit that offered him a brand of gas he recognized. He took a change of clothes with him into the bathroom and washed up the best he could, using paper towels and liquid soap from the dispenser. Maybe he should stop at a hotel tonight and sleep in a real bed and get a shower, at the very least. The urgency to get back to Tabor Heights and Max fought down that idea every time it occurred.

He bought a six-pack of Mountain Dew for the sake of the caffeine, silently grumbling at the jacked-up prices at the highway convenience store and that he couldn't find Jolt when he really needed it. He added a pack of beef jerky to his purchases. Protein and fat would help him keep going when the sugar and caffeine ran out. If he only stopped for bathroom breaks, he would be home some time tomorrow morning.
~~~~

Hopefully, Max would be so glad to see him, she wouldn't mind how bad he smelled or looked.

"Bet she'll punch my lights out," he muttered as he climbed back into his car. He envisioned kissing her—not just holding her tight—until neither one of them could breathe.

Tony grinned. That first kiss might just be worth getting a black eye or a bloody nose. And Max had to know he was serious, right?

~~~~~

Max had to go back to the hospital. She had forgotten to bring Joel the revised script, with the cuts she had made to compensate for the casting changes so close to opening night.

She knew Joel would approve whatever she chose to do, so the script was a poor excuse. She also knew her stepfather needed to talk with her, take care of little details and ask questions he couldn't ask with her brothers or his sister around.

"Please, God—things are just starting to get better," she whispered after she had put her Cavalier into park in the lot by the west wing of the hospital. "I'll be nice to her, for Dad's sake. He did ask her to come. But everything inside me says she's going to make trouble. We can't take any more."

Her eyes ached with the pressure of tears she refused to release. Max jerked the key around in the ignition, killing the engine. She jammed the keys into her jeans pocket and scrambled out of the car. She couldn't afford to sit and cry.

"Hey, Shakespeare!" a sandpaper voice called from across the parking lot.

Max swallowed a yelp of surprise, caught with one foot on the ground. She took a deep breath and turned to look. She knew that voice.

Maggie sauntered across the parking lot, dressed in black hi-tops, camouflage pants and sleeveless gray sweatshirt, and a grubby robin's egg blue stocking cap over her shoulder-length tangle of iron gray hair. The children at the Mission's daycare center loved her. Ordinarily, Max loved talking to Maggie, too. But not now.

"How's that new book of yours coming along, huh?" Maggie slouched to a stop and leaned against the post supporting the chain link fence around the lot. She reached into the army surplus backpack that hung from her belt, and drew out a can of ginger ale, dripping with condensation. "Got it just for you."

"Thanks," Max mumbled. Her throat ached for the drink. The memories aroused by the dented can hurt. When she was sick, her mother always brought her ginger ale.

"Been having it rough, ain't ya?"

"Sort of." She lifted the can to her nose, inhaling the first fireworks of
~~~~~

sparkling fizz.

"No 'sort of' about it." Maggie snorted. "Everybody's leaning on you, kid. Everybody expects you to take care of everything. They don't know they're being selfish—but that's the way people are, y'know?" She thumped Max on her biceps. Fortunately, not the arm holding the can of ginger ale. "You're a good kid, Shakespeare. Just lighten up, okay? Gotta let somebody help you out once in a while."

"Like you are right now?" Max toasted the town eccentric with the can, earning a bright grin in response.

"Just doing what the Boss says to do." She pointed upward with her thumb. "Well, I gotta meet a cat about a dog. You remember what I said, hear me?"

"Sure. And thanks." Max watched Maggie strut down the driveway and across the lawn. In another moment, she vanished into the trees and afternoon haze. When Max headed into the hospital, she could actually smile.

Maggie always seemed to arrive at the right moment. She might not make much sense sometimes. Other times, she made too much sense.

Pastor Dave, one of the associate ministers at church, was just leaving Joel's room when Max got off the elevator. The tall, bony blond man saw her and paused in the hall. He looked back through the door of Joel's room, then shrugged and grinned and continued down the hall.

"He's doing just great," Dave said as he and Max passed each other. "Says he's coming over to do his magic show for the kids just as soon as he's allowed out."

"That'd be nice, but ..." Max grinned back at him, tilting her head to meet his eyes.

At nearly seven feet tall, Dave was constantly being asked to play basketball—but only by people who didn't know him. He was as awkward as he was bony.

"I know. Got to let him make his plans. Part of healing." Dave winked and scurried to catch the elevator, waving good-bye with his dog-eared Bible.

Max took a deep breath as she turned to enter Joel's room. She did look forward to seeing him do his magic routines again.

Chapter Six

Joel didn't believe Max's excuse about the script any more than she thought he would. He smiled, flipped through the pages, and nodded and 'hmm'ed a few times.

"Looks fine to me." He handed the sheaf of pages back to her. "I don't know why I worried about taking time off. You can handle anything."

"Right." Max sank down into the chair next to his bed.

"What's really bothering you?" Joel leaned back against his pillows, not quite hiding his sigh of weariness.

"I — is it really okay that she's here?" She hated how her voice took on a whine. Max knew she sounded just like she had when her parents told her Joe was on the way, and she wouldn't understand why she couldn't go on being the only child.

"It's very okay." Memories made his eyes and voice soft. "Rose needs us as much as we need her right now. Her whole world was wrapped up in taking care of me and our father after my mother died, and then she had Morris... Surprised me a little, how much it hurt her to lose him." Joel stopped, swallowing audibly. "See, our father was Old Country all the way. A lot of guys wanted to date her, but she wasn't allowed. Our father wouldn't let her go to college. He had a husband in mind for her, and he wasn't going to let her be ruined with independent notions."

"Dad, this is the twenty-first century."

"I know. And arranged marriages are still going on all over the planet, so don't get that superior tone, young lady." He grinned and tapped the end of her nose in rebuke. "Rose obeyed and married a man she'd never met until a month before the wedding. She liked Morris and he was good to her, and when he died, she —" Joel's voice cracked. "She took it hard." He turned his head away, toward the open curtains, where the afternoon was just starting to turn scarlet and gold. "If I had lost Em... thank God for every little mercy," he said, his whisper strained.

"Dad?" Max got out of the chair and leaned into the bed to wrap her arms around him.

She needed that. She hadn't done more than touch his hands or give gentle hugs, afraid to add to the damage from the car rolling over and over. Max felt a band of tension leave her chest as she held tight to her stepfather and felt his whole body shudder with silent tears.

The sun just started to gleam in the upper right corner of the window before Joel caught his breath, wiped his face, and gently loosened Max's arms from around his chest. He met her eyes, managed a shaking smile, and gave her a playful shove back to her chair.

"It's going to be all right, kiddo."

"I know." She rubbed at her eyes, fighting tears.

"Take care of Rose. She risked a lot coming to help us. I almost didn't ask her, and then your mother said she was sure it was time..." Joel pushed himself back further into his flattening pillows. "I don't know how she got our father to let her come, but it probably cost her plenty."

"Okay, Dad. Jeremy's trying to talk her into making those nutty honey cookies he's crazy about, and she's baking for rehearsal tonight. Guess we do need her." Max hoped she looked as casual as she sounded.

"Bring some of those cookies when you visit tomorrow, okay? The food here isn't worth throwing out. And bring my Bible study books. I might as well get a head start on those classes I'm supposed to teach."

"Which ones? You have about thirty books on your study shelf now." More heaviness left her chest as she teased him. Joel was constantly buying Bible reference books and then complaining that he never had enough time to read them.

"Then it's a good thing I have time now, isn't it?"

Max dragged her ever-present notebook from her purse and wrote down everything Joel wanted for the rest of his hospital stay. At the back of her mind, she marveled at how much energy he had. She knew part of it came from all the prayers from their friends. Part of it was Joel's way of coping with his worry for Emily.

On the way home, Max wondered what kind of trouble Rose had made for herself, agreeing to help her brother against their father's wishes. What would it take to get back in that domineering old man's good graces?

Maybe the more important question was whether the nasty old patriarch knew he had two grandsons, and if he wanted to see them.

Maybe dominate their lives, like he had tried to dominate their father?

~~~~~

Rose reached out slowly with the hand not holding the phone and gripped the edge of the butcher block kitchen counter. It didn't stop the spinning sensation in her head and chest.

"Are you still there, Rosy?" Hannah asked. Her voice faded out for a few seconds, then came back strong with a crackle of long-distance static.

"Yes, I'm still here." She looked around the kitchen. Not a chair within reach. Rose took a tighter grip on the edge of the counter.

The beef stew on the back burner of the stove rattled its lid and sent up wisps of fragrant steam. The cookies for rehearsal cooled in perfumed clouds of chocolate and peanut butter. The domestic scene gave her some
~~~~~

sense of solidity, despite the certainty that the floor would disintegrate under her feet at any moment.

"I should have expected him to react like that," Rose continued. She managed a chuckle that sounded almost normal. Joel wasn't the only good actor in the family.

"But he threw all your cross stitch out onto the lawn, and your books and your clothes—in the pouring rain!"

"They're all replaceable." Her voice wobbled. Rose hoped it sounded like laughter, not the leading edge of hysterics. She hadn't been hysterical since Morris was shot, an innocent bystander during a robbery.

"Aunt Rose?" Joe hurtled into the kitchen, tugging a sweatshirt on over his tousled blond head. "How soon until we eat?" He saw her with the phone to her ear and grinned, shrugging an apology just like his father had when he was a rambunctious, skinny high school junior.

"As soon as your sister gets back," Rose said, a hand over the receiver. "Get Jeremy, would you, and set the table?"

"Sure." Joe ducked back out the swinging door into the living room.

"Are you going to be all right, Rose?" Hannah asked.

"Fine. I'm with my family now. How could I be anything but fine?"

Rose insisted, silently, she would indeed be all right. Her brother was recovering, the doctors held hope for Emily, and their sons had welcomed her with open arms. Max was another matter, but Rose understood how she felt. This was like when Morris' widowed mother came to live with them for two years before she died. Both women had been reserved and polite, making the best of it for the sake of the one they both loved.

"You have everything at your place, Hannah?" she asked, then smiled as the woman insisted, with a touch of hurt feelings, that of course she had rescued every stitch of her dear friend's belongings. "Hold them until I can send for them, would you? I don't know how long it'll be before I know where I'm going from here, but... you know how it is."

"No, I don't." Hannah let out her usual cackling laugh. "But I do know I'm glad you're finally free of that old ogre. Everybody is laughing at him behind his back. I'm surprised if anybody at all speaks to him at temple for the next few weeks. They all know how horribly he treated you and Joel and—"

"I really have to get going, dear," Rose broke in, as Max came through the back door. "I'll call you later when we know better how Joel and Emily are doing. Take care, and give my love to Abe, will you?"

"Friends back home?" Max asked, after Rose hung up.

"They're worried about Joel." Rose pulled her lips into an approximation of a smile and crossed the creaking linoleum floor to the stove to check her stew.

~~~~~
~~~~~

After the first ten minutes of rehearsal, Max let herself relax. The cast and crew had settled into the changes, and she sent up a dozen silent prayers of thanks for that as the evening went on. She also thought silent prayers of thanks every time she turned around and saw all her father's theater students who had turned out to help.

They were to do ten performances of *Taming of the Shrew*, beginning Tuesday. Joel had been director, as well as playing Petruchio. He had no understudy. Joel had never needed an understudy. Legend at the university said he was unstoppable, and Max knew that was nearly true. The General had often joked that it would take an earthquake and a tidal wave to keep Joel Randolph from finishing a theater project. Max now knew that wasn't true — it took a drunk driver at the wheel of a truck.

The only person in town who had the experience, the stage presence, and the comic flare to handle Petruchio was Dr. Daniel Morgan, the third member of the Butler-Williams University theater department trinity. Fortunately, it had only taken minor pleading and teasing to get Morgan to agree to take over the part. Max was pleased to see Lynette Teague came along to help with costumes and prompt him on his lines.

Max took over as director. She gratefully let Truman Dempsey take over coaching the many smaller parts. Jake Holt had treated half the cast to his traditional snit fit and pouting session when he found out he wouldn't be shifted from playing Lucentio to Petruchio, but he seemed to be in good spirits tonight. It irked her that she had to work around his ego. Joel had been able to handle Jake and bring out some shining moments of a true gift. Max doubted she could do that. She just prayed that Jake's ego would take a rain check for the run of *Shrew*.

A shiver of apprehension hit as she considered what would happen if Jake quit just before opening night. Joe was his understudy, and she was sure her brother could handle the sudden elevation to secondary romantic lead. The problem was, Joe wasn't sure of himself.

Rose had settled into the kitchen, found the vacuum cleaner and straightened out the living room before the cast arrived. Max knew she would have resented the way Rose acted as if she had always been there, if she herself hadn't been so busy checking lights and fuses and ropes between dinner and rehearsal. That, and the wonderful, satisfied heaviness from tender beef stew and warm brownies in her stomach.

The hairs stood up on her neck at how quickly her brothers accepted and welcomed their aunt. Yes, Max admitted, Rose was a lot like their father. That didn't automatically give her a place in their home as if she had lived there for years, did it? What happened when Rose packed up to go back home to Boston? How much would it hurt the boys when she left?

Max was grateful for the distraction and ritual chaos of rehearsal. Gretchen descended on the makeup table and costume racks, hitting them like a reverse cyclone to put everything into manageable order. She and Emily most often shared control over makeup and costumes, so there was no hitch there. Everybody was to try on costumes and makeup tonight, to give them time to make adjustments and repairs.

Audrey fluttered around, making sure everyone had updated copies of the script. It always amazed Max how she could be a little klutzy in normal life but transformed utterly as soon as she had a script in her hand, or an audience. Della glided through the usual chaos like an old-fashioned ocean liner, answering the questions Emily usually handled, giving bits of advice and direction to the tech crew as they manhandled pieces of furniture onto the stage. Steve worked well with the tech crew, having already picked up enough to anticipate what needed to be done or moved or put together next. Max thought about the second background check Joel hadn't run on him and told her apprehension to take a hike. They needed Steve right now. Maybe later, when everything settled down, she could get suspicious again and investigate him. That particular concern was so far down on her list, it had fallen off entirely.

Pastor Glenn and Rita arrived late with the picnic-sized spigot cooler from the church. They usually didn't have time to help out at rehearsals unless children from the church were involved. April meant preparations for Bible School and coordinating camp scholarships, along with the usual demands of pastoring Tabor Christian Church. Still, they found the time to help, even if it was just with costumes and cold drinks and finishing the set. Max didn't know how she could thank them properly without embarrassing them and herself. She welcomed this kind of help more than loads of food, with the accompanying casseroles and platters she had to wash and return to their owners.

She fell into her usual duties, running around with a clipboard tucked under one arm, a flashlight hanging from her belt, pens behind both ears, shouting directions over the general din. Max loved it, almost as much as she loved finishing a key scene in a script or book.

The only damper was seeing Rose running back and forth with trays of cookies and cups of tea and lemonade, serving and meeting and laughing and talking with everyone. The entire cast and crew acted like she had been part of the group for years.

Jeremy was safely ensconced in the doorway between the Green Room and box office, taking care of ticket sales, his homework, and the bookkeeping for both the theater and print shop. He was smiling, so Max assumed they would cover costs and have something to live on.

Joe stumbled out of the kitchen, clad in tights and doublet, no boots, sword tucked under one arm and his shirt hanging open because it lacked laces. He had his fourth brownie in one hand and a glass of milk in the other. Max hoped he wouldn't gain any weight before the production started, because that doublet had already been altered four times in the seven years since her mother had made it for a production of *Twelfth Night*.

"Aunt Rose!" Joe swallowed without chewing as he hurried over to the woman.

"Did you get enough to eat?" She held out the tray of cookies, her smile teasing.

"Way more than enough. You are saving my life, you know? I don't know how long we could have gone on casseroles or Jeremy's cooking or whatever Max can—"

He saw Max watching him and stopped with an audible croak. His stricken look almost made her laugh. Max smoothed her lips flat and stepped away to save him the embarrassment.

"I understand, Joe," Rose said. "Thanks. It's nice to have someone to do for."

Max knelt behind a flat painted to look like a raw stone wall, propped up longways against the end of a sofa, and spread her worksheets out on the floor in the clear space between it and the wall. It was a little shadowed, but at least she had some open space to work in and no one would find her for maybe two minutes. She felt the loose floorboard sag under her knee as someone stood on the other side of the flat.

"Jeremy tells me you're his father's sister," Pastor Glenn said. "I didn't know Joel's family was in the area."

"I just arrived today," Rose answered.

Oh, just great. The last thing Max wanted was to hear Rose ingratiate herself with her pastor. There was no way out except directly through the conversation. Max concentrated harder, trying not to listen.

"I'm sure it's a real comfort to the kids, having you here."

"Pastor," Dan Wilson said, coming in from the theater. Max could just see him in the doorway. "Can you help us with a flat that's come loose?"

"I'll be right there." Pastor Glenn chuckled. "Duty calls. Everybody here pitches in for every job."

"I noticed." Rose's voice had a rich sound, like she held back laughter.

"Well, it was nice to meet you. I'll be looking for you in church on Sunday." The board creaked as he started to walk away.

"Well, thank you—but I'm Jewish."

Silence hit, even through the din in the room. Max bit at her hand to keep from laughing. She could imagine the slightly stunned, sheepish look on Pastor Glenn's face. He was fine in the pulpit or coming to someone's rescue in a crisis. He made a great umpire in the church sports leagues and stood up to angry men twice his size and weight. But when he was caught in a flub, especially the silly ones, he stumbled and his brain froze. It made him human, but she still couldn't help laughing, even if it was Rose who did it.

"Oh, ah, well..." He coughed. "So was our Lord." The boards creaked as he hurried away. Max thought his face looked as bright red as his plaid shirt when she glimpsed him, just before he escaped into the theater.

"Our pastor is a wonderful man." Della's low, cultured voice cut through the hubbub as she joined Rose next to the flat. Max swallowed a groan and settled in for a long wait. "A little too concerned about saying the right thing from time to time, but we love him dearly."

Come on, Della — trying to tell her you don't care about public opinion?

"I'm sure he's been a great help." Rose sounded a little stiff. Max sympathized. Della was especially imposing, in costume now, as she worked herself into her "grand lady" character as the Widow.

"Yes. He and his wife are like a second set of parents to all the youth in our church. How long will you be in Tabor Heights? I think you might enjoy some of the ladies' activities in our little community. Bridge, Red Cross Society, a few art classes, literary discussions."

Yeah, Aunt Rose would just love to discuss Gone With the Wind *this summer. Isn't four summers in a row enough?* Max grinned, then choked as she realized she had relaxed enough to refer to her as "Aunt Rose," even if just in her thoughts.

"That sounds wonderful," Rose said. "But things are still up in the air. The children didn't know I was coming and—"

"Didn't know?" Della almost squeaked. Max would have loved to have seen the expression on that matronly, German governess face, but her attention clamped onto Rose's words and the landslide of implications that followed. Sometimes it didn't pay to have an overactive imagination that kept trying to write mystery novels.

"Ah... and I'm not sure if I'll stay or move on and find a place of my own. I'm sure I could find a good job as a cook or something..." Her voice faded out, making Max wonder if she had sidled away from Della. The floor sag hadn't changed, so she couldn't be sure.

"Please. If I'm prying, just tell me." Della's voice gentled. "But may I assume you have nowhere to go?"

"You may assume anything you please." Rose's voice turned to the first thin ice of winter. "I shouldn't discuss family business in public."

"Of course." Silence. Loud enough to muffle the laughter and talk backstage. Della made a soft cough. "If you'll excuse me, I have lines to rehearse." The floor sagged and bowed back as she departed.

Max sat backward, wrapped her arms around her legs and drew them close to her chest as she balanced on her tailbone. Rose had nowhere to go? She knew exactly how that had happened. A mix of emotions pressed against the resentment she had carried since Rose walked into the house; shame, sympathy, and something she feared was a little nasty glee.

No time, she scolded herself. *You have rehearsal. Think about other problems later.*

"Oh, wonderful, a free set of hands!" Rapid footsteps accompanied Audrey's breathy, panicked voice. "Can you help me? Please?"

What is this? Grand Central Station? Max nearly burst out laughing. Of course, it was Grand Central Station—it was backstage in a community theater, with a week until opening night.

"Why, what's the matter?" Rose asked. The floor squeaked and sighed as she walked away. Max gathered her papers for a quick exit.

"Could you help me? My laces snapped all to pieces!"

"You'll have to get all the way out of that dress and put new laces in. Into the dressing room with you." The calm efficiency in Rose's voice impressed Max.

Now would be a good time to exit, before anyone saw her and realized she had been in a perfect spot to eavesdrop. Max emerged from her shadowy spot as Gretchen came from the dressing room. The aging milkmaid hadn't put on her whole Katarina costume. Her patched blue jeans looked ridiculous under the top half of her costume for act one. She crossed the room, a thoughtful frown darkening her sea blue eyes.

"There you are, Max. Where have you been hiding?" Her slow, cultured voice held only a hint of her unidentifiable accent. "I like your aunt."

"Yeah, yeah, I know." Something inside Max snapped. She didn't know whether she should laugh, cry, or start throwing small, heavy objects. "Everybody loves her."

"Well, what's wrong with you?"

"Make a list and take your pick!" Max met Gretchen's stare for a moment, then looked away. Her face warmed. "Sorry. There's a lot of pressure."

"I understand pressure." She slipped an arm around Max's shoulder for a moment, squeezing. "You're doing just fine." She looked down at herself, then breathed a laugh. "Better get into costume, huh?"

"Yeah, go turn into the wicked witch." Max forced a smile onto her face for Gretchen. She hurried backstage as the woman vanished back into the dressing room.

Chapter Seven

Ten minutes later, Audrey dragged a flustered, blushing Rose out onto the stage to confront Max. The woman held a battered copy of the script as if the pages burned her fingers.

"Max!" Audrey called. "Tell her she has to help! I was going over my lines for Bianca and she knew them without even looking. You know how much I need a prompter up until dress rehearsal."

"Yeah, don't we all?" Jake called from where he lounged in the front row, dog-eared script in his hand.

"Your Aunt Rose is just the greatest!" Audrey ignored Jake, as usual. "She knows how to do everything."

"You're a regular lifesaver, no doubt about that." Max took a few steps closer.

Rose looked like she wanted to run away, but there was a light in her eyes that Max recognized. Emily and Joel both had it when they were determined to help no matter how much it hurt them, personally. It hurt Max to meet Rose's eyes.

"Ah... Dad said you always wanted to act. It wouldn't be too much trouble, would it?"

"I'd love to help," Rose said almost in a whisper.

~~~~~

"Okay, want to tell us what's going on?" Joe asked, slipping into the director's booth, backstage right.

"We're re-doing that scene because Truman forgot his props." Max barely glanced up from her script. She tapped the control for her headset. "Shane, could we have that spot turned down about two notches?" The radio crackled, blurring the response from the lighting booth.

"Not that," Jeremy said, stepping up behind Joe. "Where's our sister and what have you done with her?"

"Huh?"

"You sure changed your mind about Aunt Rose in a hurry," Joe said.

"She wants to help—we need help. Dad said she was in a lot of plays when they were kids."

"She's a great cook, but you sure haven't said anything nice about that yet."

"Well..." Max followed the script for a few lines. "How much do you guys know about her?"
~~~~~

"What's that supposed to mean?" Jeremy squeaked, his voice rising loud enough to make all three flinch.

"Joe, you're on in four lines." Max glared at him until he scurried around to the wings, stage left. "Think about what Dad told us." She waited, seeing dawning comprehension on Jeremy's face. "Isn't it weird she was allowed to come help, when everybody in Boston has ignored Dad all these years?"

"She said they wrote and—"

"I believe her." She nearly smiled at Jeremy's look of outrage at the mere suggestion Rose might have lied. "What do you think your grandfather did when she left to help us?"

"You think he threw her out?" His mouth dropped open in a little "o" of dismay. "But she never said anything about that."

"Yeah. I kind of like her for that. Della was starting to give her the third degree and she just barely admitted she didn't have anywhere to go."

"Max, you can't throw her out!"

"Who said I was?" Max took a deep breath and rotated her shoulders a little, fighting the tension that tried to bow them. "Look, I admit we need help. She needs a place. Because of us. Let's just let things ride until we know each other better, okay?"

"You got a deal." Jeremy grinned at her, then surprised her by throwing his arms around her for a fast hug. "Gotta get back to my homework," he mumbled, releasing her.

Despite the shadows, Max saw a hint of blush on his face. Her face felt warm, too. She rested her chin on her fists and let her gaze wander back to the script as her brother left.

Don't know how it's going to work out, but please, God, something has to start going right around here.

~~~~~

Three hours later, Max hunched over her keyboard, struggling for at least three more pages before giving up and going to bed. The living room was in utter chaos. She had sent everybody home or to bed, threatening their necks if they stayed to put away costumes or makeup or props. Sleep was more important than cleanliness and order right then.

Max wished she could sleep. Behind her growing headache and the way her eyes tried to lose focus whenever she blinked, she felt the pressure of all that cleaning waiting to be done. She told herself she would wait until she hit a bad block before she started straightening out the living room. Usually, that killed writer's block instantly.

In the quiet, she barely heard the creak of floorboards upstairs. Max ignored it, certain Joe or Jeremy had come to watch her struggle for a while. If she kept quiet and her back to him, maybe he would go away.

Max's sudden flurry of typing covered the creak and squeak of the
~~~~~

iron treads as Rose came down the stairs. She threaded her way through the chaos of the living room and came up behind Max, her gaze fastened on the computer screen until the typing subsided to a few half-hearted pecks.

A creeping feeling went up Max's back, into her scalp. She turned and met Rose's eyes.

"Maybe if you had Faith slap Grego's face, instead of telling him how much he disgusts her?" she offered with a tentative smile.

"Huh?" Max stared at the woman a moment, then turned back to the screen. She reread what she had just written, then her eyes widened. She typed furiously, deleting and then adding new lines.

Rose tugged over a chair, forced to dislodge a pile of leggings and boots before she could sit. She settled down where she could see the screen without looking over Max's shoulder.

"I've always wondered how you did it," she said, when the flurry of taps slowed.

"Did what?" Max mumbled, eyes on the screen.

"Put out so much work. All your books and screenplays, the contests you enter. And now these romance novels." She smiled when she got only a murmur from Max. "I've read them all. Even the ones that didn't get published."

"You have?" Max turned from the screen. She couldn't see any teasing or mockery in Rose's face. How could anyone with pillow creases and bloodshot eyes make fun of someone else, anyway?

"Oh, yes. And I'm no critic but..."

"After tonight, I can stand some criticism." She offered a smile, which Rose caught.

"Well, what *I* don't like is that your heroes and heroines act too rationally," Rose said, relaxing a little more. "They explain when they should act sometimes. I'd much rather your women break out in tears and run away, or slap somebody, or have your men solve a problem with their fists instead of their brains. Once in a while."

"Brenda and Tony say the same thing. They're writing friends. You'll meet them sooner or later."

"Will I?" She smiled wistfully.

"I haven't exactly welcomed you, but I'm not—I can't really explain everything that's been going through my head." Max let her gaze wander to the screen. If Rose made other helpful suggestions, she would be tempted to *pay* the woman to stay. "Let's keep going like we are, doing what needs doing, and we'll see how it works, okay?"

"That sounds just fine."

Wednesday, April 23

Five a.m. The kitchen door opened and Tony Martin crept into the house. He stood a moment framed in the silvery glow before dawn, rubbed at his eyes, then scratched at the three-day growth of black stubble on his jaw. He almost shut the door before taking the key from the lock. With nearly three days of driving behind him, he looked closer to forty in his travel-wrinkled khakis and baggy sweatshirt, with the computer case and black duffel bag hung over both shoulders.

Tony kicked his duffel into the corner by the swinging door and wandered into the living room, still a shambles from rehearsal. He nodded, smile widening despite his weariness. He picked up a few tubes of lipstick and an eyebrow pencil left on the dining room table and put them back on the makeup table, then fingered some doublets left lying on a couch. He straightened, yawning, and his gaze wandered to Max's computer in the office alcove. His body followed. He leafed through the pages left sitting in plain sight, then touched the case.

"Still warm, huh? That good or bad?" Tony rearranged the first ten pages into order and moved to a couch to sit. He shoved aside some costumes without looking and knocked several swords onto the floor.

Upstairs, Rose swung her legs out of bed and reached for her robe. She thought she had heard something odd downstairs and had been sitting for the last ten minutes, straining her ears to listen to the house. She knew it was ridiculous to worry. An old patchwork building like this was sure to have noises that weren't quite right, yet were perfectly normal. Now, however, she knew that clatter didn't belong.

Five steps took her out the door and down the hall. She rested her hands on the balcony rail, eyes widening as she studied Tony sprawled on the end of the couch, reading. Her hand strayed into the corner filled with bats, fishing poles, tennis racquets and other paraphernalia that had nowhere else to land.

"Aunt Rose?" Joe stumbled down the hall, dressed in torn blue sweatpants. "What're you doing up?"

Rose pointed down into the living room with the baseball bat. Joe's eyes widened at the sight of the bat. Then he looked down. He shook his head, rubbed at his eyes, then stumbled back down the hall. Rose jumped when Joe thumped once on Max's bedroom door. She made shushing noises to him. He grinned and hurried back to the room he and Jeremy shared.

"Anybody up there?" Tony called. He pushed himself to his feet and stepped backward to get a good look at the balcony. "Who are you?" He gaped at Rose in her bathrobe with the baseball bat poised over her shoulder.

"Rose Weinberg." She straightened, faintly irked. This wasn't going at all as she expected. "What are you doing here?"

"What am I—I have a key. What are you doing here?" He put down the pages and took a few steps toward the stairs. Rose shifted her grip on the bat, hefting it into a better position for swinging, and that stopped him.

"I live here."

He gave the room a second sweeping glance. "I know I'm in the right place. No place in the world looks like this house."

Max emerged from her bedroom, tugging her sweatshirt into place and stepped to the railing. Joe and Jeremy joined them a moment later. "Are you okay?"

"Fine!" She pointed at Tony. "Who is he?"

"Tony?" Max let out a shriek and stumbled down the curving steps. Joe followed on her heels.

"Tony!" Jeremy shouted. "All right!" He took the firemen's pole.

"When'd you get back?" Joe demanded as the three reached the bottom of the steps and converged on Tony with arms open, everyone talking at once as they tangled in a group hug.

"Excuse me?" Rose put the bat down and started down the steps. The four separated and watched her descend. "What's going on?"

"Tony's our friend," Joe began, "and—"

"I gathered that. But what is he doing in the house at 5 in the morning—and how did he get in?"

"Tony has a key," Max said. "He uses one of the lofts to write in."

"Another writer. Don't tell me you keep the same strange hours Max does?" Rose caught the odd looks the boys shared and smiled.

"Not lately," Tony said, shaking his head and grinning. "I just got in from—"

"Wait a minute." Jeremy grabbed his arm to stop him. "What *are* you doing here? You're supposed to be teaching."

"It wasn't for me. So, I'm home in good old Ohio. The food—"

"Since when do you care about the food?" Max gestured everyone into the kitchen. "As long as it doesn't crawl off your plate, I've never heard you complain."

"Be nice, or you don't get the presents I brought for everybody."

"What'd you get me?" Jeremy demanded, leading the way into the kitchen.

"Not before I get some answers!" Rose pushed her way into the kitchen and spread her arms, blocking the way between the table and the refrigerator. She waited a moment. All four gave her matching looks of confused innocence. "First, what's his name?"

"Sorry." Tony chuckled. He held out his hand. Rose shook it after a slight hesitation. "Tony Martin."

"Also Antonia Maxwell, depending on what part of the bookstore you go to," Max added with a snicker. She stepped around Rose and opened the refrigerator.

"Antonia—" Rose gasped. That earned grins from the boys. "This is *that* Tony? Your romance writing partner?"

"He shanghaied me." She glared at Tony in mock threat. He laughed and made to swat at her. She sidestepped him, putting the milk jug on the table, and reached for the tray of cookies left over from rehearsal.

"I've read all your books!"

"Sorry. Tony," Max said, "this is Dad's sister, Rose Weinberg."

"So you heard about the accident and came to help? Nice to meet you."

"Aren't you supposed to be in California?" Rose asked.

"That's right, you rat," Max growled. "You skipped out to come back here because you think we can't get along without you, didn't you?"

"So what if I did?" Tony crossed his arms over his chest and returned her glare.

Joe nearly dropped the glasses he had piled into his hands to bring to the table. He managed to set them down, while he and Jeremy waited, holding their breaths.

"Could somebody explain what's going on?" Rose said.

"Tony was doing a teaching gig," Jeremy said.

"He ditched a great opportunity," Max said. She sank into a chair at the table, still staring at him, but her glare had lost its heat and energy.

"Hey, you guys are my family. This is where I need to be." Tony settled into the chair next to her and slouched, offering a lopsided grin.

"It's a little early, but is anybody up to breakfast?" Rose said from in front of the refrigerator. She held up a carton of eggs. "It has to be better than all those cookies."

~~~~~

By 6a.m., the boys had washed and dressed for the day. Rose conjured a massive breakfast of pancakes and eggs, orange juice, hash browns and muffins, and two pots of coffee. Max wondered how Rose knew Tony was a coffee addict, but decided it wasn't necessary to ask. She made a pot of tea for herself. With only two hours of sleep behind her, she needed it. Tony would probably get her working on their next writing project before the breakfast dishes were washed.

The five sat around the kitchen table, talking and eating. This morning, at least, the boys wouldn't have to rush to get dressed for school at the last moment.

"Anyway, I now know that I hate teaching with a passion," Tony said, concluding a rapid-fire listing of the torments he had gone through, trying to fit into the university system.
~~~~~

"Then don't teach with a passion," Jeremy said around a mouthful of pancake.

"Somebody hit him?" Tony begged with a groan.

"That's how he got that way," Max said, and reached for the bottle of syrup for her second pancake.

"I don't have to sit here and listen to this," Jeremy grumbled.

"Then stand up," Rose said, her face perfectly calm.

"Aunt Rose, not you too!"

The others burst out laughing. Jeremy's face grew red, but then he joined in.

"So you suffered and survived," Joe said, gesturing with his fork. He grimaced when Max yanked it out of his hand, a skill necessary to survive his habit of talking with pointed objects in his hands. "Were things really that bad?"

"Not that much," Tony admitted. "I can handle the lectures four times a week. But the questions those mental midgets asked afterwards were always the same—no matter what I talked about in the lecture."

"I take it you didn't care for it?" Rose said, a slow smile growing back on her face.

"Just talking is fine. I can talk for hours." He glared at Joe and Jeremy, who met each other's gazes and grinned, but wisely kept silent. "It was the tutorials that killed me."

"Tony is an instinctive writer like me," Max explained. "It takes a lot of thinking and headaches to explain *why* we did something. We just write it and know if it feels right or not, and when we read something somebody wrote, we know if it works or not. Figuring out *why* and explaining it to them is the hard part."

"And you're the one who talked Max into writing romances." Rose shook her head.

"Still not sure I'll ever forgive him for that," she returned. "And 'talked' isn't exactly the right word."

"He told his editor he couldn't write a book without her," Joe put in. "Mr. Winters helped them gang up on her."

"Tony practically moved in when they were working on the first book," Jeremy said.

"It was either help her or get my fingers broken," Tony added, giving Max a mock dramatic look of fear.

"Max," Rose said, laughing. "I'm surprised at you!"

"I didn't say anything!" Max gave Tony and her brothers the same sweeping glare. "He came over all on his own."

"When your father said you got into writing romances reluctantly, he wasn't joking, was he?" Rose said, muffling her last few giggles.

"I enjoy a challenge, okay?" Max picked up the teapot and looked inside. She grimaced when she found it empty of all but the bags. "But me, writing romances? I still don't understand how we produced anything worth reading."

"It doesn't hurt to be flexible and show the publishers you're willing and able to work with them," Tony said.

"And that's all you do?" Rose got up and took the teapot to the sink to rinse.

"Well, I'm trying to write the Great American Science Fiction Novel... but it's not as easy as it sounds. I scribble proposals for scripts and screenplays all the time, just like Max. We met at a creative writing course at BWU and it's been downhill from there."

"I wouldn't call guest lecturing in a university 'downhill.' No matter how much you disliked it."

"Yeah, well, I knew I was needed back here," he said softly, looking at Max with a peculiar light in his eyes that made her feel jumpy. It was like he wanted to say something, and she could almost guess what waited on his lips, but her sense of impending danger told her not to ask.

"But you're back early," Joe said. "We just rented out your apartment. Steve's a great guy, but he isn't going to be real happy to have to move so soon."

"He can keep it, for all I care. It's time to find a new place. I was even thinking of buying a house now."

Tony snagged the last pancake from under Jeremy's blindly seeking fork. Rose smiled, shook her head, and took the platter back to the stove to start on a fresh batch.

"What are you going to do until then?" Jeremy asked. "Hotel bills will kill you until you find a new place."

Tony shrugged. Three sets of eyes focused on Max, who concentrated on wiping up the last bit of syrup with her pancake just to escape that unsettling expression in Tony's eyes. She felt the sudden concentration on her and froze.

"Well," Tony said slowly, "I was kind of hoping a dear old friend could help me out."

"Oh?" Max looked up, narrowing her eyes at him. "I'm not *that* old."

She groaned when Tony dropped to his knees on the floor in front of her and grabbed her hand. Her brothers laughed at the familiar routine. For the first time, Max didn't find it funny. Rose didn't know the long-standing jokes between them. What did the scene look like to her?

"Please?" Tony whined, stretching his face into his wide-eyed, begging hound-dog look. "For old time's sake? For the memory of all our good times?"

"What good times?"

"For the memories of cool, crisp fall days, walking down the street, kicking stones." He gestured wildly in the direction of the windows. "For the companionship of chilly afternoons in the bleachers at football games." His voice cracked as he stretched it into an octave range he normally didn't use.

"Games I didn't want to go to."

Tony growled at her, prompting hoots of laughter from her brothers. He yanked on her arm, sat forward, and kissed up from the tips of her fingers, heading toward her wrist. Max held still, biting her lip, fighting to keep a straight face. Tony paused at the sweatshirt cuff.

"In memory of the hard times we endured together, then," he continued. "The agony of sweating over a keyboard at 3 in the morning." He pushed up her sleeve and planted another kiss. "The tortures of rejection. The—"

"Any higher and you're dead meat, buster," Max said, plastering her hand flat over his mouth.

Joe and Jeremy howled, leaning over the table. Rose held her hand over her mouth, eyes glistening with laughter tears. Max grinned.

"Besides," she said, "I'm not the one responsible for the house." She gestured at Rose with her free hand. Tony scrambled over to Rose on his knees and captured her hand.

Rose yipped, yanking her hand free. "Yes! You can stay!" She laughed through her pretend fear.

"All right!" Jeremy yelled.

"You two have to set up wherever Tony is going to sleep," she continued. "Before you go to school, hear me?"

Joe stood up straight and saluted, prompting a sigh from Rose. Jeremy grabbed Tony by the collar and pretended to drag him toward the door.

"Watch it, will you?" Tony rasped, clawing at his collar and making a face like a stranded fish.

"Come on." Jeremy eased up but kept moving. "If we have to do it, you have to help."

Joe caught up with them and grabbed Tony by an arm. In seconds, all three were out the door and gone.

"Good friend?" Rose asked, as she and Max got to work clearing the table.

"Yeah," Max admitted slowly, after giving her a searching look. "We've been through a lot. He's like a big brother. Or a little brother."

"Oh, is that all?"

"Come on!" Max decided laughing was the better choice that early in the morning. She and Rose had come to an understanding last night, but there was no way in the world she would admit she had entertained hopes Tony would want more than best buddies friendship. Even he hadn't caught on yet that all the heroes she created looked like him.

"Romance just ruins everything," she continued, as much to convince herself as Rose. Now that Tony was home in Tabor Heights, Max had to get her thoughts back in control. "Look what it's done to my career as a science fiction writer." She watched Rose take the dishes from the table to the sink. "Are you sure it won't be any trouble having him here?"

"If there's no trouble for you." Rose rinsed her hands and dried them on her apron.

"We've done it before. Just set up a cot in the corner by the dressing room doors and some dividers for privacy. It won't be too much trouble, will it?"

"I said so, didn't I?" She chuckled. "Besides, I like Tony."

"Everybody likes Tony. That's his gift."

"I hope so. You know the saying – after three days, fish and guests..."

"Well, we've survived longer stays from worse people." Max slid the leftover muffins into a plastic bag and twisted it closed with a flourish. "We'll be fine."

Chapter Eight

"Please, God," Tony whispered as the house settled into quiet around him. "Please let Miss Emily wake up soon. Show me what I'm supposed to do to help Max. She shouldn't have to face all this alone." He groaned and covered his face with his hands. "She's never going to be alone again. But the timing has to be right, or she'll never believe me."

He lay on his back on the cot in the temporary room erected in the corner of the living room. It felt almost like home. Joel and Emily had invited him to stay other times, when he and Max were so pressed for time on a book project it was foolish for him to travel back and forth between here and his place. Right now, Rose was downstairs doing laundry. Max had left for work. The boys were at school. Tony was dead tired, and clean for the first time in two days. All he wanted was to sleep, but the feelings churning inside him just moved faster now that he had seen Max again.

Tony had nearly stopped breathing when Max hugged him. Her smile was brighter than he had dared hope, all the long drive back from California. She held onto him longer than her brothers, and he had let himself believe for two seconds that she had developed the same feelings for him that he had discovered while away. Max needed her best friend and that was all. Someone to help her keep the boys under control, to help bully some of the morons on the theater team who wouldn't listen to her because she was female.

"I'll just bet that idiot Jake has been giving her a hard time," Tony whispered into the shadows of his cubicle.

Jake had tried to put the moves on Max two years ago, when he first earned a position in the ensemble. Tony had trusted Max to know Jake was a phony. She didn't trust a single word that came out of his mouth. All right, so Max knew when beautiful words and romantic gestures were fake, and she knew how to write incredible romantic scenes. The question was if she could recognize it when a man was in love with her.

"It's a given I can't just come out and say it. Not now, not with everything she has on her plate. She hated that book, where the guy took advantage of the girl's crisis to make her fall in love with him." Tony stretched, groaning luxuriously. "With all the books we've written together, and all the scenes she threw out as hokey, I should know what will work for her. But I don't. Too bad I can't get her to write the storyline for me."

He chuckled at the imagery. Then it caught and held in his brain. He reached for the lamp next to his cot, turned it on, then dug under his cot for the trunk that held his clothes. He pulled out a notebook and pencil and scribbled his ideas.

Maybe he should present the idea to Max as a story, first, and get her reaction? However she reacted, he would use it as guidance for the next step.

Have some consideration for her family, he told himself as the plan of attack and story proposal ideas flowed from his brain to his pen. *She's got enough problems to contend with, without trying to sweep her off her feet.*

He grinned. The image of scooping Max up in his arms and carrying her over a threshold somewhere had a certain appeal. He had kept his eye on the McCafferty house across the street for more than a year now, and he liked the idea of carrying Max through the door as his bride. But not dressed in the jeans and sweatshirt she had worn when she flew out the door half an hour ago. Something lacy and soft.

No, he decided, he shouldn't be doing this. Imagining Max in something skimpy — seductive even — was not right. Not in her parents' home.

He kept seeing her tossed over his shoulder, kicking and struggling, instead of docile and dreamy-eyed. A thud from downstairs reminded him that Rose was busy with the laundry. No, he probably would end up slinging Max over his shoulder in a fireman's carry instead of the romantic cradling in his arms. That was probably how it would be, if he could ever get that far in their relationship.

Later, though. He had to see Max through this current crisis before he started guiding her toward his ultimate goal.

But could he? What if Max wasn't innocent and oblivious when it came to real romance? What if she just plain resisted when focused on her?

Tony thought back to the revelation of Saturday night's phone call. He had wondered about Max's birth father, and how anybody could walk out on Emily Keeler-Randolph and refuse to be her knight in shining armor. A few times, he had considered asking Max if she knew who her father was, and each time scolded himself to put that question away. Joel Randolph was Max's father in every way that mattered. Tony wondered now if Carlo Vincente's absence in her life had anything to do with Max's attitude toward romance. Maybe she knew a lot of details about her parents' relationship that the rest of the world obviously didn't know. Maybe she simply didn't trust men with romance on their minds because of her mother's broken career and her own illegitimate birth?

That was something else Tony was going to have to work on. He put his notebook away, turned off the light, and lay down to do some serious thinking and praying.

~~~~~

"Where's Aunt Rose?" Tony asked, coming from behind the dividers creating his guest room.

"At the hospital, visiting Dad." Max smiled, amazed she hadn't bristled at how easily Tony called Rose "aunt." Part of her relaxed feelings could stem from the two pages she had written since coming back from work only twenty minutes ago. She hit *save* on her keyboard and sat back. "I didn't wake you up, did I?"

"I can always sleep through typing." He cracked a wide grin and stretched out on his stomach on the couch across from the office alcove. With his chin resting on his crossed arms and Max leaning back in her chair, they were ready for one of their hours-long, meandering chats.

"Any ideas for the next book?" Max knew better than to try to avoid that subject, much as she dreaded it. "Have you worked on those ideas you mentioned in our last phone call?"

"A little. I had another idea. There's this guy, he's kind of dense, I guess. He suddenly realizes his best friend is a girl."

"Sounds kind of dense to me." She grinned, anticipating one of Tony's comical stories.

"He's always known she's a girl, but suddenly it hits him that she's — you know — a girl. And she's the only one for him. Know what I mean?" His voice cracked.

"Not really, but I'm sure you'll explain it to me." Max reached to close out her file and turn off her computer. She didn't need to. She often left her computer on all day, coming back regularly to write some more. Right now, though, she didn't want Tony to see her face as his story idea conjured a few images she hadn't been able to lock in the back of her imagination.

"He wants to tell her that he wants to change their friendship. Into something better. No, not better, but more to it, you know? It's great as it is, and that's the problem. What if she's scared off or the whole idea of being romantic makes her sick?"

"Does he just want sex, or a cottage with a white picket fence and a dozen kids?"

"He's pretty sure it isn't just hormones kicking in. It's her he wants, not the standard package, know what I mean? He wants what they have right now, but he wants to wake up next to her every morning and be the first one she turns to when things are bad, and the one she celebrates with. He'd really like to know what it's like to kiss her. But what if he tries and she gives him a black eye?" Tony chuckled, but it had a strained sound that made Max's heart skip a beat.

"Maybe he should tell her outright. If they're best friends already, they should be able to talk about anything, right?"
~~~~~

"There's complications."

"Yeah, no such thing as happily ever after in chapter two, huh?" She leaned back in her chair, crossed her arms, and tried to grin back at him. Daydreams of Tony kissing her kept filling her mind's eye, making it hard to see him clearly there on the couch only a few feet away.

"If he tells her and she doesn't want to go deeper into the relationship, it'll change everything. He doesn't want to lose her. After what he's started feeling about her, he's scared he can't go back to the way things were."

"Then the question is whether romance is worth the risk of destroying a really great friendship." Max took a deep breath. What was it about Tony's eyes all of a sudden? They seemed to bore straight through her with an intensity that was almost pleading, almost afraid. "We'll have to think about this one for a while."

"Yeah, kind of half-baked, huh?" He shrugged, which had to be hard to do, lying on his stomach.

Max shrugged back at him, finding it safer than trying to choose the right words. Why had Tony come up with that story idea all of a sudden? Why did he have to have it now, in the middle of all the problems in her life?

"It's okay to visit your dad, isn't it?"

"He'd love to see you." She breathed a sigh of pure relief that the subject had been dropped. "Even if he does lecture you about not sticking to a commitment."

"Wish your mom could give me that lecture," Tony said, his voice dropping to a whisper.

Max nodded. Her eyes got hot and blurry as her imagination kicked in and painted the scene. Emily would be all tease, playing the part of the never-satisfied, scolding mother—and then laugh and hug Tony and tell him she still loved him even if he was a chronic drop-out.

This is ridiculous. She wiped at her eyes and swallowed hard against a choking sensation.

"Hey, Max, it's okay." Tony rolled off the couch, knelt by her chair and grabbed hold of her hands. "We'll get through it okay, hear me?"

"We?" Her voice cracked, caught between laughter and the growing pressure of the tears.

"I will always be here. You're stuck with me for life. You never have to go through anything alone. So just suck it up and live with it, got me?"

"Got you," she whispered, then shuddered and let the floodgates go down.

Tony tugged her down to sit on his lap, cradled against him. His tight arms around her were what she needed. She had to admit that, with wracking sobs breaking through her chest. It had been too long since someone held and supported her like that. It felt like a lifetime. Tony held her, rocking her a little, until her tears had soaked into his sweatshirt and her throat hurt and her nose stuffed up. It felt good to rest her head on his shoulder and pretend she didn't have any burdens. Just for a little while.

"You've been playing the hero again, haven't you?" Tony scolded. Max tried to protest and only succeeded in producing a squeak when he took a handful of her hair and gave it a gentle tug. "Can't fool me, Maximilian. With both your folks out of it, I know who's been taking care of everything and letting everybody else dump on her. You're going to go gray before you're thirty, y'know?"

"Like you?" Max pulled back now—the flood had passed. There was no excuse to be so close, though leaning on Tony had been a taste of heaven. She slid off his lap, nearly falling until she got her legs under herself and slid back into her desk chair.

"Ought to make you pay for that." He braced himself on the desk, pulled himself to his feet and cocked his head to one side, studying her. "I'll just wait until the pressure builds up again and make you let out another gusher in public, where everybody'll see you."

"Try it." She wrinkled up her nose at him and shoved her chair back a little further into the alcove.

"Okay." Silence sat between them for a few seconds. Tony looked away, glancing around the room. "I really missed this place."

"It *must* have been awful in California."

"Horrid. Nobody knows how to make spicy curly fries the right way." He gave her his usual cocky grin and continued before she could retort. "What's up with the fellowship? Any news yet?"

"You mean about..." There was no way she could force that name onto her lips right now. Not when everything felt so fragile.

"Yeah. The change of leadership."

"According to the last piece of correspondence, I have to turn in outlines for four possible scripts to work on during the next year and they choose the one I'll write." Max relaxed, glad to get onto safer territory. "They keep sending mail to 'Mr.' Keeler, even though I must have written 'Maxine' at least twenty times in all that paperwork I had to fill out."

"At least you're one step safer from news hounds, if people think Max Keeler is a man," he offered.

"That's what I told Chuck, but he thinks I'll just get in trouble later on if I let the misconception continue." A sigh gusted out of her. Too late to go back and change that particular decision. "All the reporters pestering us think Max is a guy, too, and my name should be Maureen. So I don't have any problem saying Max Keeler isn't around, when they call."

"Your folks probably figured this would happen with that pen name."

"I thought I could handle it. I guess I'm just a nasty little brat at heart. I had this dream of getting the Academy Award, and stepping up there and—I don't know—payback time. Despite everything Mom told me, I still think all those good friends in Hollywood just abandoned her. Couldn't have cared less when she left."

"Not that way now?"

"You should read some of the stories in all the links Chuck keeps forwarding me." She shook her head. "Tony, I really need your help. What am I going to propose for my four scripts?"

For the next hour, they talked writing; Max's participation in the Gabrielli Screenwriting Fellowship program, Tony's ideas for the next book in their series, Max's troubles with her current book, and things that needed to be done before rehearsal that night.

Rose came back from the hospital by way of the grocery store. When she stumbled into the kitchen burdened with four bags, Max and Tony ran to help her. They unpacked with companionable chatter that amazed Max, considering her reservations toward the woman just the day before. Then Tony again asked about visiting Joel in the hospital.

"You'd better get to him before the boys stop by after school," Rose said, pulling out the mixing bowls for more baking. "They'll wear him out, and your father won't let it show."

"Space things out, huh?" Tony nodded. "Sounds good. You want to drive, Max, or you want me to?"

"You might as well earn your keep and play chauffeur." Max sidestepped Tony's attempt to swat her with the dishcloth and stuck her tongue out. "It'll help us hide from the newshounds. They know what my car looks like, and there's no way I'm taking Dad's car. Some bozo will try tailgating us and we'll end up in a fender-bender." She shuddered at the idea of any damage to Joel's prized vintage black Mustang.

Max ran ahead to check the mailbox at the end of the driveway while Tony pulled his car around from the private family lot. She sorted out the mail after she got into the car, putting mail for Joel on the seat, the rest in her purse.

"Speak of the devil," she said with a snort of laughter. She held up an envelope so Tony could see the return address—Gabrielli Fellowship. It only took her a few seconds to open and read the letter, along with the small saddle-stapled, color booklet, introducing participants to the board of directors and staff they would be working with for the next year.

Her stomach knotted, and Max was glad she hadn't eaten lunch.

Be sure your sins will find you out.

"What's the news?" Tony stopped at a red light and leaned over to try to read over her arm.

"Just details of the awards ceremony and the writing workshop." Her voice threatened to crack as she shoved the booklet into her purse.

"What's that?" He reached for it.

"Waiting for a better color?" She slapped his hand away and gestured at the traffic light, which had been green five seconds.

Tony opened his mouth to retort, but the car behind them honked. He grimaced and took his foot off the brake.

"What are you hiding from me, Max?"

"Huh?" She didn't look at him as she folded the letter and crammed it back into its envelope. The picture of Carlo Vincente's family had been burned into her retinas. When she closed her eyes, it was still there: Carlo, his wife, Jeannette, posed in a happy family portrait with their three sons, Nicholas, Raymond... and Steve Coheny.

"Something's bugging you. And don't deny it. We know each other too well to lie or hide problems."

Steve Coheny was a liar—and her half-brother.

"It's just..." She took a deep breath, feeling as if the car seat swayed underneath her. Tony knew part of the truth. The question wasn't if she *could*, but if she *should* trust him with the rest of the ugly surprise. What would he do when he met Steve tonight at rehearsal, knowing his real identity? In a moment, she decided. One crisis at a time. "Carlo Vincente is a lot more involved than the last guy doing his job. He's going to be at every event involved with the fellowship."

"You knew you'd have to face him someday," he offered. There was only sympathy in his voice and face.

"I know. I just didn't plan on it being so soon." She took a deep breath. "Well, with everything going on, I'm definitely not going to L.A." Max waited, but Tony didn't scold her, didn't tease her about being a coward. She dared to take a sideways glance at him as they headed down Sackley toward the hospital. Their gazes met, and she saw only understanding.

What would she do without Tony in her life? The weight on her shoulders had dropped in half since he walked into the house that morning. He was her hero, her energy source, her anchor. Max fought down the hungry surge and the wailing inner voice that wanted so much more than best friends. Now was not the time to grumble, when she knew she should be grateful for so much. Her parents were alive. The play would open on schedule. She had broken her block in her book. And Tony was home, to hold her hand and let her cry on his shoulder and understand when nobody else could. What more could she ask for in life?

~~~~~

At the hospital, Joel was delighted to see Tony for about ten seconds. He scolded him, but Max could see he was genuinely glad Tony was staying at their house and helping.

When Tony went down to the snack bar on the next floor to get contraband juice and cookies for Joel, Max showed her stepfather the Gabrielli letter. Joel nodded, but didn't catch on. She held her finger under
~~~~~

Carlo's name and waited for him to read it.

"Oh." He frowned, cocked his head to one side, studied her for a moment, then took a deep breath and sat back against his pillows, squaring his shoulders.

"Please don't lecture me, Dad." She decided not to show him the photo of Carlo Vincente's family. She would have to think long and hard before she decided whether to confront Steve at all with his identity. When to do it could be figured out later.

"Who said I was going to?" Joel grinned sheepishly. "Well, maybe a little. You're going to have to face him sooner or later as your career grows, kiddo. And with the name you're using, well, it's a dead giveaway."

"Actors and writers don't come into that much contact, even at those legendary Hollywood parties. Which you couldn't *pay* me to attend." Max tried to put a mocking tone into her voice.

"Well, I'm sure Chuck will shield you, just like he did your mother." Joel nodded, carefully watching her face. "You're not a little girl anymore, Max. Your mother and I won't always be there to turn on the light and scare the monsters away from your room."

"Dad—"

"He's not that bad. He couldn't be, for your mother to still love him after all these years."

"If she still loves him, how come she hasn't contacted him? How come she never told him about me?"

"Why don't you tell him, then? She gave you permission a long time ago."

"What? And get myself disqualified?" she joked.

The joke fell flat. Max felt sick to her stomach.

"What did you think would happen when you chose your writing name?" Joel whispered. He caught Max's hands in his and squeezed gently.

Chapter Nine

"I don't know, Dad. I really don't know," Max whispered.

"Then you'd better pray about it, and think hard about it, because you're going to have to face that question head-on, no matter what you do."

"Just not right now, okay? Let me face one crisis at a time." She squeezed his hands to hide the trembling in her own.

When Tony came back to the room, Max left the two men talking about California. She tried to visit her mother every time she came to the hospital, even if all she could do was whisper a prayer, kiss her forehead, squeeze her hand, and tell Emily she loved her.

When she reached ICU, Max didn't bother signing in. The nurses there all knew her. The two on duty at the desk smiled and waved for her to go through. Max tiptoed through the long room, silent but for the gurgle of respirators and the humming and beeping of monitors.

"Hi, Mom." She leaned on the rail of the bed to reach through the bars and brush her mother's hair off her face. The hair that hadn't been cut away or hidden under the bandages wrapped around her head was loose and soft. Max suspected someone had washed it that morning. She appreciated those little details. The doctors said Emily was aware of everything around her, even if she couldn't respond.

Whispering, Max told her mother all the little details of what had happened since her last visit; Joe and Jeremy getting antsy for the end of the school year. Rose's arrival. Her ambivalent feelings about the woman. She hesitated to tell her mother about the Gabrielli competition and Carlo Vincente's addition to the board.

"Dad's talking about Joe playing George in *Our Town*, just like you suggested. Jake'll probably quit if he has to be Joe's understudy," Max said. "I wouldn't miss him at all. He's not right for George, anyway. Not innocent enough. Joe is sure innocent, isn't he, Mom? He gets all goofy when you even mention Karen and..."

Max stared at the hands neatly crossed on her mother's sheet-draped chest. The left one had twitched, hadn't it?

"Mom?" Her voice cracked. "Mom, are you in there?"

An eyelid twitched. Max picked up her mother's hand and squeezed it. She waited, holding her breath. She felt just the slightest tremor of tension move through that soft, limp hand.

"Oh, please, God. Please... Mom, can you hear me?"

"Max?" Beth Mason, the duty nurse hurried up to the bed.

"She moved!" Max blinked hard, then rubbed the threatening tears from her eyes with her other hand. She refused to let go of Emily.

"I know you think—" Beth gasped as Emily's head turned to the side and her lips twitched into a frown. "Don't you move," she said, pointing a threatening finger at Max, and then scurried to the door.

"Mom? Squeeze my hand. I know you can hear me. Don't you want to come home? We miss you so bad. Aunt Rose is great, and I hope she stays, but we really need *you*, Mom." Max held her breath. Tears instantly blinded her as her mother's hand slowly tightened around hers.

Then the doctors descended. Beth caught Max by the arm and led her out into the waiting area. She moved in a daze, all her attention focused on the low babble of voices coming from around her mother's bed. Then she heard Beth say something about calling her father.

"Dad! I gotta get him!" She flew to the stairs, refusing to wait for the elevator. She didn't care when Beth burst out laughing.

Dr. Holland came upstairs with Joel and Max, pushing Joel's wheelchair. He was a family friend and insisted that he could get them through the barrier of doctors and nurses faster than even putting the wheelchair up to ramming speed. Tony came with them, but stayed out in the hall. Only so many people allowed in Emily's room at one time.

There was no one in their way when they reached the ward. The crowd around Emily's bed had vanished. Beth stood lone guard, smiling. Max wanted to run ahead, but she stayed with Joel, one hand resting on his shoulder. He trembled under her touch.

"Em?" Joel's voice cracked. He frowned and grabbed control of the wheelchair and pivoted himself up closer to the bed. Dr. Holland's fussing wasn't fast enough for him. "Emily, honey? Can you hear me?"

"Mmm hmm," Emily moaned. Her head turned toward his voice. She frowned. It took forever for the twitching eyelids to open.

"Sweetheart, I've missed you so much." He reached through the railings and caught hold of her hand.

"It's good to have you back, Emily," Dr. Holland said. He patted Joel's shoulder, grinned at Max, and turned to walk out.

"Back?" Emily blinked sleepily and twisted her head to look around. "Max? You—you were here before?"

"I'm still here, Mom." Max wedged herself between Joel's chair and the nightstand.

"Do you remember what happened, honey?" Joel whispered.

"Wilder." Emily sighed and her eyes drooped closed. "I wanted Joe to play George. Jake isn't right."

"You're absolutely right." He paused, glanced at Max, licked his lips.

"What else do you remember?"

"That's... it. Did I fall asleep on the way home?" She struggled to open her eyes again.

"Something like that." He pushed himself up in the wheelchair and tugged Emily's hand close enough to kiss the palm. "I love you, Em. Don't you ever leave me."

"Don't... want... to," she murmured, smiling a little.

"So, should we tell the boys or keep it a secret until they go visit Mom?" Max asked when Joel had been safely returned to his hospital bed. She laughed when he turned a puzzled look at her.

"Oh. Sorry. I was thinking..." He shrugged and nodded. "I'll tell them when they get here."

"What are you thinking, Dad?"

"Well... you know how your mother said she wanted Joe to play George, and she doesn't remember anything else? We talked about *Our Town* at least half an hour before the accident. I'm glad she can't remember anything beyond that. It's God's mercy, more than we deserve."

"Yeah," she whispered. "God's mercy."

~~~~~

Brenda stayed after rehearsal that night to get Tony's opinion on her latest short story. She and Max hung up costumes while he read. Max knew better than to watch him and try to predict his opinion from his face. Brenda hadn't learned that lesson yet, and she kept running into Max because she didn't watch where she went.

To make matters worse, every time they ran into each other, Brenda contorted her face, obviously trying to communicate something without speaking. Finally, Max caught her by the arm and led her around the shelving to give them a little privacy.

"What?" she whispered.

"He loves you." Brenda smirked and crossed her arms and leaned back against the shelving full of glassware.

"What?" Max barely remembered to keep her voice down.

"You said that if Tony really loved you, he would jump on the next plane and come back from California. And he did that, didn't he?"

"He drove. No plane."

"Details, details." She slid an arm around Max's shoulders, drawing her closer. "So? How was it?"

"How was what?" She couldn't seem to get her brain to keep up with Brenda. Maybe that was a good thing?

"The kiss." Brenda groaned and shook her twice. "I figure when a guy confesses his all-consuming passion, that demands a great kiss. So, was it great?"

"He didn't confess anything. And the way he smelled after driving all
~~~~~

that way without stopping... no way was I going to offer." Max shivered, remembering how close she had come to kissing Tony. If her brothers and Rose hadn't been there, she suspected even the aroma of dirty clothes and hair wouldn't have stopped her.

"He didn't..." She scowled. "Well, did you confess to him?"

"Are you nuts?"

"No, but I think both of you are hopeless." Brenda sniffed, turned sharply on her heel, and stalked back to where Tony read and waited.

"Well, it's a good start," Tony said, raising his head. He leaned back against the sofa, sitting on the floor because every couch was full of props and costumes.

"A good start?" Brenda gave Max a mocking look of terror. "Is that good or bad?"

"A good start is crucial. You don't want to lose the reader's interest in the first four paragraphs." He chuckled and looked at the hand he had been waving in time with his words. "I really ought to buy a pipe to gesture with while I'm lecturing, you know?"

Max stepped over to the office alcove and tugged out the two rolling chairs. Giving one a shove to aim it at Brenda, she steered the other over to the bit of open floor space by Tony. "There's no way I'm getting down on the floor this late in the day."

And no way would she ever make a fool of herself confessing to Tony how she felt about him. After all the books they had written together, Tony should know it was the man's duty to confess love first.

"Getting old."

"Look who's talking."

"But is it going where I want it to go?" Brenda demanded. She plunked down on the floor next to Tony, her back against the sofa. Her multiple braids rattled and clicked.

"I don't know," he said, giving her a half-smile. "There are so many possibilities, it's hard to know which trail you're following. Or are you following all of them?"

"All of them?" She snatched the pages from his hand and shuffled them into order. "Here. Rico's point of view. I'm following his story."

"Which one? The disease he's probably going to catch, or the chance to join the gang, or the scholarship his mother wants him to apply for? And what about Kera and Jake?"

"You see stories for them?" Brenda glanced up at him without raising her head. If she wore glasses, she would have been looking between her eyebrows and the frames.

"You've sketched them all as real people, so yes, they have stories of their own." Tony chuckled and stretched his arms to the ceiling, turning the movement into a long, luxurious cat-like stretch. "Is this supposed to be a short story, novelette or *War and Peace*?"

"How about a mini-series?" Max squawked and ducked when Brenda reached for a pillow trapped under a pile of swords. Fortunately, she couldn't budge the pillow to throw it.

Friday, April 25

"Hey, Max?"

Tony paused in getting out of his car in the parking lot behind Homespun and glanced at the spot where Max's car belonged. It was empty. So who was calling her when she wasn't around? He didn't recognize the voice. He almost looked around, to find the speaker and let him know Max wasn't there, but he remembered just in time her complaints about paparazzi and nosey reporters trying to spy on the goings-on at Homespun. It was better to ignore intruders than get into a fight with one. Gathering up the handles of five bags of groceries in his back seat, he stepped back, kicked the car door closed, and headed for the back door of the house.

"Hey, are you Max Randolph?" A flicker of movement caught Tony's attention, despite his resolve to practice quantum physics and hope the power of his belief would make the intruder fade away.

He looked around and saw the source of the voice, immediately pegging him as a not-quite-there-yet photographer, bohemian wannabe, dressed all in black, with silver piercings in his eyebrow and nose. Tony prayed there wasn't a piercing in his tongue. Who could eat with that in the way? He had two cameras slung around his neck, and a fanny pack that sagged with the weight of what was probably more equipment.

"Nope." Tony continued to the back door.

"Where is he?"

"Work, probably."

"Who are you?"

"Somebody close enough to the family that if I call the police and make a complaint about trespassing, it'll be legal." He nodded toward the big sign that Joel had installed five years ago, when patrons of Homespun Theater kept trying to come in through the kitchen door. It clearly said the back parking lot was private, for friends and family only, and politely asked all others not to trespass.

"You one of his brothers?"

Tony sighed and bit his tongue to avoid asking aloud what part of "close enough to the family" didn't this bozo with his Captain Jack Sparrow eyeliner understand.

"Definitely not."

"So... what'll it take to get an invitation inside?" The paparazzi raised his camera.

"Buy a ticket for opening night." Tony breathed a sigh of relief when he reached the back porch. He heard the crunch of footsteps on the gravel and put down the grocery bags with a synchronized thud. Pulling his cell phone out of his pocket, he turned and glared at the photographer. The guy kept coming, so Tony hit a speed-dial number. "Hey, yeah, Dispatch, it's Tony over at Homespun. Got another intruder complaint to make." The photographer stopped short. "Hold on a second." Tony didn't bother to hide his smirk as he held out his camera and pressed a button. "Say cheese." He wondered what kind of drugs this paparazzi was on, that he just stood there and stared, his eyes getting wider with every second. "Yeah, I even got a picture of the guy to add to the official complaint. I can get his license plate number if you hold on for a second."

Now the intruder ran. Tony held still, listening, until he heard the roar of an engine gunning and the rattle of gravel as the car pulled out of the lot. A moment later, he saw the red Jeep, which he had thought belonged to one of the college volunteers, race down a side street. If there were any justice in the world, a Tabor Heights patrol car would be close enough to get the guy for speeding in a residential zone. Sighing, he clicked the red phone icon, cutting off the voicemail message he had been leaving on Max's cell phone. Tony hoped they would be able to laugh about the trick he had pulled. The bottom line was that he would do anything to protect Max's family.

He wondered if he would have to resort to pretending to be Max Randolph, to do that. It would throw the really persistent newshounds off the trail for a little while, at least.

~~~~~

Rose sighed in complete satisfaction and looked around the living room. It amazed her how everything could look like a mess on the surface and yet be so organized. She had taken Gretchen aside last night before rehearsal and asked her to explain how to tell what was in use and couldn't be moved for the duration of the play, and what could be moved. Now Rose knew how to clean the room without causing problems for the cast and crew. And the living room was finally cleaned to her satisfaction.

The kitchen, bedrooms, and bathrooms were easier to handle because there weren't forty people using those rooms and leaving their possessions and tools lying around. Rose had taken control of them yesterday. It was also nice, she reflected, to have the house completely to herself. The only time it was ever this quiet, according to Joel, was around 4a.m..

The kitchen door banged open. Rose stiffened and checked her watch—the boys weren't due home from school for another hour. Max was at work. Tony had gone to get some clothes and books out of storage.
~~~~~

Unless some new minor disaster had struck, no one should be home. Shaking her head, Rose scurried into the kitchen to investigate.

"Tony?" She stopped short, almost letting the swinging door come back and hit her. "What in the world?"

"Groceries." Grinning, Tony hefted net bags of groceries and set them down on the table.

Rose stepped up to the table and with two fingers, tugged aside the paper of one bag enough to see the contents. The warm, crisp aroma of fresh bread, the sweetness of fresh cookies and sweet rolls rose up to slide through her nose and down her throat, making her mouth water and her stomach growl.

"We go through a lot of food during rehearsals," Tony said.

"You didn't have to do this," Rose began.

"Yes, I did. I'm eating all your fantastic cooking, right?" He set down the bags and started unpacking.

Nothing was in plastic or prepackaged, Rose noted. The meat was wrapped in paper, the fruits and vegetables in paper or net bags. Wherever Tony had found his groceries—she meant to find this store immediately—everything was top of the line and green-minded.

"But you already help with the dishes and you took out the garbage after I asked Jeremy. And I notice you scrubbed the shower stall this morning," she added with a smile and a sigh. Rose hadn't been looking forward to that chore, but knew it had to be done some time.

"I'm living here, I ought to pitch in. Besides." He paused with a bundle of celery in his hands, still sparkling with drops of water. "This is all the family I've got."

"Where are your parents?" Rose picked up a net bag bulging with three different colors of grapes and stepped over to the refrigerator.

"Heaven." The light tone of his voice made her think he was joking for a minute. Tony paused to stow four paper-wrapped packages marked 'sirloin tips' in the bottom of the freezer. "Plane crash eight years ago. If it wasn't for Max and her folks..." Rose saw a tiny flicker of remembered pain in his eyes. "I have to be here for them."

"With groceries and badgering Max into writing." She chuckled, despite the aching lump in her throat. "You still didn't have to do this. Though I appreciate it. I dread seeing the receipt for all this."

"Who says you will?" He slid a box of sesame crackers into the cupboard.

"I know quality, young man, and these few bags must have cleaned out your wallet."

"I'm independently wealthy."

"Tony..." She sighed when he just smiled cheekily and reached for the first empty grocery bag to fold it up. She picked up another. "Seriously?"

He leaned back against the cupboards. "My folks spread their money out, so if one investment failed, they wouldn't lose everything. Annuities, fidelity bonds, stocks, different portfolios. I pretty much live off the dividends and I bank or re-invest the bonuses. My books give me something to play with. Or help out folks who are like family to me."

"Well, if nobody remembers to say so, I want you to know I appreciate all this." She looked at the groceries still waiting on the table, and chuckled. "It's a little hard to believe Antonia Maxwell just bought groceries for me."

"Oh, please..."

"I gather Max wasn't thrilled about being a romance writer. At least, not at first. Is that why you two write together, and under a shared name?"

"She's more uptight than I am about people finding out she writes romances." He chuckled. "You ought to see her squirm when we get to kissing scenes." His smile faded, making Rose wonder what was going through his head. "It's fun to keep it clean and still keep the reader's attention. Challenge is good for you."

She nodded, picked up a box of spiral noodles and a jar of spaghetti sauce, and took them to the counter next to the stove. "Joel told me how grateful he is that you're here for Max."

"Yeah. Grateful." Tony sighed and looked around the room. "But no matter how grateful he is, I bet the father in him hopes I don't live here too long, huh?"

"Well..." She had expressed the same worry just yesterday and Joel had laughed even as he set her straight on Max and Tony's relationship. "Joel let me know you're about the only young man in town he does trust with his daughter."

"Is that supposed to be good news or bad news?"

Despite the sparkle in Tony's eyes and his easy laughter, Rose wondered if there wasn't a great deal more to his words than appeared on the surface. It struck her for the first time that maybe Joel *should* worry. After all, Tony had abandoned his teaching position in California and drove cross-country to be here for Max and her brothers. Maybe he had done it for Max, alone, and not just because they were best friends?

She was going to have to keep her eye on that young man. And maybe nudge Max, to open her eyes to the treasure right under her nose?

~~~~~

"Dad, don't you think Aunt Rose should come to church with us?" Jeremy asked, leaning against the railing of his father's hospital bed. Joe was upstairs visiting Emily, and soon it would be Jeremy's turn to go up.

"I suppose." Joel cocked his head and studied his son a moment. "Have you asked her?"

"Not yet."
~~~~~

"Not today, he means," Max said from the doorway, having just arrived from work. "He's asked her every day since she got here, and she always says she'll think about it when she's a little more settled."

"Why won't she say yes?" Jeremy insisted.

"She's giving you the brush-off and being nice about it. Is Joe with Mom?" When Joel nodded, she headed down the hall.

"Max doesn't care about Aunt Rose at all. I think she still hates her."

"Max never hated her. In fact, I think she cares enough to leave her alone," Joel said.

"Huh?" Jeremy's elbows slipped off the railing. "But Dad, Aunt Rose can't get saved if she doesn't hear Pastor Glenn preach."

"Who says? If we have to wait for a preacher to talk to us, a lot of us would never get saved. Your mom and your sister did more for getting me to know God than any preacher ever did." Joel reached over to the bedside table for his coffee. "Did you ever think that just living with us might make the difference?"

He laughed, nearly sloshing his coffee, when Jeremy screwed up his face in a horrified look of embarrassment. Joel struggled to put the cup down. His laughter turned into coughing that shook his whole body. Before he caught his breath again, Joe and a nurse had run into the room to check on him.

"No, I'm okay," he insisted, still gasping a little. "Needed that, I think." A few chuckles escaped him when he caught sight of Jeremy's concerned, pale face.

"Maybe we should limit you to one visitor at a time, like Emily," the nurse said, even as she smiled and straightened his blankets. "Too much stimulation around here, I think."

"That's one way of putting it." He reached for his coffee again and took a sip.

"Dad?" Jeremy half-whispered.

"I'm okay."

"You sure?" Joe asked as the nurse left the room. He grinned when his father nodded. "Good, because there's this magic trick—"

"I was talking to Dad," Jeremy half-wailed.

"Ease up, Jeremiah," Joel said. "If your aunt doesn't want to go, badgering her isn't going to do anyone any good."

"Is he bugging you about that now?" Joe gave his brother a nudge with his hip. "Go see Mom, will you? We only have a half hour before we have to go home and get ready for rehearsal."

"You know those lines?" Joel asked.

"Perfect, Dad, but I keep messing up that coin trick you taught me."

Jeremy sighed and stomped out of the room, prompting his father and brother to burst out laughing.

~~~~~

"Mr. Winters?" Gloria stood from her desk as Chuck Winters came into his office. Her face was flushed, eyes bright. "You have a v-visitor."

The thick cream sauce from his linguini at lunch curdled in his stomach while his mind raced over who it could be. Whoever had come in and decided to wait during his lunch meeting, it couldn't be someone angry and dangerous. Not if Gloria looked like she had been offered the keys to heaven.

"In my office?" he guessed, since the waiting room was empty. He didn't wait for her frantic nod before he opened the door.

Carlo Vincente sat on the edge of his desk, looking through a portfolio of location shots the agency was putting together. He lifted his head and regarded Winters a moment, then a slow smile spread across his weathered Mediterranean features.

"Chuck, it's nice to see you after so long. How are you doing?" Even after forty years in Hollywood, Carlo still had a soft trace of accent that gave dignity to the elder statesman and patriarch roles he played nowadays.

That dignity and a touch of disappointment stayed in his large, dark eyes. His smile never reached them. He stood and held out a hand, which Winters shook.

"Keeping busy. You're looking good. Just in from golf?" he asked, gesturing at the sky-blue polo shirt and tan slacks Carlo wore. Winters wondered, yet again, how the other man could stay looking so trim and youthful despite the silver frosting his close-cropped black curls.

"No. Jeanette and I just drove in from Palm Springs." Carlo watched Winters settle in at his desk. "It's been too long since we've seen you. I wonder why, now."

"Busy." Winters tried to smile. He knew what was about to happen. He wished he could predict *how* it would happen, to ward off as much damage as possible.

"Too busy to return my calls? Or because they concerned Max and Emily Keeler?" He settled in the chair facing the desk. "I find it rather curious you're representing Emily's son."
~~~~~

Chapter Ten

"Let's take this one step at a time, Carlo." Winters settled back in his chair and took a deep breath. "First, I've been in contact with Emily since she left. Why didn't I ever tell you? Well, you never asked about her when you returned from France. That's all there is to it."

"And her son? It wasn't hard to put the pieces together. He lives in the same city where Emily lives. As chairman, I have access to all the forms for the Gabrielli judging. Grace remarked on the name coincidence when Emily was injured. Then I saw the boy's birth date."

"Uh huh." Winters grinned wider despite the tension running through his body.

"Max Keeler is Emily's son."

"Nope."

"I don't know what kind of a joke you think you're pulling—" Steel cooled the usual warmth in his voice, thickened the Italian accent.

"It's no joke, Carlo. It's very serious."

"That big grin of yours says otherwise." He sat forward, leaning his elbows on the front of the desk. "Max is my son."

"Wrong again." Winters took a few deep breaths, staring down Carlo, willing his expression into neutral. It amazed him that he wanted to laugh. Finally he relented. He had to say something before the accusations gleaming in his visitor's eyes spilled out in words they both might regret. "You ask for so much information on those forms, but do you ever ask about gender? Even just for statistics?"

"Gender?" Carlo shook his head, clearly confused.

"Max is short for Maxine. Emily's *daughter*. I told her she was headed for trouble if she let that misconception continue."

"Misconception. Interesting choice of words," he murmured.

"Carlo, before you go any further, listen. I watched Max grow up. When she showed talent, I made sure I was there to help her. That girl is going places, and I'll make sure nothing and no one gets in her way."

"Yes, I can tell. I've read her script three times." A faint smile tugged at his lips and reached his eyes at last. "I'm glad you stood by Emily. Knowing her family, I doubt anyone did. Except Aunt Maxine, of course."

"Like glue."

"Why didn't Emily tell me? Did she ever tell you?"

"She never talked about it." Winters took a deep breath and started to relax. "At the beginning, I didn't want to hurt her. Then, as the years went by, I didn't think it was important. She was happy. Max was happy."

"Do they need my help? Is there anything I can do? Will they let me help?" He paused and took a deep breath, and for the first time couldn't look Winters in the eye. "Is Emily going to live?"

"She woke up yesterday. She'll be fine. I'll tell you, that Max is something special. The way she's kept things going after Joel and Emily were both hurt, she makes me proud, and she isn't even my kid."

"Yes, and we go back to that question."

Winters had an urge to get down on his knees and beg Carlo not to disturb Max's life, now that things were finally settling down again.

"I've been living in memories and regrets since Emily appeared in the news. Even before that—when I read Max's name on the fellowship roster. I looked up the Homespun Theater web site and read Max's name and saw Emily's picture. My past and my mistakes are coming back to haunt me, in ways I never anticipated. Be sure your sins will find you out. The Bible is right, isn't it?" Carlo smiled wistfully, and Winters could only nod. "I want to know more about her, help her career. If she'll let me." He straightened and rubbed at his eyes.

"You should realize I'm rather protective of that girl," Winters began.

He had dreaded the day Carlo would come into his office, asking his questions. Even knowing the day might come, Winters hadn't prepared the right words. What could he say? He remembered how Emily had asked for his help twenty-six years before. She never asked him to lie, but it was implied that she depended on his discretion and protection.

"I've had my suspicions over the years. Nobody ever denied or confirmed my... hints, you understand." He swallowed hard, finding the next words a little difficult. "I've harbored some resentment for you. I blamed you for Emily running away, the problems she faced. For a while."

"A while?" Carlo prompted, voice soft.

"You never knew Emily was pregnant, did you?"

"No. If I had known..."

"We wouldn't be having this conversation right now." Winters surprised himself by smiling. "Emily didn't want you to know, evidently. Did you think she might not want you to know now?"

"Max Keeler *is* my daughter," Carlo half-whispered.

"Randolph. Joel adopted her."

"Then Keeler is her pen name?" He frowned, pausing a moment. "Why would she choose that name?"

"I thought maybe she wanted to get attention, using Emily's name, but the way she's been avoiding the media..." Winters shook his head. "I just don't know. I doubt she's going to be very happy learning you're on the board now."

"Indeed. You think she knows I'm her father?"

"Emily wouldn't keep that a secret from Max, even if she kept it from you. Max was all she had, until Joel came charging into their lives like a white knight."

"He's good to them. I'm glad."

"I wouldn't have let him get within a mile of them if I didn't think he'd be good for them." Winters sighed, feeling more tired than anything now. This pivotal moment had gone rather better than he had anticipated.

"I only want to help them." Carlo waited until Winters nodded that he believed him. "I have a responsibility toward Maxine, at the very least. But if I acknowledge our relationship, I could hurt her very badly."

"The fellowship?"

Carlo took a deep breath. "There is a rule against participants being relatives of the judges or anyone involved with the fellowship, no exceptions."

"Max won, didn't she?"

"The winners haven't been decided yet, but she is premiere among the finalists."

"And she could lose it all if people know you're her father." Winters shook his head. "You can't just hold off on the family reunion for a few years, Carlo. No matter when you make the connection, somebody will look back and claim it was a set-up. It could kill her career. Think you can keep your relationship a secret forever?"

"No. I wouldn't want to. I want Max to meet her brothers and Jeannette. I *need* to confess to my peers what a fool I was as a young man. And..." A genuine smile eased across his face. "And, I must admit, I want to brag about my talented daughter, even if I had nothing to do with her upbringing."

"Then it's up to Max now, isn't it?" Winters whispered.

"I need your help. Like you helped Emily."

~~~~~

Joel watched Joe practice the sleight-of-hand trick he had taught him only a few days before the accident. His son scowled, all his concentration on manipulating the coins balanced on his fingertips. The coins slid, and in trying to catch one, he lost control over all five. They tumbled to the blankets of the hospital bed, thudding dully against the hard surface of the cast. Joe grimaced and picked them up to start again.

"It takes time to get it right." Joel grinned despite a dull ache in his temples — a sure sign he was getting to the end of his strength.

A flicker of irritation flared up at the thought of the nurses fussing over him, giving him pills, checking his temperature and making sure he rested. That, in turn, made him smile. Only a few days ago, he hadn't been strong enough to *get* irritated.
~~~~~

"Yeah, but it'd be nice to get *something* right," Joe retorted.

"Up to visitors?" Pastor Glenn peered into the doorway.

"Depends if I'm getting a condensed version of Sunday's sermon, or just lectured for missing," Joel said with a grin.

"Neither. Hey, aren't you supposed to be getting ready for rehearsal?" he asked Joe as he stepped up to the bed and shook hands with Joel.

"Guess that's my cue to leave," Joe said with a sigh.

"Tell your sister to check with me before she leaves," Joel said, and gestured at the chair nobody in his family seemed to want to use. "Have a seat, Pastor."

"How about a wallet?" Joe asked, holding up a beat-up brown wallet in two fingers.

Pastor Glenn paused, halfway down into the chair. His eyes got wide behind his silver-rimmed glasses. He felt three pockets, then his surprised gape flattened into a rueful grin. He held out a hand and Joe deposited the wallet into his open palm. "You've been teaching him magic tricks again, haven't you?" he accused, turning to Joel.

"I thought it was for a good cause." Joel made a shooing gesture at Joe. "Get out of here, you delinquent." His son just laughed as he hugged him and hurried out the door. "My past is coming back to haunt me," he said with a chuckle. "I could have been a pretty good pickpocket, if Emily and Max hadn't dragged me off to church. Joe's picking up the talent." It was funny, yet bittersweet, how the slightest mention or thought of Emily could shake him. The relief he felt that he hadn't lost her was almost like falling in love all over again.

~~~~~

Max came downstairs to find Jake had arrived early for rehearsal. He stood in the office alcove, bent over her desk, reading papers from her organizer baskets. She fought a tightening in her gut from a sense of invasion. She didn't mind if her brothers and Tony helped themselves to her latest writing. She drew the line at the theater's cast and crew.

Not all of them, she amended. Max wouldn't have minded if Audrey, Gretchen or Truman read her stories. Or even Steve, despite knowing he had lied to her. He had proven himself reliable and able to anticipate needs, so she practically never had to ask him to do something during rehearsals. Jake irritated her enough she would have hesitated to perform CPR on him in a crisis. He had grown arrogant as his talent smoothed and strengthened under Joel's tutelage. He mimicked other members of the cast when they made major flubs during rehearsal. His classically handsome face wasn't made for twisting into caricatures of other people.

"What's up?" she said from halfway down the winding stairs, to give him fair warning. If he didn't move back from her desk, then she would get a little more direct.
~~~~~

"You going?" he asked, turning around and waving a sheet of pale blue paper at her.

It took a moment to remember the paper held a revised schedule for the Gabrielli Fellowship seminar. It had come in the mail along with the announcement of Carlo Vincente joining the board. Max had read the listing of workshops, social events and industry professionals who would be present with a mixture of regret, longing, irritation and fear. Irritation took the majority of her feelings now. Then fear—where had she put that booklet with the pictures? She didn't need Jake finding it, recognizing Steve, and trying to schmooze his way into a Hollywood connection.

Not that she would mind Jake vanishing to the other side of the country, but she would have a hard time explaining to Steve that she knew who he was and had chosen not to confront him. If she pretended she didn't know he was lying, then ugly secrets wouldn't be revealed.

"You know, it's understood there are boundaries down here." She crossed to Jake and snatched the paper from his hand before he could tighten his grip. "My office and the theater records are private. You do know what privacy is, don't you?"

"Yeah, but are you going to that seminar? A lot of big directors and other hot-shots are going to be there." Jake slid down onto the nearest couch and stretched out his legs. He grinned at her. "I'd go if I could write more than my name on a check."

"I have too much to do here."

"You're being stupid, Maxi."

She turned her back to him and folded the seminar invitation into a small packet. Max hated being called "Maxi," because it reminded her of her past weight problems. She couldn't figure out if Jake did it to irritate her, or if he was just plain dense.

"It's *my* life."

"No, it's your career. I mean, look at that list of bigwigs who'll be there to make connections. And all those old friends of your mom's. Use their sympathy to get a leg up in the business. What's his name, that one she was in that war movie with? He's going to be there."

"Carlo Vincente?" The name slipped from Max's lips without her really wanting to say it.

"Yeah, that's the guy. Get him to feel sorry for you. Make those business connections." Jake got up and sauntered over to the alcove. "Don't be stupid and give up everything for a hick town like Tabor Heights, like your—"

Max turned to face him and he stopped short in mid-taunt. She hoped her glare hurt Jake, just like his words hurt her.

"Like my parents?" She shoved the folded paper into her pocket and pushed Jake aside. "The people who created opportunities for you? The people who have helped you polish your talent? I have work to do for tonight, and you'd better rehearse your lines again, don't you think?" She forced her mouth into a stern, flat line, refusing to show her relief when Jake nodded quickly and hurried out into the theater.

Max sank down into her desk chair and swallowed hard. She wanted to go to that seminar, just to meet other writers. Yet, Carlo Vincente might be there and she couldn't take the risk of seeing him—and him seeing her. She had always been glad she looked so much like Joel that nobody ever questioned that they were father and daughter. Unfortunately, she looked enough like Carlo that people with a hint could see the resemblance between them, too.

Sunday, April 27

"Yeah, just about ready to pack up," Mr. McCafferty wheezed, settling down in the rocker swing on the deep-set porch of his ranch house. He gestured across the street at the Homespun Theater, a bright blur in the afternoon sunshine compared to the deep shadows of his tree-filled front yard. "Gonna miss those folks. Always been good neighbors."

"They'll miss you, too. Have you told them yet?" Tony tried to relax his death-grip on the glass of lemonade. He swallowed hard to keep from laughing at his own nervousness.

"Nah. Not with all the troubles those poor folks are going through now. I'll just stop over to say good-bye and wish them luck and give them my sister's address in Arizona." He nodded and rubbed at the stiff white bristles of his beard, which made his dusky skin even darker by contrast. "You haven't changed your mind, have you?" He chuckled when Tony nearly dropped his glass. "Nope, guess you haven't. How long have you been waiting for me to move out of this place so you can have it?"

"Oh, come on," Tony groaned. "We only started talking about my buying it this winter."

"I know. Kind of makes me glad I don't have to fuss with realtors and strangers tramping through my place. My Gloria, she put her heart and soul into this house. She'd want you to have it. Kind of big for a young, single guy like you. Probably rattle around like a lone pea in a pod. Gonna get you a roommate, at least?"

"I plan on it." Maybe he should test the idea of marrying Max on McCafferty? No matter his reaction, the old man would keep his mouth shut. Besides, Tony sensed he would approve.

Monday, April 28

Tony heard the kitchen door open and sat up quickly. The creak-thud of the door swinging back into place masked the creaking of the cot.

Who was out there? Max and the boys were visiting their parents on the way home from school and work. Rose was downstairs, trying to mend a costume that had been altered so many times the much-abused fabric kept splitting. Even now, faintly through the antique ventilation, he heard the whirring of the sewing machine.

Who could have come into the house through the back door? Max or the boys would have called out to either him or Rose. Queries on performances and tickets went through the box office, where hours were clearly posted. Anybody asking about Joel and Emily would call.

The paparazzi had calmed down since the hospital released the news that Emily was awake, and most of them had vanished back wherever they came from. Tony didn't think anyone was sneaking in to try to get that elusive scoop after a week of frustration and being led in circles by the friendly, supportive people of Tabor Heights.

Maybe a thief? What was there to steal?

Max's computer. The cash from advance ticket sales that had been put on Joel's desk and not counted yet. The intruder wouldn't know where the money was kept.

Stealthy footsteps crossed straight to the office alcove. This was someone who knew exactly where to go.

Tony slid to his knees on the floor and grabbed the walking stick he had been decorating for Morgan to use as Petruchio. It would probably break, all the plastic gemstones scattering to the four winds if he had to hit somebody with it. But it would do the job, if needed.

He looked around the dividers set up around his impromptu bedroom. Jake Holt stood in front of Max's desk, going through her stacked organizer baskets.

He wasn't rifling her desk. Tony knew rifling. Jake searched methodically. Moving carefully, so no one could tell the desk had been searched. He put down the stack he was going through, in two piles. He took several papers over to the copy machine tucked into the corner behind Joel's crammed desk and turned it on. Tony shook his head at the man's denseness. Didn't he think anyone would hear the noise of the machine warming up? For being such a talented actor, Jake was several fries short of a common sense Happy Meal.

What was he up to? Tony thought hard as Jake made copies of the papers he took off Max's desk, then put the originals back into the stack, and the stack back into the basket it had come from. Then, moving just as stealthily, he went back through the kitchen door and outside.

The only way to find out what he had copied was to get those copies.

What were the chances Jake would come to rehearsal with the incriminating evidence in his pocket? Knowing Jake Holt's arrogance, the odds were in Tony's favor.

Tony decided to have a little talk with Joe before dinner. He had learned a long time ago to take advantage of every talent God put in his path. Including the talents of others.

~~~~~

"Can't figure this out," Joe muttered as he settled down next to Tony in the back row of the theater that night. On stage, Jake and Audrey simpered through the courtship scene.

Despite his dislike for Jake, Tony had to admit the man did have talent. He could turn on the charm so it blazed like a chandelier.

"Figure what?" he whispered. Then he grinned as Joe slid a sheaf of folded papers into his hands. "You are a genius."

"Yeah, a pickpocket genius. Why did Jake take this stuff from Max's desk? He can't write a postcard, let alone a script."

"What?" Tony unfolded the papers and could barely make out the first few lines in the shadowy auditorium.

"He took all the stuff Max got about writing seminars and invitations to all the parties and workshops and things hooked up with that fellowship she placed in. Why would Jake want to go to those?"

"I don't know."

"She's going to be ticked."

"Definitely." Tony thought fast. "Let's not tell her. At least, not until things settle down, okay? Until we figure out what good old Jake is up to."

"Sounds good." Joe slid out of the seat. "I'm on in a few minutes." He grinned and scurried down the aisle, tugging at his tights.

Tony grinned and said a prayer of thanks that he had no acting talent and would never have to go through dress rehearsal.

Why was Jake so interested in Max's business? Tony read as best he could in the dim light of the auditorium. His confusion increased when he saw information on that screenplay option offer Max got in the mail that day. Why would Jake need to know about that?

"Is there some reason why you're encouraging juvenile delinquency?" Steve muttered, leaning down to rest his arms on the back of the seat next to Tony.
~~~~~

Chapter Eleven

For three long seconds, Tony held his breath and fought a surge of hot irritation that surprised him. He understood Steve was new and it was just smart to try to be everywhere, see everything, to get up to speed. He appreciated how the new guy was always there, willing to do anything necessary to get the production together.

But did he have to watch Max all the time, as if he was trying to read her mind? Did he have to sit and study her as if he analyzed every word she said, every move she made?

You're not jealous, Tony scolded. He was reasonably sure Max was just as oblivious about other guys as she seemed to be about his feelings for her. At least, he hoped Max was oblivious to other guys' interest.

That didn't do anything for Steve's side of the story. It didn't explain his intense interest in Max.

"Jake's slime, so I don't think you're picking on him," Steve continued. "What's up?"

"What's your interest in all this?"

"I like these people. They're having a rough go right now." He shrugged. "I want to help." A soft laugh slipped out. "Besides, I've caught Jake about a dozen times trying search the office. If he just kept going when he saw me, I wouldn't have been suspicious. For all he's a pretty good actor, he doesn't have the brains to realize that sudden changes in direction are a giveaway."

"He's taking papers from Max's files." Tony sighed. "I want to know why." He handed the papers over to Steve. It took only a few moments for him to glance over them.

"I assume Joe's part of the spy team. What do you want me to do?"

"Watch Jake when I can't. Make sure he can't replace those papers."

"Jake was boasting to one of the kids from the U that he has photographic memory. He might not need to get them back." Steve tapped his temple. "He might have it all upstairs already."

"Great," Tony sighed.

"So... is she going to the fellowship doings?"

"Nope." That was one thing he was sure of, at least.

"Yeah. Too much going on here." Steve offered a lopsided grin. "With all the reporters trying to dig into things around town, to find out about Miss Emily and such, Max sure wouldn't want to go put herself in the center of the bull's eye."

"Max isn't afraid of the gossip rags. She's staying here because she's needed."

"Must be nice."

"What is?" Tony sat up and really turned to look at him.

"Having a family like hers."

"What's your family like?"

"Oh... complicated." Steve offered a shrug. "Dad. Step-mom. Two half-brothers. You know how it is."

"No... but Max does."

"Yeah. Funny, isn't it?"

Tony thought about that, and the wistful rasp in Steve's voice, after he left to take care of a problem with the turntable. He knew it was stupid, but his irritation quotient went up another couple notches, realizing Steve and Max had that much in common.

Tuesday, April 29

Rose scurried around in the kitchen, starting her day's cooking and making pancakes as fast as she could to keep up with Joe and Jeremy's forks. Tony was already hard at work in the theater making last-minute adjustments to the lighting. Max wasn't out of bed yet.

"Whatever that is, Aunt Rose," Joe said, "it smells great. Is it for lunch?"

"No. And that reminds me." She stirred the soup base once more and turned down the heat. "Your lunch is on the top shelf in the refrigerator."

"Leftovers?" Joe sounded so eager, that made her laugh.

"I swear, I've never seen a boy so concerned with food." She reached for a towel to wipe her hands. That reminded her of the dryer load and she went out, through the living room, through the theater, to the stairs to the tiny basement.

"Joe," Jeremy whispered, "loan me five bucks?"

"No way — you've got plenty of your own."

"But I don't have enough to get Aunt Rose some flowers for tonight."

"Why?"

"It's opening night. Tradition."

"We get *Mom* flowers." Joe scraped syrup off the plate and checked the covered dish for another pancake. He speared it, giving his brother a wary glance. Jeremy didn't notice.

"But Joe —"

"No way. If we get flowers for anybody, it should be Max, and you know how squirmy she is about getting flowers from anybody. You want flowers for Aunt Rose, you dig up the money yourself."

Jeremy opened his mouth to argue, but Rose walked back in. He concentrated on his plate, scraping up the last crumbs of pancake.

"We're really glad you're here, Aunt Rose," Joe said through a thick mouthful. He grinned, embarrassed.

"At least you won't starve now." She chuckled.

Joe wiped his mouth and stood, putting his plate in the open dishwater before dashing out the door and upstairs. "Leaving in ten minutes, Jeremy," he called amid the banging of his feet on the iron stairs.

"I'm ready," Jeremy muttered. "You're the one who's always running late." He flipped a pancake onto his plate and proceeded to devour it in huge bites, his gaze unfocussed.

Rose added a few more shakes of pepper to the soup, then pulled out ingredients for her next recipe. Max stumbled into the kitchen, hair mussed, wearing the same green sweats from the day before. Her eyes were only half open. She sank into a chair at the table and stared blankly at the syrup bottle.

"So what are you making next?" Jeremy asked, turning to watch Rose at work.

"Stroganoff."

"Is that Jewish?"

"I think you mean kosher. No. Morris wasn't as strict as your grandfather. He asked me to cook things that would have given the rabbis a heart attack. Or heartburn."

"Good." His face warmed when she gave him a puzzled look. "I mean, I was worried about eating and... if you still..." He shrugged, his face wrinkled with the effort to find the right words. Rose just laughed and reached for a bowl and spoon.

"Want a taste?"

"Yeah!" Jeremy reached out to take hold of the spoon she used for stirring the pot.

"You'll be sorry," Max mumbled.

Jeremy glared at his sister. Rose shook her head, smiling.

"For what? And good morning to you, Max." She went over to the stove and turned on the burner under the griddle.

"Mornin'." Max yawned and gave her a grin of apology. "Don't get him started tasting everything. He'll eat it all while your back is turned."

"I will not!" her brother yelped.

"Opening night of *Snow White*. You ate every cherry tart Rita brought. You got so sick..." She snorted. "It's a good thing *Dopey* didn't have a big part. He spent more time in the bathroom than he did on the stage."

"I heard about that." Rose nodded and winked at Max so Jeremy couldn't see. "It's tradition for Jeremy to get sick on opening night."

"No fair!" Jeremy tried to pout, but he watched Rose turn the fresh pancakes and the aroma made him smile instead.

"No yelling," Max groaned. "Is there anything ready? I have to shower and scramble to work. Tony kept me up writing until 2:00. I hate him! He only got a few hours of sleep and he's hammering away on the stage like he went to bed at 8:00." She groaned again, smiling, as Rose brought over a fresh plate of pancakes. "Plan on running the box office alone tonight, Jeremy. Roger is doubling on lights again, to try to catch that short that keeps popping up."

"When have I ever goofed up the box office?" Jeremy said with scorn wrinkling his face.

"My brother, the wolf of Wall Street." She speared a single pancake and lifted it onto her plate. Jeremy reached for the other three.

"You're always grumpy when you have writer's block."

"Hardly." Max stopped him, grabbing at his wrist with one hand and squeezing syrup onto her pancakes with the other hand. "How many of those have you eaten?"

"Not nearly enough. Aunt Rose—"

"Six," Rose intervened. "And that'll be seven, eight and nine. Save some for your sister. I need you to run a few errands for me on the way home from school. More groceries for tonight's opening night feast."

"Ah—" Max stopped with a forkful of pancake between her lips. She gestured while trying to swallow quickly.

"I know the tradition, Max. Eat and run."

"And eat and run," Jeremy added with a chuckle.

"And *you* are going to run for me." Rose reached into the pocket of her red-checkered apron and pulled out a long slip of paper and a thick fold of dollar bills, which she handed to Jeremy. "Here's the list and money. And none of your famous penny pinching. Get the freshest and the best."

Jeremy nodded, eyes gleaming. Max frowned at him, eyes narrowed in suspicion.

"You just loosed a monster," she mumbled, reaching for the milk pitcher. "Give Jeremy money and free rein and you're headed for trouble."

~~~~~

Jeremy had his plan in place when he walked into the grocery store after school. When Rose's list asked for a fifteen-ounce can, he settled for twelve. When she specified extra-large eggs, he bought large. He kept track of the difference in prices and calculated he had saved nearly $12. He pocketed five as his "commission."

He had called the florist from school to order the corsage for Rose. When he got home, he would have to scramble to open all the cans, put away the eggs, and otherwise hide the evidence of his penny-pinching
~~~~~

before he went out again to get the corsage.

No one was in the kitchen when Jeremy got home. He grinned at the butterfly feeling of relief that scrambled his insides, then shifted into high gear. In moments, the cartons were open and tossed into the trash, with the receipt on the bottom. He dumped the fish and the beef cubes into two colanders and rinsed them in cold water, just like his mother did. He shoved the wrappers showing the weights down into the garbage. He put the eggs in the rack in the refrigerator and the carton went into the garbage. He opened the pineapple into a wire strainer over a mixing bowl. The can followed the egg carton. Other containers and their incriminating labels were soon hidden in the trash. Phase one complete. Jeremy grinned when he heard the footsteps approaching the kitchen door.

"Back so soon?" Rose said, smiling when she walked into the kitchen. "You must have gone through the store like a whirlwind."

"I go shopping for Mom all the time." He dug into his pocket. "Here's your change."

"Sweetheart, you keep it. Boys always need pocket money, and you've saved me goodness knows how much time."

"Thanks." Jeremy stuffed his hand back into his pocket. "Can I help with anything?"

"Not right now. Later on, when it's time to set up the table." She shooed him out of the kitchen with a smile.

"That was easier than I thought," Jeremy muttered.

Somehow, he didn't feel as pleased with himself as he had been when he made his plans. Maybe it was just opening night jitters. After all, this was the first opening night in the history of Homespun Theater that his parents hadn't attended. That was all it was.

~~~~~

"Where're you running off to?" Tony demanded, when Jeremy tried to slip out the kitchen door while everyone else got to work, preparing for opening night.

Jeremy sighed and let the door close with him still inside the house. In the last forty minutes, he swore every person in the building had stopped him. He had only been able to taste half the dishes Aunt Rose had made. Usually by this time on opening night, he had tasted everything. Twice.

"I gotta get up to McKay's before they close at six," he explained.

"You'll never make it." Tony looked Jeremy over and shook his head. "You feeling okay? You look like you went through finals week."

"I'm fine!" he snapped. Then he wished he hadn't. His head throbbed. "I'll make it—only ten minutes on my bike. That leaves five minutes to get the flowers."

"Flowers, huh?" His eyes went unfocused for a few seconds.
~~~~~

"Sometimes I don't think my head is attached. I'm just about as hopeless..." He sighed, shifted his gaze to Jeremy, then grinned. "I don't think opening night flowers for Max will make her forgive you if you don't open the box office on time."

"But—"

"I'll drive you. Let me get my keys and I'll meet you at my car." He didn't wait for Jeremy to react before heading back into the other room.

Jeremy ran. He didn't care that running made his stomach woozy. Those opening night jitters were worse than anything he had ever known.

When he met Tony at the car, he asked him how the new book was coming along. Tony's enthusiastic chatter kept Jeremy from thinking about anything else for the ride up to the florist. He was startled when Tony went into the store with him. A surge of jealousy shot through him when Tony ordered a big bouquet of irises and carnations, and then ordered a dozen yellow roses to be sent over to the hospital for Emily, and didn't flinch at the price the woman at the counter gave him. Someday, Jeremy swore, he was going to have enough money so he wouldn't have to worry about prices and making sure he had something for later.

The only problem was that his parents wouldn't let him play the stock market, his duties for the theater didn't take many hours, meaning the pay was low, and he didn't have enough in his savings/checking account to earn interest. It just wasn't fair the bank wouldn't pay interest until he had $5,000 in his account. He was still stewing over his inability to make money hand-over-fist when he climbed back into the car with Tony.

"Not to criticize." Tony eyed the tiny pink roses in the clear plastic box. "Those aren't exactly Max's flowers. She likes carnations and irises."

"It's not for Max," Jeremy mumbled, head bowed and gaze on the clear plastic container in his lap. "For Aunt Rose. She's doing all the cooking and stuff."

"Oh." Tony put the car into reverse, but didn't pull away from the florist's shop. "There's still time."

"For what?"

"To get Max something. It's her opening night, too."

"I don't have any money left." Jeremy half-hoped Tony would offer to lend him some. He wondered where his brain had been, not to get Max something.

"Hey, tightwad!" Tony slapped his arm. "I know better. And you're making a big mistake, leaving Max out. She's still not comfortable about your aunt staying at the house."

"Aunt Rose is great!" His head pounded at his volume, but Jeremy didn't care. How could anyone not like Aunt Rose?

"That may be why." Tony pulled out of the parking lot. "You guys treat her like she's always been part of the family. You notice Max doesn't call her aunt all the time? Maybe she's feeling left out. Or jealous."

"Max? Jealous?" Jeremy would have laughed, but his stomach churned again. "Naaah."

His stomach felt worse when he got home and gave Rose the corsage. He blamed his discomfort on the way Rose got teary-eyed and hugged him. Jeremy wished he could have missed the blank look Max wore or the quiet tone of her voice when she complimented Rose on the flowers. Jeremy was glad to retreat to the box office, pull out the cash box and ticket folders, and open the shutters.

Then he thought about that big bouquet Tony had hurried into the house after Max left the kitchen. What did he say about Max and flowers? The idea that tried to climb into his brain stunned him. After a second, Jeremy shook his head and bent over his work. There was no way in the world — Max and Tony?

~~~~~

Chuck Winters was familiar with the backstage area of Homespun. He was grateful for that when he drove up behind the theater and parked his rental car between Max's Cavalier and Joel's Mustang. Right where he always parked. He came in through the back door. Anticipation of meeting up with Steve Vincente did give him some trepidation he hadn't felt in years. He was determined to get some answers from that young man, but not at the cost of Max's opening night.

"Excuse me? That door isn't for the public." A little gray-haired woman stepped away from the stove, holding up a wooden spoon. Winters didn't doubt she would clobber him with it.

"You must be Aunt Rose." He held out his hand and turned on the charm. "I'm Chuck Winters, Max's agent and a friend of Joel and Emily. I don't suppose anybody warned you I always come for opening night?"

"Chuck!" Tony paused in the doorway. "I completely forgot. I bet Max did, too. Aunt Rose, this is —"

"Max's agent. I just heard." Rose managed a flustered smile and put down the spoon in the rest on the stove. She gestured through the swinging door into the Green Room. "Good luck catching up with Max. Nice to meet you," she added, blushing a little, as Tony guided Winters out of the kitchen.

"Nice to meet you too, Rose. I look forward to tasting your feast." Winters waited until the door closed behind them. "Bad?"

"The usual chaos. I honestly don't know if Max was worried about you showing or not showing." Tony gestured at the backstage door. "If you want —"

"There's the face I was looking for. Go on without me." Winters sent up a silent prayer of thanks when Bekka Sanderson walked into the Green Room, consulting a clipboard as she walked. He was grateful Max had
~~~~~

sent him a few photos of Bekka, so he knew his newest client on sight. Any excuse to avoid revealing his secondary mission. "Bekka? I'm Chuck Winters. Nice to finally meet you."

Five minutes later, he followed Bekka into the dimness of backstage and took his usual chair tucked into the corner by the director's booth, where they could talk. After a few moments of being flustered, she had been business-like and professional. He approved when she put her opening night duties ahead of making a good impression on her agent— which just meant she made a very good impression. Bekka explained her duties as assistant to the director as she checked off the items on her clipboard. He spotted Steve darting around on the catwalk with two other stage technicians, checking cable connections, and kept an eye on him as he and Bekka talked. Winters was relieved, however, when a small crisis at the prop table on the other side of the stage drew Bekka away. He got up and headed over to the ladder Steve would have to climb down. He didn't have long to wait, and held his peace until his target had both feet on the ground.

"Steven." Winters didn't bother hiding his smirk when his voice, coming out of the shadows, made Steve jump about five inches. The young man stared, then looked around, gesturing Winters to silence. He gestured with a tip of his head and walked to the Green Room, and Steve followed him. They went out the front door, for some relative privacy.

"Are you going to tell my father?" Steve asked.

"Hmm, no questions about what I'm doing here, or why I'm here. Did you think I came looking for you?"

"That'd be kind of arrogant, wouldn't it?" He managed a crooked smile. "I'm guessing you're a friend of the family." He put extra emphasis on the last word, and something clutched at Winters' heart.

Did he know the truth? Carlo had given no indication that he knew his oldest son was here, spying on Max and her family.

"Why are you here?" Winters asked, and didn't care about the weary tone of his voice.

"Checking out suspicions. Looking after people." He wrapped his arms around himself, then leaned back against the house. "I remember Miss Emily from when I was a kid. I really liked her. I blamed her when Dad went to France and didn't take me with him."

That childhood connection had never occurred to Winters. He guessed that he had forgotten Steve ever knew Emily.

"Why are you here? Did your father send you?"

"Dad thinks I'm working on an indy film out where there's no cell phone access."

"Which brings me back to my first question."

"Is Max my sister?" Steve whispered, without looking Winters in the eyes.

"You'll have to ask Emily." He mimicked Steve's pose. "What are you doing here, Steven? Besides using your mother's maiden name?"

"Helping out where I'm needed right now. Don't worry." He grinned. "I won't cause trouble. These are nice people. I like them a lot."

"Is that your way of asking me not to tell your father what you're doing?"

"They don't need any more problems right now."

"That's true." Winters closed his eyes, wishing he had arrived earlier, so he could have taken a hotel room. No, scratch that—so he could have visited Emily and Joel. He would do that tomorrow before he headed home. "Okay, here's the deal. I'll hold my peace and trust you to look after everybody here and report to me if there's even a hint of trouble. Got me?"

"Just like they were my own family." Steve held out his hand to shake and seal the deal. His expression was deathly serious.

~~~~~

Max finally started to relax ten minutes before the curtain went up. Opening night was the usual ordered chaos. She would have worried if preparations had gone too smoothly. The only thing missing was Joel moving through the house and theater in his usual benign tornado style, bellowing happily and tweaking everything into perfect running order, while Emily maintained a center of calm that people could run to with the slightest problem. Chuck Winters had come for opening night, as promised. He had offered to sit behind stage and help, but Max had refused. Tradition demanded he sit front and center and give his usual helpful feedback on the performance. No one could take her parents' place anyway, no matter how hard he tried.

She sat in the living room, a headset strung around her neck, checking her clipboard. Rita sat with her, handling a few bits of last-minute mending on costumes needed later in the play. Half the actors were behind stage, helping each other rehearse lines or taking peeks at the audience. Full house—it would have pleased Joel immensely to see that. The rest of the company was either in the lighting booth, walking the catwalks making last-minute adjustments to the lights, or in the dressing rooms.

Rose walked out of the kitchen with a platter of chicken and gravy on rice and set it on the dining table. It had been expanded with all its leaves and two folding tables added to it to hold the opening night buffet. Max admitted Rose had done a wonderful job. She remembered how her mother took such enjoyment in all the fussy little details for opening night. For once, those memories didn't hurt. Max almost smiled, but her gaze kept straying to the corsage Jeremy had given Rose.

"Well, that brings back old times," Rita murmured. She gestured at
~~~~~

Rose. "You're accepting her a lot faster than I thought."

"That's from Jeremy." Max bent her head back to her work. "The little skinflint stuck a crowbar in his wallet."

"Jealous?"

"That'll be the day!" She glanced up, relieved to see Rose had vanished back into the kitchen. "I swear—it's like she's cast a spell over the boys. One of these days, she'll suggest they go home to Boston with—" She stopped short, remembering that overheard conversation between Rose and Della. Max knew her fear was irrational, but she'd had nightmares of finding herself alone in the house. "Forget it. Opening night jitters."

"You think she'll steal the boys?" Rita gave her an incredulous smile.

"She doesn't have to try so hard."

"Well, I think you're wrong. Rose is just a nice person who needs to be needed."

"Not that she isn't a help." Max's face heated. "Overreacting?"

"Just a little." The pastor's wife leaned closer and studied Max's face, her blue eyes sympathetic. "How much sleep have you had lately?"

"Rita!"

"I'm serious. You need a good, long rest after everything you've done the last week."

"Just let the first performance go all right, and I swear I'll sleep like a baby tonight." Max managed a weary smile and raised her arms to the ceiling, stretching the kinks out of her back. "I think my problem is that she does everything so well. There's nothing to complain about. Does that make any sense?"

"It means you're human, Max, not super-daughter." Rita squeezed her hand. "Your parents will be so proud of you when all of this is over."

"If it's ever over."

"How often do you talk about it with God?"

"Not often enough." She shook her head and stood up. "I have to get going. I have a curtain to raise in two minutes."

"We're all praying, Max," Rita whispered, as she hurried through the door into the backstage darkness.

Please, God... Max couldn't finish her prayer. That was the way a lot of them were going lately. An unfinished plea, a longing mixed with fear. She just had to depend on the certainty that God knew what she really wanted and needed. He knew what was in her heart and mind, even if she couldn't put it into words for herself. And no matter what she thought, He would make sure the best outcome for everyone resulted.

Chapter Twelve

Jeremy closed up the box office half an hour into the performance and came through the front door into the living room. He took the cash box, properly counted and all the tickets accounted for and logged, and went upstairs to the safe hidden among the props in the loft. For a few seconds, he couldn't remember the combination, and that frightened him a little. His head throbbed when he scurried down the winding stairs to the living room again.

By the time he got to the bottom, he was sweating and his stomach had decided enough was enough. The women's dressing room was closest.

Fortunately, it was empty. After Jeremy's stomach was also empty, he sat a long time on the chilly tiles, leaning his head against the cool metal side of the stall. He felt hollow and weak with relief. Only the sour taste in his mouth could prompt him to move. He needed root beer. When he reached the door of the dressing room, he had recovered enough to have the sense to inch the door open and make sure the coast was clear.

Rose fussed over the table, refilling the coleslaw bowl. Max came out of the kitchen, her water bottle clicking with ice and dripping a little.

"Max, you haven't eaten anything," Rose said with a chuckle. "You can't be that nervous anymore. The performance is going wonderfully."

"Yeah," she murmured and headed for the door backstage.

"Joel will be delighted. He won't be surprised, though," the woman continued. "He's been saying for years that he could turn everything over to you without a worry."

"Good thing I was ready, huh?" She paused in the doorway and glanced back.

Jeremy saw and he felt his empty stomach twist when Max's gaze rested on Rose's corsage. Maybe Tony was right. He should have bought flowers for Max, too.

"Max, what's bothering you?"

"Nothing. Everything is great."

"I haven't been here long, but I know when you're not telling the truth." Rose gasped softly. "I'm not really part of things yet, am I?" Two bright spots in her cheeks matched her roses. Jeremy hated that corsage.

"The guys love you. They'd be lost without you."

"How about you?"

"Look, I have to get back." Max tugged on the cord of the headphones she wore slung around her neck. "Bekka is handling things, but—"

"I'm doing everything I can to help here, Max, but it's useless if we can't work together."

"We are." She opened the door to go back behind stage.

"No." Rose darted around the table and caught hold of Max's sleeve. From Jeremy's vantage point, it looked like the move startled them both. "Max, why do you resent me? I just want to help. Joel's my brother. *All* of you are my family."

"Especially the boys. I bet if you could talk them into going to visit Boston with you, it'd get you in good with your father again, wouldn't it?"

"With my—" She gasped as if she had lost her breath. "I would never do anything to hurt my brother. Least of all hand over his sons to that bitter old man."

"Look, I'm under a lot of pressure right now. This is the first opening night without Mom and Dad—Jeremy got you flowers—those are Mom's flowers—"

"You think I'm trying to take her place?" Rose shook her head. "I would never do that. I'm never going back to Boston, even if that vicious old man got down on his knees and begged."

"I know. I just—Jeremy is such a skinflint, it shocked me to see those flowers. I kept thinking he robbed a bank." Max gulped and rubbed at her eyes. "I've been stupid, okay? I'm sorry." She yanked the door closed behind her.

Jeremy released the breath he had been holding, louder than he expected. Rose turned and looked directly at the door to the women's bathroom.

"Come on out, Jeremy," she said very softly, with no emotion at all in her voice.

He came out, head hanging.

"You heard all that, hmm?" Rose slowly reached up to unpin the corsage. "Where did you get the money, Jeremy?"

"You gave me..." He felt cold deep inside as she took off the corsage and delicately laid it among the opening night flowers sitting in the middle of the table.

"I didn't give you enough for flowers. I was so delighted to have them, to think that you accepted me—"

"You're family, Aunt Rose. You belong here."

"Not if my being here causes problems. Not if it prompts you to dishonesty. Your father told me about your tricks to save money. You pinched pennies, didn't you?"

"It's tradition," he whispered as he nodded.

"Honesty is a better one, dear." Rose turned to go back into the kitchen. "What bothers me most is how much you hurt your sister. You really should have given her flowers, first. She's doing the hardest job."

"I'm sorry."

"I know." She paused in the doorway to the kitchen. "I think you'd better apologize to Max, too."

Jeremy didn't question, though he stayed where he was until the swinging door slowly settled into place again. Then he went backstage and found Max. He watched her, waiting until she smiled at something someone in the tech crew said over the headphones. Then he went to his knees next to her chair and wrapped his arms around her waist.

Max nearly jumped out of her chair. For a moment, Jeremy thought she would hit him. Then she sighed and wrapped her arms around him.

"It's going to be okay, brat-fink," she whispered. "Just let me get my head on straight."

~~~~~

"Emergency," Steve hissed as he passed Tony, heading for the ladder up into the side loft. "Audrey's getting flowers tonight." He tipped his head toward the corner where Max and Bekka took turns monitoring all the backstage chatter and handling emergencies.

Tony stood for several moments, staring at the table and the two dark heads bent over the clipboard with the lighting and sound cues before he realized what he *didn't* see. The paper-wrapped bouquet of Max's flowers had vanished. He had put it there after the curtain went up, while Max helped Lynette sew up a last-minute tear in Morgan's costume. He had exchanged a grin with Bekka, pressed a finger to his lips for silence, and went to his first duty station.

Something told him Max hadn't stashed her flowers when she found them. Because she hadn't found them.

Tony put down the stool he had brought over to the wings, set it out of the path of traffic, and trotted around behind the curtains to the door into the Green Room. Then it occurred to him to wonder how Steve knew those flowers were from him, specifically. The newcomer paid too much attention to the comings and goings in the theater. Especially anything having to do with Max.

He found the bouquet sitting at Audrey's usual seat in the long row of makeup tables. A torn piece of paper with her name scribbled on it was tucked into the folds of the paper wrapping. Tony would recognize Jake's scrawl anywhere. Eyes narrowed, he carefully tugged the paper out, crumpled it and put it in his pocket, then unrolled the paper wrapping. His card for Max was still inside, among the stems and baby's breath. Not only was Jake a thief, he was a sloppy thief.

What was ironic was that the flowers wouldn't soften Audrey toward Jake at all. He seemed to think that since he was the handsomest guy in
~~~~~

the cast and Audrey was the prettiest girl, it automatically meant they belonged together. After nearly two years of productions—and Jake being slapped down consistently every time he made a claim on her—Audrey's irritation had congealed into disgust. And Jake appeared totally oblivious to Audrey's attitude toward him. Tony supposed that appearances were more important to Jake than being with someone who actually liked him.

He enjoyed the thought of Jake's consternation when those flowers showed up on Max's table again.

"I'll keep watch," Steve said, when Tony returned backstage.

"Thanks, but Bekka can do that." He offered a grin and fought down the image of Steve being there, holding the flowers to hand to Max when she returned to her station after the latest emergency. It was ridiculous to think Steve would try to get into Max's good graces through lying, but what did he really know about the guy?

"I wondered where those went," Bekka whispered, when Tony put the bouquet down. A shout erupted from onstage and they both paused a few moments to watch the action as Morgan chased Gretchen around the stage, both of them snarling and hurling Shakespearean quips at each other, to the delight of the audience. "Do I tell Max they're from you?" she said, when the scene came to an end, Gretchen slumped to the floor, dazed, and Morgan strutted offstage with the audience roaring applause.

"How well can you imitate Sergeant Schultz?" He hated that momentary blank look on Bekka's face. Nothing like throwing out a cultural reference and realizing that no one caught it because it was before their time. Tony happened to love *Hogan's Heroes* re-runs.

"*Sieg heil, mine Kommandant,*" she muttered, in a passable German accent. "I know nuthink!"

Tony sauntered over to his next station. It gave him a good vantage point to watch when Max came back to the desk to see the bouquet. Then the pantomime of Bekka playing dumb and gesturing all around backstage, indicating she hadn't seen the flowers arrive. There was just enough light backstage for him to see Max's sudden stillness and her smile when she found the note from the secret admirer with the flowers.

Maybe just hinting that someone cared was a slow start, but Tony knew better than to drop the bombshell of his feelings on her while all her energy went to getting her family through this crisis. No reason not to let Max know she was admired and someone cared about her.

Next step: drop hints about marriage and the two of them being a good pair beyond writing books together. Having a house ready for their new home would prove to Max that he was serious.

Wednesday, April 30

Max, Rose, Joe and Jeremy went to the hospital together around noon to report to Joel on opening night.

"I admit, I had a white-knuckle grip on my blankets, wondering how it was going. Then I figured if I didn't hear from you, everything was fine. You'd only call for an emergency," Joel said, chuckling. "The reviews in the papers were all great. I'm proud of you, Max."

"Thanks, Dad." She shrugged, feeling that mix of relief and delight and guilt she always got when something she had thought would be a disaster went well. "I had a lot of help." She braced herself to turn to Rose. "If you weren't there, I don't know what I would have done half the time."

"Oh, you would have done just fine," Rose said, shaking her head, her cheeks pink.

"Uh huh," Joel murmured. His grin grew wider. "Well, not that I have any doubt about your ability to handle things, but I think I should get home as soon as possible."

"That'd be great," Max said, perching on the end of the bed. "How?"

"All arranged." He leaned back against his pillows with a grin. "Ambulance is waiting, plus all the gear I need to make life livable until I get out of this thing." He slapped at his cast. "If you don't mind me sitting around backstage for the next few nights."

"You're kidding—you're not kidding, are you, Dad?" Joe blurted, dropping the tangled mess he had made of the string trick he was always practicing.

"Nope." He looked around at his stunned family. "I'm allowed to come home, I hope."

"Sure—but everything's kind of a mess," Max began.

"When isn't the house a mess?"

"How do we get you up and down the stairs in that cast?" Rose asked.

"I'll stay downstairs. The parole agreement includes a hospital bed and wheelchair."

"Tony's staying downstairs," Max said. "It's crowded with everything else going on backstage. With two of you? Sardines!"

"Give him your mother's and my room."

"But Dad—" She decided to give up before she sounded any more helpless. It was what she had been praying for, wasn't it?

~~~~~

Rose stopped in the kitchen doorway, stunned. She had left the lunch dishes soaking, intending to get the kitchen cleaned up, start on dinner, and make a double batch of cookies when she got back from the hospital. Now, though, all the dishes were washed and put away, the counter glistened, that cherry pop stain on the floor scrubbed—and all her baking supplies put away.
~~~~~

Tony had struck again.

She had jokingly told him that he was to stay out of her kitchen or suffer a broom to his backside. Obviously, Tony had taken her mild threat *as* a joke and ignored the order.

If he weren't so nice about helping out around the house, Rose would have strangled him. There was something very wrong about a man of his age being so overly helpful. As if he were trying to impress someone.

The ambulance driver and his assistant pushed Joel's wheelchair up the impromptu ramp to the back porch and the kitchen door, and Rose now had to get out of the way. She propped the door open wide and made a mental note to talk to Tony a little more seriously. Maybe with a rolling pin in hand.

She hurried ahead to hold open the swinging door into the living room. That, at least, looked a little more normal. Max and the boys had gone to visit their mother while Rose waited with Joel to process the release paperwork and then ride home in the ambulance with him. The three had returned home ahead of them to push aside couches and costumes and rework the living space downstairs. The dividers for Tony's temporary bedroom sat to one side, his cot and storage chest removed. A torch lamp that used to sit in the corner by the makeup table now sat to one side of a wide swath of empty floor space, where the hospital bed would sit. Max plugged the telephone into the extension cord and set it on a high table next to the lamp when Rose walked into the room.

Joe, Jeremy and Tony were conspicuous by their absence. Rose opened her mouth to ask why none of them were downstairs helping Max when she heard Jeremy yelp, and the sound of something heavy being dragged upstairs.

"Ready?" she asked.

"Ready as we'll ever be." Max looked beyond her and slapped a hand over her mouth, barely smothering a chuckle.

Rose turned and found the two hospital workers staring at the organized chaos of the Randolph backstage household. What made her want to laugh with Max was the realization of how quickly she had grown used to it. After all, what was wrong with having Shakespearean costumes hanging along one wall, twenty pairs of boots and swords and hats lined up in the costume rack, a long makeup table filled with jars and tubes and more brushes than an art school — all in the living room?

Joel looked around the familiar mess with a wide grin. "This is more like it!" he said, loudly enough to stop the sounds of struggle upstairs.

"Dad's home!" Jeremy shrieked.

"I don't suppose the doctor gave you anything to keep him quiet?" Max asked Rose, both of them grinning.

"Enough of that, kiddo. Somebody help me out of this thing!" Joel twisted around in the chair to address the two men delivering him home. "Can you help me out before you leave?"

Jeremy scrambled under the banister and slid down the pole, nearly missing the cushions waiting at the bottom. Joe rattled and thumped down the winding steps, with Tony right behind.

"Are you sure you should get out of that, Dad?" Max detoured around a box of costumes to reach his side.

"What do we do now?" Tony demanded. He looked from Max to Joel to the hospital workers.

"I don't know if I *should*, but I know what'll feel a whole lot more comfortable—that lumpy old couch right over there. Give me a couple pillows and a cup of coffee and I'll be just fine." Joel pushed himself across the room to a four-man couch full of scratchy brown cushions.

Rose opened her mouth to protest, partially delighted in her brother's high spirits. Then she saw the slight tremble in his hands, the smears of dark under his eyes. Joel was a very good actor, but he couldn't fool her. The ride home had worn him out and only the family stubbornness kept him going.

"If that's what you want, Joel." Rose sighed, pretending resigned frustration. "But I want your word, once you're on that couch you'll stay out of our way for a few hours. If you don't rest, I'll make you drink hot milk until it comes out your ears and you'll sleep through the performance. You hear me?"

"Yes'm." Joel grinned and played meek.

His grin faded, though, when the two men showed the boys how to slide him from the chair to the couch. Rose watched his hands tighten on the blankets covering the cast and noticed the fine sheen of sweat on his forehead. He didn't resist when she settled pillows behind him, pulled the blankets up to his chin, and ordered him to be quiet and close his eyes. He was asleep before they had finished putting the sheets on the hospital bed.

"You read him like a book, don't you?" Max whispered, coming up behind Rose when she stooped to check on him.

"I was ten when he was born. Mother died when he was four, so I guess I raised him." Rose shrugged and met Max's eyes. "Can't you tell when he's bluffing you?"

"Mom's the only one who can." She sighed and rubbed at her eye with a grubby fist. "Good thing you're here."

She managed a lopsided smile and turned back to adjusting the furniture and the traffic pattern in the room. Rose watched her, feeling a little better. Not that she didn't worry about Joel, convalescing amidst the chaos of a Shakespearean production, but if that was what her brother wanted, what made him comfortable, then he would get it.

~~~~~
~~~~~

"So, Max, how does it feel, being the boss while your parents are in the hospital?"

Tony stopped short, just before coming around the corner to the front of the theater. So did Max and Steve. The three of them carried gardening tools, to do some quick work on the landscaping around the front door and the sidewalk from the parking lot, before tonight's performance.

The male voice asking the question came from around the corner. Max's frown showed she was just as confused as Tony. Steve moved first, taking two steps to the corner and looking around it. He looked back, scowling, and gestured for Max and Tony to step up next to him.

"I should have known," Max muttered.

Tony repressed a growl and silently echoed the sentiment. Jake stood on the front steps of the theater, very obviously giving an interview to three strangers with cameras and tape recorders.

"You can't let him get away with it," Steve said.

"He's right." Tony exchanged a glance with Steve. What was the next step for Jake? First digging through Max's private paperwork and now pretending to be her and giving interviews to the paparazzi who wouldn't take a hint and leave.

"The last thing I need..." She clenched her jaw, nodded sharply, and stomped around the side of the theater to the front step. "Jake, why aren't you getting into costume and makeup? You have some lines to go over. You don't want to mess up your scene in act three again, like you did *last night*, do you?"

Chapter Thirteen

"Who's Jake?" the first man said. He glanced back and forth between Max and Jake, who turned dark red, shaking his head and sputtering.

"He is. Jake Holt. He's part of the ensemble here at my family's theater. Right now he's playing Lucentio in *Taming of the Shrew*. There are still tickets available, if you're interested in some culture." She took up a wide-legged stance on the grass, arms crossed, holding pruning shears in one hand and a garden claw in the other.

"Your family?" the woman in the trio said. She held out a tape recorder. "So you're the mysterious Maureen?"

"No, that's *Maxine*. Maxine Randolph. I'm the oldest, named for my mom's Aunt Maxine. My brothers are Joseph and Jeremiah."

"But the woman over there said your name was Maureen." She gestured in the general direction of Mrs. Pluch's house.

"Don't pass it around, but she's a couple bricks shy of a full load." Max raised the weeding claw, just in time to mess up the photo the man on the right tried to snap of her. Tony muffled a chuckle at her impeccable timing. "Jake, what are you doing standing there when I gave you an order? I'm the director, remember?"

"Only as long as your dad is in the hospital," Jake snarled.

Someone in the trio laughed, and made no effort to muffle the sound. Tony decided now might be a good time to join Max for some moral support. He stepped up next to her before he realized Steve had stayed around the corner, in hiding.

"Just shows you're not up on the news," Tony said. "Joel came home today. Ah, no," he hurried to say, when the three paparazzi turned as one and took steps toward the front door of the house, "nobody is allowed in the house. The big boss needs his rest before tonight's performance. Which you need to get ready for," he added, glaring pointedly at Jake.

Tony hated that little smirk and nod that Jake gave him as he turned to head into the theater. The point he made was that he listened to Tony, but not Max. The three intruders clearly caught on to the power play.

"Who are you?" the woman asked, holding her tape recorder nearly in Tony's face.

"Tony Martin. Max's writing partner. We write romance under the pen name of Antonia Maxwell." He muffled laughter when the interest that sparked at his second statement died as soon as *romance* left his lips.

Ten minutes later, the three left in three different vehicles after asking several pointed questions about Max and Tony's non-writing relationship and how many times they researched love scenes before they wrote them. Tony took the questions because Max refused to speak, just standing there, glaring, her arms crossed. She didn't even wait for them to vanish down the street before she flung her weeding hook down into the flowerbed.

"What I wouldn't give for a couple photon torpedoes right now!"

Steve burst out laughing as he came from hiding and joined them.

"Coward." Max glared at him, turned, and stomped up the steps and into the theater.

"That didn't go well," Steve said, and bent to pick up the gardening tools.

"You vanishing into thin air, or the gossip rags digging into our lives?" Tony said.

"Max, denying there was anything between the two of you."

"She didn't say anything."

"Exactly. If she had argued, like you did, or if she had laughed, there'd be some hope for the two of you, wouldn't there? It's the old Gertrude syndrome."

"Gertrude?"

"From *Hamlet*. 'The lady doth protest too much.' Max's silence says... well, I wouldn't be too discouraged, if I were you." Steve clapped Tony on the shoulder.

"Discouraged over what?" He stared at the door of the theater where Max had vanished. Why wouldn't she open her mouth to defend their friendship?

"Well, from where I'm sitting, you're completely focused on Max, but she's too busy with the rest of her life to notice you."

"Ya think?"

"Not that my opinion matters, but you two are good together. Just hang on until the crisis is over."

"You haven't been here long enough." Tony managed a chuckle as they settled down to work on the weeds. "There's always a crisis of one size or another." He decided to be encouraged. For all he knew, the intrusive questions would put the image of the two of them being romantically involved in Max's head.

Thursday, May 1

Something odd was going on between Tony and Steve. Max had suspected it, catching glances the two shared, a nod, a frown, a tip of the head by one, followed by the other going in that direction a moment later.

She watched for it during that evening's performance. Tony passed Steve, heading for the left wing, and nodded his head toward the Green Room door. When Steve immediately changed direction, Max followed. She made sure everything was going smoothly on stage, then stepped into the Green Room doorway. She took a step back immediately when she spotted Steve in the shadows of the shelving, staring at the office area.

That got her hackles up. She had caught Jake doing a bad imitation of casually leaning over her or Joel's desk one time too many and now felt protective to the point of being paranoid. What was Steve doing, giving her desk the eagle eye?

Steve stomped on the creakiest board of the doorway — it had to be deliberate, because she had seen him avoid it with the grace of a dancer, even going at full speed. She saw him crack a grin as he crossed the Green Room. She followed, cautiously.

Jake stumbled over Joel's swivel chair and staggered for the refreshment table. Max leaned against the shelving, watching how Steve adjusted his path, looking far more convincing. He nodded to Jake, snatched one of the paper cups of ice water Rose kept filled for the cast, and continued to the men's dressing room. Jake nodded to him, almost spilling the cup of water he snatched off the table. Max fully expected him to mess up his costume. He wasn't due back on stage for ten minutes.

Plenty of time for him to try to dig through her desk.

What if he got into the business records for the theater? She and Joel had nothing to hide, and the sensitive information like passwords were locked up, but the principle of the thing irritated her.

She counted slowly from the time the men's dressing room door closed behind Steve. At eleven, Jake tossed the half-emptied paper cup into the trash and headed back to the office alcove. Max wondered how he could be so oblivious not to look around to make sure he wasn't being watched. Or was it arrogance?

Jake didn't dig through her papers sitting in the filing boxes like he had the last three times she caught him invading her privacy. She shivered when he opened the bottom drawer of her desk. There was nothing in it but her fellowship information and invitations to speak at various writing conferences across the country, as a Gabrielli finalist. Max choked down a shout when Jake pulled out a folder and opened it on her desk.

"What's your excuse this time?" she spat.

"Aren't you supposed to be directing?" Jake shot back, going dark red under his makeup. She swore if he sweated and ruined all that makeup, she'd boot him and give Joe his role on the spot. Joe could take over as Lucentio tonight, if she had to undress Jake herself and stuff her brother into his costume.

"You're supposed to be paying attention to the play." Max stomped over to her desk and flipped the folder closed. "What part of privacy don't you understand?"

"Gee, give a guy a hard time for being a little supportive." Jake chuckled, but a dangerous spark lit his eyes.

"Digging through my desk isn't supportive. It's invasive."

"Just want to know what's going on with your writing. I want a chance to act in a movie you wrote. That's what pals are for." He reached out to pat Max's cheek and laughed when she slapped at his hand, yanking it away before she could hit it. "You should really learn to relax and be friendly, Maxi. That's the name of the game. Looking out for each other, being friends, giving a guy a break. If you don't play nice, you never know when somebody'll stab you in the back."

"Sounds like a threat to me," Steve said, somehow managing to materialize only five feet away from the office alcove.

"Mind your own business, techie," Jake snarled.

"*My* business is backstage. Where's yours?" He rocked back on his heels, arms crossed over his chest, and stared down Jake.

"You're on in five minutes," Max said.

She counted to fifteen, while Jake stared back and forth between her and Steve. Then he slapped the desk, stepped back, nearly tripped over her desk chair, and stalked across the room to the backstage door.

The only thing that could have made this latest confrontation with Jake worse was if he had yelled, Joel heard from his post in the wings, and he came wheeling into the living room to find out what happened. He was so happy being back in the thick of things behind the scenes, Max didn't want any worry to distract him. Not until later, at least.

"That guy just doesn't learn," Steve muttered, watching Jake leave. "Mind my asking what he's after?"

"An excuse to tell me how to live my life—or in this case, run my career." Max flipped through the folder, though she wasn't quite sure she would know if Jake had taken something out of it or not. She barely managed to flip it closed before she came to the booklet with the Vincente family photo. Did Steve know about the booklet? No, he couldn't. If he did, he would know his cover had been blown the moment she received it. She needed to keep the secret to protect herself.

"Seven more performances with the creep. Think you can stand it?"

"I was this close to booting him and giving his role to Joe," she admitted.

"The problem with a guy like Jake is that he won't see the warning. He'll consider it a violation of his rights, and he'll quit to punish you. I've seen it happen too many times. Guys like him..." Steve shrugged.

"You and Tony have been keeping an eye on him, haven't you?"

"Hey, that's part of the stagehands' creed—protect the boss like he, or she, is family." He winked at her. "Any way of putting some barbed wire around this place when someone can't be back here, standing guard?"

"I'll do better." Max hurried into the kitchen, where Rose was stirring something that smelled of tomatoes and spices in an enormous stockpot. She had noticed that Rose didn't smile when she saw Jake moving around the Green Room. She could ask the older woman to play guard dog because Jake was digging in her desk, no further reason needed.

Friday, May 2

"I don't suppose you'd consider directing from back here?" Max asked, breaking the companionable afternoon quiet between her and Joel.

Joe and Jeremy were still at school. Rose had agreed to attend Della's literary society meeting. Tony was out somewhere. Max and Joel were in the office alcove, working on bookkeeping and their plans for the next production, *Our Town.* They had three-quarters of the cast chosen already from their regular ensemble. The biggest job would be choosing from the summer interns due to arrive in two weeks, to fill the remaining spots in cast and crew.

"What?" Joel lifted his head from studying the theater's general ledger. He started to laugh, but her serious expression stopped him. "What's wrong? Dr. Holland said I was making great progress. All this wheeling around is good for me."

"I know. I'm glad you're taking back the directing. You have no idea how glad," she said, putting a grumble into her voice. As she wanted, the worry lines relaxed around Joel's eyes. Max would have given anything to avoid adding to his burdens.

"Okay, kiddo. Are you going to tell me what's up, or do we play twenty questions?"

"I've caught Jake poking around back here. I can't catch him taking anything, but he keeps snooping and digging through my papers even after he's told to stay away. Everybody else abides by the privacy rules." She raised and dropped her hands in frustrated defeat.

"Does he say why?"

"He *says* he's interested in my career. He keeps saying he wants to read my winning screenplay, and he acts like I'm depriving him of his rights when I say no."

"Why don't you let him?"

"Because, unlike everyone else around here, Jake demands. He doesn't ask. It's the principle of the thing."

"Maybe he's finally taking you seriously," Joel offered. "It galls him to admit he was wrong, so that makes him ruder than usual." He reached for his jumbo coffee mug and sat back.

"Jake can't get any ruder than he already is. Could you talk to him? He respects you. He's still a sexist jerk, no matter what manners you and Mom beat into him."

"Sure, I'll talk with him."

~~~~~

"Hurry it up, you wimp," Tony called, watching Jeremy struggle through the logjam of students leaving the high school across the street. He opened his car door and got out, waving his arm to urge the boy to move faster. "We got errands to run before the performance tonight."

"Who are you again? Max or Tony?" a vaguely familiar voice said from behind him.

Tony groaned and turned to see the taller of the photographers from the day before, standing by the passenger door of his car.

"Yeah, that's right. You're Tony." He sauntered around the front of the car and looked at the flood of students. "Tell me something. What's with you two?"

"I have no idea what you're talking about." For a split second, Tony thought about announcing that he planned to marry Max someday. The problem was that she would punch his lights out for reading in a gossip rag that they were engaged. At the very least, she would never take him seriously when he told her he loved her.

"Yeah, that's probably true." The photographer chuckled and pulled out a cigarette case and lighter from his back pocket.

Jeremy escaped the current of departing students and crossed the street to Tony's car.

"Tell me something. Is Max really her name?" He tapped the business end of the cigarette on the case and slipped it between his teeth. "Or do you call her Max because of her size?"

"Hey—" Jeremy yelped, and stopped, mouth dropping open as Tony swung, his fist connecting with fluid grace with the reporter's gut. He folded, dropping cigarette, case, and lighter. The cigarette and lighter rolled under Tony's car. "That was great!" the boy crowed and stomped up to the reporter. "Don't you ever talk about my sister like that!"

The photographer glared at Jeremy and opened his mouth to say something, then he snarled and backed away from them, his arms wrapped around his middle.

"Jeremy..." Tony sank into the driver's seat, watching the photographer until he got into another car, another thirty feet up the street.

"You are my hero." Jeremy scooted around to the passenger side and slid through the open window.

"Do me a favor? Don't tell Max."
~~~~~

"Why not?"

"Just..." He thought about that wide-eyed look of admiration showing up on Max's face. Okay, maybe it was egotistical, but he decided he could use all the brownie points he could get. "On second thought, might as well get the true story out there, before we read about it in the supermarket."

~~~~~

"Okay, tell me what I'm supposed to be stealing," Jake said, drawing himself up to his full height. He threw his wide shoulders back and straddled the lighting tree stand he was repairing. Half an hour after the audience had left, most of the cast and crew were still in the theater, re-setting the stage for Saturday night's performance.

Joel envied him, just for a few seconds. It seemed like forever since he had been able to take a stance like that. He felt small and old, sitting in his wheelchair, his leg straight out in front of him, looking up at everyone—even Jeremy. "She didn't say you stole anything."

"She didn't have to." He dropped the wrench he was using on some loose nuts holding the base plate to the pole. It crashed down into the toolbox. "You know, boss, I was really glad when you came back. All that power was going to her head."

"We're not talking about Max and how she does her job," Joel said, keeping his voice gentle. Max was right—Jake was a sexist jerk who couldn't handle a woman in authority over him. "We're talking about you poking around in a restricted area."

"Like I told her, I was just looking. Any law against reading what's laying out for everybody to see?"

Joel's throat hurt and he ached all over. It was hard to believe only a few minutes ago he had been so "up" from tonight's performance. "Opening file drawers and folders doesn't fit the definition of 'laying out for everybody to see.' I don't care what book you're looking in."

"She's not getting anywhere staying here. Did you know she's been invited to talk at seminars, just because she's a finalist?"

"She got invited because of her mother," he corrected, speaking slowly to fight his growing irritation with Jake. He wished Tony was there. They had all laughed at dinner over the story of him decking the photographer that afternoon. Joel liked the idea of Tony having a temper. Especially when it was in Max's defense. When would she and Tony take the hint that their relationship went deeper than friendship? "Max doesn't want to trade on her mother's unwanted publicity. Besides, she's staying here because I need her."

"That's the stupidest bunch of reasons I ever heard." Jake kicked the toolbox lid closed.

"Jake, just stay away from the office. Don't make me set a guard until you learn to follow rules."
~~~~~

"What, you don't trust me?" Jake grinned.

"Don't give us a reason not to trust you." Joel kept his tone mild, hating the fire he saw behind the other man's humor.

"Who do you think you are, talking to me like I'm a stupid kid?" he roared, his voice bouncing off the acoustic tiles and the flats. Even the thick, new black velvet of the flies couldn't muffle the volume and bite.

Faces of crew members taking care of lights appeared in the shadows of the catwalks. Other faces peered through the curtains from backstage, their attention drawn by Jake's bellow.

"I'm the owner, operator and director of this theater, that's who I *think* I am," Joel said, keeping his voice at a steady, gritty level that brooked no nonsense. "If you want to keep working here, you obey the rules. Talent doesn't make you exempt."

"Yeah? How about if I just don't come back? How'd you like to find a new actor with a week to go?"

"Joe's your understudy. He's ready to handle it." He smiled, both at Jake's jaw-dropping chagrin at his calm response, and the mental image of Joe's mixed panic and euphoria at being handed a major role halfway through a production.

"Maybe I should just leave now. Suit you?"

"That's your choice. I didn't fire you."

"Yeah, that's what *you* say."

"Keep in mind, Jake, everything is based on reputation in this business." Joel waited, but the other man didn't react to the warning. "No matter where you go, on either coast, do you think you can just walk up to any agent, any production company, and get handed an audition without references?"

Joel sat back in his wheelchair, pressing hard to make his shirt absorb the sweat seeping down his back. He hated talking like this, even to the arrogant snot standing before him. Emily had warned him to be careful of Jake's pride and ambitions. Remembering that gave Joel the steel he needed to handle him now.

"You're not so hot around here. Tabor Heights is just a little hick town in the middle of nowhere," Jake growled. He wiped his hands on his jeans and looked toward the door to leave.

"Why have you been wasting your time here, then? Why would agents and producers waste their time coming to every opening night?" He took a deep breath and said a quick, silent prayer for control over his temper. "It all hinges on what you want to believe, I guess. Finish out your commitment here, you'll get a decent reference. If you walk out, then I'll be forced to tell people you have talent, but you can't be depended on because your ego is bigger than your common sense." Joel tilted his head back, meeting Jake's blazing blue eyes, and waited.

For a long time, the loudest sound in the theater was Jake's heaving, slowing breaths. Joel sensed everybody listening. If Jake realized that, he would walk out and not come back, just to save face.

"I'm finished here." Jake gave his hands one final swipe on his jeans. He turned on his heel and stomped down the steps and up the aisle to the doors at the back of the auditorium.

Joel slumped a little in his wheelchair and more sweat ran down his back. He hated the cast holding him down, because right now he needed to get up and pace and kick something out of his way.

The clanking, dragging, rattling sounds of people hard at work backstage and on the catwalks rang through the theater again. Joel caught himself grinning. There was always one rotten apple in the barrel, but the rest of the cast and crew were reliable, ethical, hard-working people. He tugged on his beard and tried to recall where Joe would be right now. Who could he move into Joe's role, so his son could take over as Lucentio?

Saturday, May 3

"This sounds good," Max said. She folded the newspaper so the "apartment for rent" section was on top and handed it across the table to Tony. The boys were still asleep. Rose was eating breakfast with Joel in the living room, leaving her alone with Tony.

"Yeah, the price is right, at least." Tony barely glanced over the ads, including the one Max had circled with a red marker. "You know, with all that money I've had sitting in the bank and the interest rates going down, I could get a house now." He put the paper aside and returned to attacking his half-grapefruit.

"You don't like anything you've looked at, do you?" She wondered if she would have to take Tony by the hand and drag him out to inspect every apartment building or house for rent in the entire Cleveland area.

Maybe she could talk Steve into offering to share his apartment with Tony. Maybe she could offer to help Steve find a new apartment, so Tony could move back into his own apartment.

After getting the inquisition from those three reporters, and then hearing how Tony clobbered that photographer he met up with at the high school, the sooner Max got him out of the house, the better. Tony was her best friend, but sometimes there was just too much togetherness. Especially when her thoughts kept drifting into wishing for something that had obviously never entered his mind. And yet, why did he punch that photographer?

No, better to get Tony out of the house before she lost all her dignity and common sense and told him she wanted roses and violins, and that white picket fence.

"Everything that comes near to suiting me is either too expensive for the size, or too far away from here." Tony put aside his grapefruit and picked up his toast. "Guess I'm spoiled."

"Oh, really?" Her face grew warm from the heavy sarcasm in her voice. Max wondered why it irritated her so much that Tony was picky about finding a new place. His attention to details was what made him such a good writing partner.

"It's been great, being so close, being able to work on our book or just talk about things whenever we feel like it."

"Whenever *you* feel like it," she retorted. Max picked up her glass of milk. "I have to admit, it's nice not having to call you and hope you're at home when I need to talk."

"I don't want to lose that convenience, I guess."

"You don't want to lose the good cooking around here."

"Yeah, that too." He shrugged and took a bite of toast. He grinned, eyes sparkling.

"What?" Max wanted to thump him when he just grinned wider, shook his head and finished chewing and swallowing.

"We should get married."

Chapter Fourteen

"What?" Max flinched at her near-shriek and hunched down in her chair, darting worried glances at the door into the living room. "Are you sick or something?"

Had Brenda broken every rule of confidentiality in the battle between the sexes and *told* him that Max wanted a white picket fence?

"No, I'm serious," he said. "Then we can be together all the time and work on our writing whenever we want. If I get an idea in the middle of the night, I don't have to wait until morning to tell you."

"Anybody who wakes me up in the middle of the night to work on a story is going to get a black eye." Max hated the heat in her face. "Besides," she forced herself to say over the sudden racing of her heart, "there isn't even enough room in my bedroom for me, let alone you."

"You move in with me when I get my new place," he said with a shrug.

"If you ever get a new place. You're the most finicky man I've ever met."

"Does that mean you won't marry me?" He twisted his face into a mournful mask.

"That's the most ridiculous—until this moment, I doubted you even knew I was a girl!" Max picked up her milk to drink and cover her flustered feelings. It was a mistake, with her hand shaking and her face growing hotter.

"Oh, yeah. I've noticed for a long time." The laughter had left Tony's voice. She was afraid to look at him.

Now's the time, Tony. Just three little words. Are they so hard? You're the man, the hero. It's your job to say them, not me.

He cleared his throat. "Makes writing some of the slop we do a little difficult, you know?"

"How?" she challenged, forcing herself to meet his gaze. *Slop*? That said a lot. All bad.

"It's—some of the things we—I'm writing from a guy's viewpoint and—there's just some things guys don't like talking about in front of girls, you know?" His face turned pink.

"No, I don't know. Want to tell me about it?" Max took her dirty dishes to the sink while he stammered and finally refused. She grinned as she rinsed the dishes and congratulated herself on turning the tables on

Tony. For once.

And yet, what if he wasn't totally joking?

Should she ask? Would he laugh at her? Or had she already ruined things by acting like his suggestion was a joke?

The mental image of waking up next to Tony for the rest of her life made her lose her breath. And yet it also gave her a sense of stability and comfort she hadn't felt since before the accident. She remembered how safe she had felt when he held her while she cried. She had felt complete, even as she emptied herself of her pain and fear and three-quarters of the moisture in her body. Just because Tony held her.

Did he mean it, when he promised she would never be alone again?

Did he mean it in all the ways she wanted him to mean it?

Or was she mistaken, reaching out in desperation for something stable?

"It wouldn't be so bad, would it, Max?" Tony murmured, and slipped out of the kitchen before she could even turn around.

"Not when you're driving me crazy," she said, so softly she could barely hear herself.

She had been trying to prod him into finding a new place to live without actually telling him to get out of the house. How had he managed to turn things around on her like that?

The very idea of spending the rest of her life with Tony made her feel dizzy. Yes, he was handsome and fun to be with and her best friend. The idea of kissing him made her feel weak and shivery—forget anything more intimate. If anything could convince her not to daydream about marrying her writing partner, this last week was the best argument in the world. The idea of being able to work on their writing at any hour of the day or night was nice as long as it *stayed* a dream. Turned into reality, it became a nightmare.

Tony staying for an overnight cram session on a crucial part of a book was one thing. Tony living in their house, always reminding her of the work they had to do and their deadlines, was something else altogether. The difference between an occasional workout on the gym's rowing machine and being chained to a bench in a Roman slave ship.

He was still her best friend. Max knew that would never change, no matter how much she wanted to take his notebook computer and shove it down his throat.

She would talk to Joel about Tony. Just for advice. She couldn't ask him to leave. Rose liked him so much and depended on him. After how she had treated Rose when she first arrived, Max didn't want to hurt her by sending Tony away. If she *could* send Tony away.

Sunday, May 4

That night, Max was alone in the kitchen, filling glasses with ice cubes, to take out to the living room. It was tradition to have a pizza-and-movie night on the Sunday break in the middle of a play run. She had broken her block on her book, every last trace of paparazzi in town was gone, and Tony was busy elsewhere, giving her some breathing room. The only thing that could make tonight better was if her mother was settled on a couch with Joel, waiting to put the first DVD in the player.

BJ Marshall tiptoed into the kitchen and climbed up on the stool that always sat at the end of the counter. The four-year-old and his mother had come to visit Emily when Max, Joel and the boys were at the hospital. When they went home, it was natural to invite Jeannette and her son to join them. Homespun Theater was as much a home to BJ as the hallways and classrooms of Tabor Christian. He spent just as much time in both places. That familiarity made him bold.

"What are you doing, short stuff?" Max growled, as he reached for the bowl of ice cubes.

"Nothing, Aunt Max." The little boy giggled and picked up an ice cube in each hand, eyes sparkling with mischief.

"Nothing? And just what do you think you're going to do with that ice?"

Some boys loved worms or snakes or toy soldiers. BJ loved to sneak ice cubes and put them down people's collars. Max suspected Jeremy and Joe had taught him that method of torture.

"Nothing." He squealed when she picked him up around the waist and swung him back down to the floor. Giggling, he ran out into the other room, triumphantly carrying his ice cubes.

A loud thumping on the back door stopped Max when she was about to pick up the tray of glasses and follow the boy. The pizza was getting cold, after all. Who could be coming by at this time of the day? Maybe she was wrong, and all the paparazzi hadn't fled back into their slime pits. She took a deep breath to fight down a surge of temper when she reached the door and saw Jake scowling at her through the glass.

"I want my paycheck," he announced as she pulled the door open. He jammed his thumbs into his pockets and rocked back on his heels. "I'm taking a job that pays a lot better than this place and starts right away."

"Oh. Really." Max fought for a neutral expression. No way would she give him the satisfaction of reacting to his disparagement of Homespun. Expressing how glad she was he had quit would only take her down to his level. "Well, good luck. If you want to have a seat, I'll check with Dad. We wouldn't want to keep you in town one minute too long, would we?" Max's hand shook as she shut the door, but from Jake's lack of response, she knew he hadn't seen.

He had probably expected her to beg him to come back and finish out the run of *Shrew*. Max peered through the sheer curtain, half-expecting to see him kick a chair or even stomp down the steps from the back porch, angry enough to leave without his check. To her disappointment, Jake threw himself down into a lawn chair. Sighing, she braced herself and went into the living room.

"What's up?" Joel asked as Max came through the swinging door. BJ was on the floor, wrestling and giggling with Joe and Jeremy. From the squeals, there was still enough ice to torture someone in that pile.

"Jake's here for his last check." She went to his desk to pull out the checkbook and the payroll register book, then brought them over to the couch where he sat with Rose.

"Last check?" Joe echoed and popped up from the pile of boys, turning ghost white. "As in... he really is gone?"

The game and noise had stopped, and Joe had regained some color by the time Joel wrote out the check and recorded the figure. Max took the check and headed back into the kitchen. She didn't think her stepfather looked disappointed at all to see the last of Jake Holt.

Jake took his time getting to his feet when Max opened the door again, and she hated every inch of his perfectly shaped, athletic, graceful body. He didn't say anything. He didn't have to, disdain shining bright in his eyes. He took the check she held out, then bowed with a grand flourish, almost touching the ground with his fingertips.

"I don't stay where people accuse me of stealing." He slid the check into his pocket and turned to leave. A little too slowly.

"Nobody accused you," Max said, knowing he was trying to stir up an argument, but unable to resist. "We only asked that you keep your nose out of private property."

"You just keep right on telling that story. Maybe somebody will believe you." A grin sliced across his face. Jake stepped closer, looming over her without actually crossing the threshold into the kitchen. "Just about the only story you'll get anybody to listen to ever again, little Maxi. You're blowing your biggest chance, and you're too stupid, too busy playing dutiful little daughter to realize it." He turned on his heel, jumped off the porch and strutted down the flagstone path to the parking lot. His rear end and his back-tilted head made tempting targets, but Max had nothing to throw.

"Good riddance," she whispered as he drove away. Yet knowing he was out of their lives, she didn't feel better.

She returned to the living room in time to hear Joel say, "I think maybe you're ready to play George when we do *Our Town*. How do you feel about it?"

Max wouldn't have traded anything for that moment, watching the panic on Joe's face transform into disbelief and then glee, his eyes bright, mouth dropping open, and color returning to his cheeks.

Monday, May 5

Joel settled down into the lawn chair on the back porch, closed his eyes and let out a sigh of contented weariness. It would take some getting used to, moving around with crutches, but he was up on his feet now, navigating with the much lighter, smaller cast the doctor had put on him at his checkup this morning. It only went from his ankle to halfway up his thigh now, instead of toes to hip. He could put up with a little clumsiness just for the sheer luxury of being able to move without anyone's help. In another week, maybe he could trade his crutches for a cane. With the doctor's approval of course.

For now, he would relax in his new lawn chair, enjoy the afternoon warmth, and rest up for tonight's performance of *Shrew* as the run of the play resumed. He looked forward to actually being able to see Joe on stage tonight, instead of just listening to him from behind the scenes. His oldest son had taken over the part of Lucentio without a hitch. True, Joe had been on his knees in the bathroom until five minutes before the curtain went up that first night, but he had come through like a trooper. Emily had been so proud of him. That alone had been worth the inconvenience and unpleasantness of Jake walking out in the middle of the production. Dr. Holland confided in Joel that being able to see their son on stage in his first big role might be the boost Emily needed to get her home. Maybe one more day.

The thought of possibly having his wife safely at home by this time tomorrow made Joel's cup of thankfulness overflow. He closed his eyes, feeling the dampness from threatened tears, and wasn't ashamed at all.

"Lord, You've gotten us this far in such a short time... Thanks. There's so much ahead of us, and a pretty big hill to climb, but I know You'll get us through." He sighed and rubbed his eyes with the heels of his hands. "Thanks. A thousand times. If I had lost Em, I don't know what I would have done."

Sighing, Joel slouched down further in the lawn chair and kept his eyes closed, enjoying the warmth, the quiet. The novel sensation of losing half the weight from his leg. The absence of the gnawing aches throughout his body that had haunted him for the last week.

The screen door from the kitchen creaked open. Joel smelled fresh chocolate chip cookies and heard the clink of ice cubes in glasses. He grinned and chuckled.

"I hope you aren't coming to make sure I'm taking a nap," he said.

"Since when do you or your boys sleep through fresh cookies?" Rose said.

"My momma didn't raise no dummy." He opened his eyes. Fresh lemonade in two glasses and a plate of cookies graced the tray in her hands. "Want me to hold that for you?"

"Please."

She waited until he had a good grip of the round metal tray, then reached around behind him and pulled over the wobbly white plastic end table with the melted leg that had sat too close to the gas grill the summer before. Rose set the tray on the table, then settled down on the steps next to him, smoothing her green, daisy-print dress under herself.

"Lovely," she said with a sigh as she gazed out over the back yard.

It was only twenty feet by forty feet, but the grass was luxuriant and dark green, and the entire area was enclosed with thick, tall bushes and pines to enforce privacy. The only gap in the wall was a six-foot section where the path led to the gravel parking lot and the scene shop.

"This is just May, Rosy. Wait until you see Tabor Heights when summer is in full bloom."

"Do you think I'll still be here?" She kept her profile to him, a wistful smile making her look tired.

"Of course you will. Where else would you go?" He coughed, not liking how that sounded. "The kids would send the police out after you if you abandoned us. You're family."

"I know." Rose turned to look up at him. She patted his knee, chuckling when she got his cast. "I don't regret for a minute leaving Boston."

"But?" he prompted, knowing that look of weighty problems in her pursed lips and narrowed eyes.

"But ... there's Max ... and Tony."

"Max and Tony? Something going on I don't know about?" Joel knew he was taking less pain medication, so he couldn't have been in that much of a fog.

"I wish something was!" Rose picked up a cookie from the plate and toyed with the edge, smearing chocolate on one fingertip. "I swear, that boy is in love, but despite those books he's written, he doesn't have clue one on how to let Max know how he feels. Joel!" She glared at him when he burst out in roars of laughter.

He laughed so hard he started to choke. Rose's anger faded into concern. She scrambled back to her feet and stepped behind him to pound on his back until he got his breath back. Joel snorted, struggling to stop laughing, and picked up one of the glasses of lemonade to sip it.

"Sorry—but you—" He snorted again, then coughed when the

lemonade went up his nose, burning. "Rosy, if you only knew—" Joel shook his head. His mouth ached from grinning.

"I wish you'd share the joke with me." Despite her tone, she smiled back at him and picked up the other glass.

"Some boys never grow up, Rosy. Maybe I'm making up for thirty years of not picking on you. Then again, maybe all this enforced closeness finally got my two favorite writers thinking in the right direction."

"Joel Aaron Rubenstein..." Rose whispered. A delighted smile crept across her face. She leaned back against the porch railing. "Are you playing matchmaker?"

"I've *been*, but that little girl of mine is convinced no man in his right mind would look twice at her."

"So you picked Tony as a future son-in-law?"

"Low blow." Joel chuckled and raised his glass in a toast to her. He certainly had missed Rose all these years. Letters just hadn't been enough. "You know..."

"That look in your eye is definitely trouble."

"Help us out, Rosy? Sit Tony down and have a talk with him?"

"Why me?"

"I have the feeling that getting romantic encouragement from someone he doesn't know like family—yet—will go down a lot easier than coming from his future father-in-law."

Rose gaped at him. He grinned and reached for a cookie and saluted her with it. That first big bite was more wonderful than anything he had tasted in a long time.

A car engine cut through the momentary quiet of birds chirping and a lawn mower buzzing on a lawn far in the distance. Max's blue Cavalier pulled into the private parking area. She got out of the car, looking in every direction as she headed for the house.

"Tony gone?" she asked, smiling.

Joel couldn't help it. He burst out laughing and Rose joined in. In light of what he and Rose had just been discussing, Max's words made his thoughts go in a totally new direction. Maybe she wasn't jumpy because Tony was everywhere in the house, and she couldn't complain because he was so useful. As in Tony being available to take Joel to his checkup so Max could go to work. Maybe she was jumpy because she felt something more for her long-time best pal, and she didn't know what to do about it, despite—as Rose had said—writing all those romance novels.

Max looked back and forth between them as their laughter faded. "Dad, what's going on?" Her confusion faded to a frown when his answer was to chuckle harder. "Aunt Rose, can't you get him to act his age?"

Joel choked on his laughter. Rose stopped short, her grin softening, tears in her eyes. Max had called her "aunt" without any hesitation or awkwardness.

"I was just telling Rose that I wish Tony could stick around forever. Join the family." He smirked at his sister and she shook her head.

"Yeah, well, there's joining the family and then there's joining the family." Max half-raised her arms in a gesture of frustration and stalked into the house.

"Are you thinking what I'm thinking?" Rose whispered.

"You know how long I've been praying for this?"

"Okay." She nodded, once, sharply.

"Rosy?"

"Give me time to think of what to say. I'll have a talk with that boy."

Chapter Fifteen

Tuesday, May 6

"Looking for Max?" Rose said when Tony stuck his head into the kitchen and looked around.

"She's at work, isn't she?" He stepped into the room far enough to let the door swing closed. "Anything you need done, Aunt Rose? Any errands? I thought I'd go over to see Miss Emily, maybe bring Joel home if he's tired, so Max can spend more time with her mom."

"You're trying too hard."

"Huh?" He hesitated when she gestured for him to sit down.

"You're trying too hard, Tony. There's a fine line between being someone's hero and taking over her life."

"Taking over—" He sat down hard, stunned when Rose slapped her little hand over his mouth and kept it there.

"Hothouse flowers are lovely, but they don't last long in the real world." She took the chair next to him at the kitchen table and then removed her hand from his mouth.

"What do hothouse flowers have to do with... I'm lost."

"You're so intent on proving to Max that she needs you in every part of her life, you're scaring her. That's why she's been avoiding you the last few days." The sympathy in Rose's gaze made it easier to endure the smile that threatened in the twitching corners of her mouth. "Have you ever considered just telling Max you love her?"

"She knows I love her," he grumbled, and looked around the room. What he really wanted was for one of the boys to bomb into the kitchen and interrupt, but it was too early in the day for them to be out of school.

"You know, Cyrano de Bergerac had the same problem. Think of all the trouble he could have saved himself and Roxanne if he had just said he loved her, instead of making himself miserable by proving it to her."

"Cyrano put his words in someone else's—" Tony started to correct her, until she raised her hand as if she would slap it over his mouth again.

"You know what I mean. If it's any consolation, Joel and Emily approve heartily."

"They do?"

"Cyrano had a rival," Rose continued.

"I don't."

"Yes, you do. This theater. Max's sense of duty. The fact that she's so intent on giving herself to others, she won't think about herself. If I didn't know better, I'd think that girl was hiding from something. Keeping so busy she can't think about it, or even think, period."

Tony sat up straight as a picture snapped together from a dozen fragments in his mind. It made so much sense now. Max kept busy so she wouldn't have to think about the problems waiting for her in Hollywood, with Carlo Vincente and the Gabrielli Fellowship.

"Thanks, Aunt Rose." He patted her hand as he got up. "I think I just figured out a few things."

"Take the traditional approach." She sighed when Tony stopped, his hand on the kitchen door, and gave her a blank look. "Roses. Music. Get down on your knees. Make her feel like she's a princess."

"There are a couple dragons to slay before I can do that." He winked and pulled the door open, just as the phone started ringing.

First step: finalize things with Mr. McCafferty. Then roses. The other steps could wait, but not much longer. Tony chuckled as he hurried around the back of the house and headed for the house across the street.

"Tony!" Rose leaned out the door and waved for him. "Wait!" She gestured for him to come back. "Can you go to the hospital to meet Joel?"

~~~~~

"Beth?" Max backpedaled out of the hospital room where she expected to find her mother. She had come over straight from work to pick up Joel, who had been there all morning visiting Emily. They had a dozen errands to run before they prepared for tonight's performance. "Where are my folks?" The sight of Emily's empty bed hadn't been that frightening, because her mother could get out of bed now, with help, and even managed to walk to the lounge at the end of the hall on Sunday.

What worried her was the total absence of Emily's books, her sewing, and other little personal items, among the greenhouse's inventory of flowers and potted plants that filled the room. Max refused to let her mind pursue the implications.

"In the lounge." Beth stepped around the side of the nurse's station and wrapped her arms around Max for a quick hug. "Isn't it great news?"

"What is?" She tried not to let her voice rise, but it was hard.

"There you are." Tony bombed out of the elevator, pushing an empty wheelchair. "Good. I'm running out of room in my car."

"Room for what?"

"I'll take all the flowers, and you can take your folks. Or maybe your dad can't sit in the back seat with that cast on?" He frowned as he hurried past her, heading for Emily's room.

"Room for what?" she demanded, turning to follow him. She had a hard time processing most of what he had just said, for some reason.
~~~~~

Maybe it was the panic that made her heart race.

"Max!" Joel called, leaning out of the door of the lounge. He beckoned with his cane. The joy brightening his face lowered her apprehension, but Max still shivered a little as she hurried down the hall to join him.

She nearly wept when she saw Emily sitting up in a wheelchair in the lounge, looking serene, with good color in her face — and dressed in her favorite dusty blue sweatsuit and sneakers, instead of her robe and slippers. It was the sight of the neon yellow scarf wrapped around her head, hiding the bandages and most of her hair, that made something click in Max's head. She dropped to her knees next to the wheelchair and grabbed her mother's hands.

"You're coming home?" Max wasn't ashamed when a few tears escaped.

"Yep, time for another gusher," Tony muttered, when they went down in the elevator together a short time later, both of them pushing borrowed wheelchairs full of flowers in vases and pots.

"I don't know what you're talking about."

"Promised you when I got back. Next time you need to let go of all that pressure. You, me, and a big sponge on my shoulder."

"How about a big punch in that smart mouth of yours?" Max sputtered, caught between laughter and the tears that kept threatening.

"Naaah. How about a big, sloppy, romantic kiss?"

"Romantic kisses are not sloppy." To her relief, the elevator doors opened and they were in the lobby. She hurried to push her wheelchair load of flowers away, just in case Tony decided to pursue that ridiculous topic. Correction: kissing Tony wasn't ridiculous, but the way he had brought up the subject made her feel achy and want to run away.

And it just proved to her yet again that Tony definitely didn't think of her in that way. Of all people, he had to know the right words to say if he loved her.

They finished up Emily's paperwork just after 3p.m., carefully loaded her and Joel into Max's car, and drove the few miles home to Tabor Heights. Followed by multiple trips out to both cars to unload the flowers, and phone calls to let all their friends at church and the university know Emily was home. The house was immediately flooded with people, bringing more flowers and bakery and casseroles. And then the chaos of rearranging the furniture, moving Tony back downstairs to the Green Room so Emily and Joel could have their room again.

Max was too overwhelmed with all that, and preparations for that night's performance, to feel anything more than mild shock when Chuck Winters walked through the kitchen door.

"We have to talk," he said, then took off his jacket, rolled up his sleeves, and dove in to help bring some order out of the chaos.

~~~~

"Smashing success, like always," Winters said, raising his cup of coffee in a toast.

The cast and crew laughed wearily as they moved around in various stages of removing costumes and makeup and cleaning up after the performance. Max, who had collapsed in her office chair in the alcove, laughed with the others. The remains of the celebration buffet littered the table before him.

Emily nodded and smiled. Her laughter hadn't been heard much, and she mostly sat still in her nest of pillows in the living room and let Rose and Della and Max hover around her all during the performance and now the party. Which had been provided by Winters. Still, her presence had given everyone extra energy tonight.

The performance had not suffered, despite people constantly vanishing to sit with Emily and nearly miss their cues. Joel never lost his temper, even though he and Max ran themselves ragged keeping track of cast and crew.

All in all, there was nothing to mar the glory and excitement and satisfaction of the evening. Max loved sitting and watching her mother, back in her place as the center of the home and the theater.

Nothing to mar it but her growing curiosity over why Chuck Winters had showed up that afternoon. He certainly hadn't known Emily was to be released from the hospital today. So what had brought him to town without warning?

"No, folks," Winters continued, "I know I say it every time I come here, but this time is a special occasion. We're all grateful and relieved to have Emily home." Applause interrupted for a few minutes. "God's timing is perfect, like always. What better gift could He give Emily than to let her see her son on stage?" More applause. Winters glanced around the room until he found Joe, sitting on the bottom step of the stairs, talking to Truman, who sat four steps above him, and Morgan, who leaned against the wall next to the steps. "Here's to the next emerging talent in this household. To Joe Randolph, with his mother's stage presence and good looks. Fortunately," he added after a momentary pause.

The laughter this time was louder and longer. Joe turned bright red.

"I think I've been insulted," Joel called from his perch on the wide arm of Emily's couch.

"No, Dad—I have," Max said, getting up to join Winters at the table. She picked up a strawberry and turned to face her stepfather. "Everybody says I look like you." She grinned when another wave of laughter rewarded her and popped the strawberry into her mouth. Joe gave her a grateful look.

"Got a minute?" Winters asked her when the conversation around
~~~~

them split and drifted in ten different directions.

Max nodded and led him over to the office alcove. Short of going outside, which would necessitate stepping over people sitting on the floor by the doors to the stage or kitchen, or out the front door, it was the closest they could get to a private conversation.

"Somebody's playing games in Hollywood." His jovial expression faded into a pensive, weary one.

"And?" Max prodded, when he paused a little too long. She settled down on the edge of her desk and gestured for him to take her chair. She was too relieved to finally get an explanation for his surprise visit to tense up over the subject matter immediately.

"I called the Gabrielli people about the schedule for the seminar, since I'll be representing you at the awards and I haven't received my paperwork and passes. According to the front office, they got a letter last week saying you were coming to the seminar and awards after all, despite my telling them you couldn't come because of everything going on here." He gestured around the Green Room. "They sent your passes and tickets and schedules, all the information, to a box in L.A., three days ago."

"Let me guess. Just a number? No name on the box?" This felt like a ploy out of one of her own books. Albeit, one that hadn't sold.

"Pretty much. The strange thing is that the letter also said you had split your representation, and I only handled your book contracts now. Everything dealing with your screenwriting is to be handled through a new agency."

"What's the name?" Max asked. She congratulated herself on her calm tone, when ice had taken root inside her stomach and reached up to her brain. This was even worse than the threat of losing her fellowship money. Someone was stealing her career before it had even gotten off the ground.

That begged the question of how someone got enough information to try something like that. Her gaze went to the file drawer directly behind Winters' chair. Everything someone needed to steal her identity and her career was right there. Max barely heard him answer, as she fought a falling sensation while the answer came clear to her mind.

"Doesn't matter. It's a new operation and when I contacted them, they were frightened out of their socks." Winters chuckled, with a vicious edge to the sound. "They showed me all the paperwork, including the letter with your forged signature and mine, transferring rights of attorney from me to them."

"I never signed any rights of attorney." It was a battle to keep her voice just loud enough Winters could hear her, but no one could overhear. "How well forged?"

In her mind's eye, she saw all those documents she had left in her baskets, waiting to be filed. Documents with her signature, his, contact information for various production companies, seminars she had been invited to be a teacher, and contracts with her social security number.

"Somebody obviously had samples of your signature and my signature, but they didn't do a very good job. The Max Keeler who talked to them on the phone was a man. I offered to bring you up to meet them, with your birth certificate if they wanted proof. They were more than agreeable about straightening things out."

"What about the Gabrielli people?" Max kicked herself for being so relieved that one very large blight in her life had left town. Obviously, not soon enough.

"They know. I straightened out that mess, and said I'd get a letter from you verifying that I was still handling all your representation. They're pretty angry. Made me look like I was on Valium. They've kept things quiet, but there's been some deep-seated trouble the last few months, requiring a complete reshuffling from the inside out." His eyes narrowed. "That's why Carlo Vincente is the new head of the board."

Max didn't react. She couldn't react, her thoughts swirling with useless strategies to resolve this problem without having to go to Hollywood. A vague, growing sense of impending doom made that fried chicken do a dance in her stomach.

"Anyway, since we can't figure out how much information this imposter has, I thought I'd check with the folks at Pelican, since your option check is supposed to be coming any day now." Winters paused, prompting her to fill in the gap.

"Same thing, huh? Who was the check supposed to go to?"

"That's the funny part." Winters didn't smile. "The fake Max is having a friend come in and pick up cash for him, as soon as the agency lets him know the check has arrived. But you don't have anything to worry about. They're giving him the silent treatment, and they'll call the police if he gives them any trouble." He tipped his head, studying her. "You're a little too calm. Stunned, or do you have an idea who's doing this?"

"Stunned, and feeling like an utter moron. And I don't have an idea — I know who's doing this. Jake Holt."

"What's Jake doing now?" Tony demanded from behind her. He grasped her shoulder as he stepped into the alcove to join them.

"I've caught him searching my desk, reading papers. Including fellowship documents. I guess he made copies of our signatures, too."

"What did he do?" His fingers dug into her shoulder and his voice took on a growl.

A little thrill shivered through her chest. Funny, but she had never seen Tony as a cave man before. Certainly never on her behalf.

In a few moments, Winters brought Tony up to speed on the problem.

"He's going to show up at the fellowship seminar and awards, isn't he?" Tony guessed. "And probably try to take Max's money."

"That just shows what an idiot he is," Winters said with a snort. "They don't hand out checks at the awards ceremony. Certainly not checks for that much money. But that gives me an idea." He thought for a few moments, his gaze shifting back and forth between Max and Tony, while he rubbed his chin. "Okay, if he has vital information, the only way to stop him from continuing to impersonate you is to make a big, public splash. Embarrass him, and make sure a lot of people are witnesses to who is the real Max Keeler, the daughter, not the son, of Emily Keeler."

"No. I won't trade on Mom's name to get ahead." Visions of Carlo Vincente descending on Tabor Heights made her feel as sick as Joe had looked when he realized Jake had quit. She made to slide off the edge of the desk, but Winters stopped her with a hand on her shoulder.

"Your mother would go on television and radio and take out ads in newspapers to protect your career. You know that." He met her eyes, waiting until she conceded with a nod. Around them, the party continued without pause.

"Can't you just have people waiting at the seminar, to quietly arrest Jake and take him away, and then do a nice, dignified PR blitz?" Tony offered. "Let Max stay home? If you make her face down Jake and publicly humiliate him... that's just descending to his tactics."

"True," Winters said slowly. He leaned back in his chair. "Dignity might just be the best tactic." He narrowed his eyes in thought again, then nodded decisively. "Do you trust me?"

"Of course. Always," Max said. She managed a smile, and was proud her voice didn't shake. That had been a close call. The thought of going to Hollywood and facing Carlo Vincente as well as Jake was just too much to handle, after everything else that had happened today.

What would she have done if Tony hadn't been there? He understood why she couldn't go there, and offered a solution while she was still trying to process everything. How could she show him how grateful she was?

She thought of that booklet hidden deep in her file drawer. Tony knew one deep dark secret. She could show her trust in him by sharing another one. He might laugh, or he might get even angrier on her behalf, when he knew Steve Coheny's true identity.

Max kind of liked that idea.

As the celebration wound down and Max helped Rose clear the buffet table, she caught sight of Joel and Emily and Winters deep in conversation. She swallowed down a surge of resentment. What right did Winters have involving her parents? A moment of thought told her Winters didn't consider it his right, but his responsibility. She was Emily and Joel's little girl. He felt it was his duty to help them protect her.

Still, she didn't like that grim tightness that settled around Joel's mouth or how the glow left her mother's face. Things were starting to feel like normal again, then this had to happen.

~~~~~

Tony breathed a sigh of utter exhaustion as he came out of the men's dressing room and padded across the littered Green Room to his re-assembled temporary quarters. It was long past midnight, and everyone had finally gone home. Morning would come far too soon.

First thing tomorrow, he was going to see Mr. McCafferty and find out how soon he could take possession of the house. Not that he didn't love the energy that constantly filled this house, and not that he didn't love the people who lived here, but he needed his own place to run to and get some quiet and alone time. Max needed a place where she could get away from everyone even more than he did. He liked being able to offer her that.

"Hey." He stumbled when he came around the divider wall and found Max sitting on the end of his cot.

Not that he didn't like seeing her there. The truth was that he had entertained far too many images of Max in his future home, just the two of them alone together. Writing together. Cooking together. Curled up on the couch watching old movies together. And Max asleep next to him, in his bed. Seeing her in her old gym shorts and T-shirt, sitting on the cot, was a little too close to his imagination to bear.

He licked his lips and considered taking Rose's advice. Just tell Max he loved her right now. Forget about waiting for the perfect staging, the right timing.

Would she laugh or take him seriously? Get angry or be happy?

Would she punch him... or would he get his first goodnight kiss?

"What's up?" He hated how stiffly he moved as he continued into the makeshift room and settled down on the cot next to her.

"We need to talk." Max handed him that ivory and gold-speckled booklet he had seen her take out of the mail last week.

"About what?"

"Just look." She stood and backed away when Tony dropped the booklet on the cot and reached for her. "You'll figure it out in a second. I just felt you should know this. You know everything else. You're about the only person I'm not keeping any secrets from," she added with a shaky little laugh.

Tony wanted to wrap his arms around her, but he could see how much this meant to her. He nodded, opened the booklet, and read the introduction from the Gabrielli Fellowship. Then the short paragraph under the picture of Carlo Vincente's family. He started to turn the page, wondering what Max wanted him to see, when a familiar face caught his attention. He studied the photo again.

"He's your brother." He looked at Max, then at the photo, with Steve
~~~~~

Vincente, not Coheny, smiling from the back row of the family photo. Tony could almost laugh at how oblivious he had been, not seeing the resemblance between Max and Steve until now. "So... I'm guessing you haven't faced him down yet."

"Not for anything in the world." She scrubbed at her face with her fists, then frowned. "What's that big grin for?"

"I'm just... relieved, I guess." Tony handed the booklet back to her. "All this time, I thought he was getting ready to make some moves on you. Trying to impress you, be your hero."

"Nope. You're the only white knight in my life." She let out a gusting sigh. "Just like you were tonight. I couldn't think straight, after everything Chuck told us. I probably would have agreed to go to Hollywood, if you hadn't been there. Thanks. You keep rescuing me."

"Any time. Forever."

Just a few minutes later, after Max had hurried up to her bedroom and Tony turned off the lights and finally stretched his achingly exhausted body on the cot, he groaned.

Yet another perfect opening he had missed, to tell her how he felt, promise he would always be her white knight, her hero, and that he loved her.

What made him think he could write romances?

Thursday, May 8

Max came home for lunch, surprising her parents in the middle of a discussion of what to do about her imposter. They agreed with Chuck Winters: eventually Max would have to go to Hollywood. Convincing Max to go and figuring out how to cushion the shock of meeting her father and revealing her identity to protect her career would be the hardest thing they would ever have to do. They had just agreed to call Pastor Glenn and bring him in on the whole long, old story and get his advice, when Max came home. She stormed into the room, dropped the mail on Joel's lap, and settled down in the couch facing them with a large manila envelope.

"I'm seriously considering some violence," Max offered as she shuffled through the stack of papers from the envelope.

"To who? Doing what?" Emily asked.

"Jake Holt, or else this character in my book who isn't behaving. I figured I'd start out with tar and feathers and work up from there."

"Sounds like fun," Tony said, coming in through the kitchen door. He chuckled when everyone jumped at his sudden entrance. "Who are we maligning this week?"

"Never mind," Joel said. He had to stop this before it got anywhere near out of hand. "You look awfully cheerful."

"I ought to be." Tony flopped down onto the couch next to Max and tugged his Club Paradise shirt away from his chest. "Hot out there. I'll miss the air conditioning."

"What's that supposed to mean?" Max hitched a few inches away from him, her expression turning wary even if she still smiled.

"The McCafferty place across the street is being sold."

"Huh?"

"Old Sam didn't say anything to me about that," Joel said. "When did this happen?" He glanced up as Rose came into the room with the iced tea pitcher.

"Actually, we've been talking about it since last winter." Tony glanced around, eyes sparkling. "The place is too much for him to handle and I want a place close by — "

"You're buying it?" Joel blurted. He burst out laughing and scooted forward, holding out his hand. Tony grinned and nodded and got up to shake hands. "Welcome to the neighborhood!"

"How soon is Old Sam moving?" Emily asked. She beckoned and Tony leaned down for a hug.

"Yes, how soon?" Rose asked. "How much help do you need moving?" Her tone was light and convincingly casual. Almost.

"You mean how soon am I getting out of your hair?" Tony slid back into the couch and made a show of putting his feet up on the box of costume boots to one side.

"I wouldn't put it that way."

"I would," Max said. She put her back into the corner of the couch among all the throw pillows.

"Guess I've been a royal pain, huh?" Tony kept smiling.

"Kind of hard to strangle somebody who's so helpful," Joel said.

"I know." A muffled snort of laughter escaped him. "It was great, watching you all fighting to be nice and polite and not tell me to mind my own business. Max, I thought you were going to burst a few times."

"Oh, really?" Max said, her voice like syrup.

Joel smothered a chuckle. He saw the way she slowly reached behind herself for the throw pillows, the tight thinness of her lips, the deadly sparkle in her eyes.

Chapter Sixteen

"Guess we really are friends if you go to that much trouble to put up with the garbage I was dumping on you," Tony said.

"But Tony, how could we really get mad?" Rose said, her voice a mixture of laughing and wailing. "You were always so helpful!"

"I know. I just love playing with people's minds."

"It helps to have one of your own," Max growled.

"Hey, Max—"

The rest of his words died in a grunt and the thuds of pillows Max slammed down on top of him. Rose snatched up a green pillow like a rolled sausage and joined in with a few thumps on his legs. Yelping with mock fear, Tony tried to fend off Max. He grabbed at her and they rolled off the couch, kicking aside boxes and knocking over a pile of old scripts.

"I'm really going to miss him," Joel said, which earned a dirty look from Rose and a sigh of laughter from Emily. "Come on, let's let these two battle it out between themselves."

He levered himself up from the couch and held out an arm to help Emily up. Leaning on each other, they made their way into the kitchen without any help from his cane. It was somewhere on the floor, in the danger zone where Tony and Max thumped each other with pillows, laughing and yelping, and scrambling to stay upright. The noise didn't dim much when they and Rose put the kitchen door between them and the battle.

"Take it easy!" Tony yelped, when a round blue pillow split open, sending a rain of foam rubber pieces across the floor.

"Why?" Max dropped the pillow and picked up a square red one with gold pompons. She knew from experience it gave a good, solid wallop.

"If you kill me, you have to finish the book by yourself."

"Horrors!" She dropped backward onto the couch, clutching her chest in mock heart attack.

Tony flopped down next to her, gasping for breath. For several seconds they lay sprawled there, grinning, sweating, and catching their breaths.

"You know," he said, after swallowing hard a few times. "I really will miss having you around all the time."

"Yeah—now you have to shout across the street instead of up the stairs."

"No, I mean it. It's a good feeling, knowing you're always around."

"Wish I could say the same for you," she returned, smiling sweetly.

"Guess I earned that, huh?" Tony chuckled. He put his back against the arm of the couch, knees up, feet on the cushions only a few inches from her leg. "So, that means no, if I ask you to marry me again?"

"Tony!" She reached for a pillow, then decided the effort was too much.

He grinned at her. If he was joking, why did his words put that strange, achy feeling in her chest? Too many of her dreams lately had been about Tony kissing her.

"Besides," Max hurried on, "I couldn't put up with your snoring."

"What snoring?"

"Should I have Jeremy put a tape recorder under your pillow tonight? When you were in Mom and Dad's room, the sound used to rattle my windows."

"I don't snore!" He made a move to snatch up a pillow and restart their fight.

"Besides, I don't do laundry."

"Who said I was looking for a housekeeper?" He settled more firmly into the couch. "I think I proved I'm pretty easy to live with."

"Oh, yeah? We were ready to strangle you."

"Well, it's different when it's your own place."

"I guess." She tilted her head to one side and studied him. Why did Tony look different, all of a sudden? Why didn't he look like he was laughing, despite the grin? "How soon do you move in?"

"Saturday."

"That soon?"

"Sam has already sent what he wants to keep to his sister in Arizona. Everything else gets hauled to second-hand stores and Salvation Army."

"That's awful fast."

"I know." Tony cracked a grin. "Think you can put up with me two more days?"

Sunday, May 11

"You have no idea how much I appreciate this," Tony said, puffing a little as he led Max up the steps to the front door of the sprawling, ranch-style house. They both carried plastic bags of books from his massive library.

Steve had declared that he wanted to stay in Tabor Heights, and he agreed to take over Tony's apartment lease. He would take most of the furniture. Tony kept the bookshelves, dishes and linens, and planned on hitting all the used and discount furniture stores to furnish his new place around what Mr. McCafferty was leaving behind for him. Max and Tony had been packing books into both their cars and hauling them to the new house since right after church and a fast food lunch. It was now nearly 3p.m.

"Yes, I do. If I had this many books, I'd be on my knees begging someone to help me move them," Max said. She winced as another drop of sweat rolled into her eyes.

"Feel like going shopping when we're done with all this?" Tony asked.

He paused to fumble the key out of his pocket, balancing his bag of books against the wall with one arm. He almost lost his balance and his grip on the bag.

"For what?"

"I need a new bed, for one thing." He let out a gasp of triumph as the lock clicked and the door slid open. He tripped over the threshold and stumbled across the living room, footsteps echoing in the empty rooms, off the hardwood floors. All that space, all that solitude, all his to enjoy.

Max was jealous. Every time she looked at all the space and privacy Tony could enjoy now, she felt twinges of envy and self-pity. And she couldn't help thinking about all Tony's off-hand comments about how they should get married. All this space would be hers, too—if she could take him seriously.

What if Tony had been serious? Even just once?

Did she really want roses and fancy speeches and all those upside-down, hormone-driven feelings that only seemed to get people in trouble? Sure, the idea of Tony kissing her for purely physical reasons made her insides twist in a pleasantly nauseous way—but that was no reason to ever hope he would ask her in total seriousness.

Keeping my mind on track would help, Max scolded herself and resolutely pushed those daydreams out of her head before they got her in trouble. She followed him to the corner of the room where all the bags and boxes of books waited for unpacking into the bookshelves.

"I want you to help me pick everything out," Tony said, after they had put down their burdens and hurried back outside for another load from their cars.

"Why?"

"Because nobody else can be suckered into it?" He skipped backward, laughing, when she swatted at him. "Seriously, Max, this is your place, too. We're partners, in everything." Tony lifted the trunk lid on his car and let out a sigh as he surveyed the few bags still waiting to be lugged into the house. "Thank You, God, it's almost over."

"Maybe you should consider donating some of these things to the

Friends of the Library sale," Max called, as she pulled another box from the back seat of her car.

"Heresy!"

"Well, at least get rid of the stuff you don't use anymore, before you move again."

"I promise you, I am never moving again. I am settled here for the rest of my life." Tony thumped the trunk closed with his elbow and started for the house again. "Whether you marry me or not, everything I've got is yours when I die."

Max bit her tongue against asking if that was a threat or a promise. Two more trips emptied both their cars and brought the total count to twenty-eight grocery bags, fifteen copy paper boxes, and nine milk crates of books. She hoped she never had to move that many books again for the rest of her life. She had been leery of the whole e-book revolution, but Tony had jumped wholeheartedly into buying everything he could in electronic format. He had four e-book readers, and at last count, he owned nearly 500 ebooks. Max shuddered at the thought of how many more bags and boxes they would have had to haul if those books had been printed on paper, instead of taking up a couple flash drives.

"Everything is in great shape," he said, as they stood in the living room, staring in weary triumph at the empty shelves. "I won't have to paint or caulk or do anything to the outside until spring. That means I can spend all my free time fixing up the inside."

He led the way into the kitchen. The refrigerator hummed, all the appliances left plugged in and operating. Tony yanked it open and took out two bottles of apple juice from its well-stocked interior.

"That is a dangerous look in your eyes," Max said. She nodded her thanks and twisted the bottle open. "I'd go easy on all that spending, if I were you."

"Why? I have plenty of money, just saving it for something like this. It'll be fun."

"What if your stocks go bad or the book contract falls through and you don't get the money you're planning on?" She drank and winced as the icy juice hit her overheated system.

"I'll go nice and slow on my spending, I promise." He saluted her with the bottle before taking a long drink. "That's another reason why you have to help me with all this, Max. You'll keep me from going crazy."

"You're already crazy." She yelped when he pressed the icy beaded bottle against her hot, sweaty neck.

~~~~~

"Come on, Max. Get into the spirit of things." Tony looped his arm through hers and half-dragged her through the door from the mall into Kingsbury's department store.
~~~~~

"Spending money you don't have yet?" she groused. Shopping was fine, but she found she didn't really enjoy helping someone else spend his money on furnishing and decorating a house she wanted for herself.

"Spoilsport." He slid to a halt in front of the store directory. "Linens. Upstairs. Escalator's this way." He started off again and Max had to keep up to save her shoulder from being dislocated.

The afternoon shopping traffic wasn't thick enough to be troublesome. Max usually liked shopping with Tony. Usually he stuck to the book, music and computer stores. Now he had a taste for furniture, dishes, and interior decorating.

He was in entirely too jovial a mood, which only made her depression darker. Max couldn't seem to write her way out of her hero's current difficulty—not without spending twenty pages on talking heads. Avoiding facing her computer screen was really the only reason she agreed to come shopping with him.

At the top of the escalator, she saw an escape. From Tony. Temporary. But any escape was welcome.

"You go on. I have some shopping to do." Her mouth cracked into a smile for the first time since Tony made her spend half an hour comparing border patterns in the wallpaper store just outside the mall.

"Yeah, you'll just run out to the bookstore and leave me stranded here. I know you too well, Maximilian." Tony shifted his grip from her arm to enclose her shoulders. They stepped off the escalator and moved aside to let the people behind them pass.

"I have to pick up a few things. I promise, cross my heart and hope to die, I *will* catch up with you."

"How about if I help you?"

"I don't think so." She waved in the general direction of the lingerie sign hanging from the ceiling. Max muffled a giggle behind her hand when Tony balked.

"Okay. But if you don't show up in fifteen minutes, I'm coming looking for you." He gave her a shake, released her and walked off toward the linens department, just past kitchenware.

She waited until he disappeared behind a display of cake pans and decorating accessories, then turned and walked past the girdle display to the nightwear side of the department. All she had at home besides gym shorts to sleep in were flannel pajamas, and the nights were too warm.

A display of lacy, string-strap nightgowns with matching robes caught her attention. Max stopped and lightly ran her fingers down the front of a knee-length sheath all in red lace with black edging.

She could wear something like that now, with all the weight she had lost in the last year. If only she had someone to wear it *for*. How would Tony react if he saw her in it?

"Hey, Max, how're you doing?" Steve said, coming up behind her.

She turned to face him, just barely stopping herself from accusing him of following her and Tony. It was a ridiculous accusation—wasn't it?

Unless he had figured out that his father was her father, and he had decided to confront her about it?

Max immediately shook aside that ridiculous idea. He wouldn't choose a department store for something like that.

So why was he here? Not the mall, but Ohio in general, Tabor Heights specifically. What had brought him to town?

The only problem was that she couldn't demand answers without revealing some truth of her own, in exchange.

"What are you doing here?" Max thought she had spoken soon enough to keep the silence from being awkward. She tried to step backward, trapped by red lacy outfits. The hangars banged against the display next to the rack. The only way out of the corner was to push past him. Max didn't like the idea of getting that close to him. Knowing he was her half-brother just made her feel even more oogy at the thought of touching him, even casually.

"I was walking through the mall and saw you go by, and I thought I'd just catch up with you. Maybe see if you wanted to hit a movie." He shrugged, giving her a lopsided smile. "You're usually so busy, it's hard to spend any goofing off time with you, just getting to know you."

"That sure doesn't stop all the questions you've been asking."

"Uh... yeah. Sorry. Occupational hazard. I was thinking of being a private investigator for a while."

"How about a reporter? You'd fit in great with all the news hounds pestering us. Not much difference."

"Maybe." Again that grin, that sparkle in his eyes, like he knew some big, important secret and it just made his day to keep it away from her.

Maybe he knew the truth, but he thought she didn't?

All the help he had given Tony and Joe in protecting her from Jake didn't make up for that. The creep was acting like... a real brother.

This whole business with so many secrets exhausted her.

"No maybe about it," she blurted, to keep from letting everything spill directly from her thoughts. "Ever think about becoming a writer? Maybe some of those grimy tell-all books."

"Nah. My dad is the one with the gift for words, not me." He stepped back, almost running into a display rack of violet satin nightshirts. "You should meet him some time."

"What do you want?"

"Just to talk. Get to know you better."

"Why?"

"I think you're interesting." He snorted. "I still have to figure out how

Buddy never caught on that you were a girl."

"Uh—Duh! Max isn't exactly a girl's name." Despite herself, Max had to mirror his grin. She remembered that confused look on his face that day he first showed up.

"Anything in particular you're looking for?" he asked, gesturing at the bits of confection hanging all around them. "Maybe I could help you?" He grinned, waggling his eyebrows like Joe or Jeremy would do to make her mad. Max almost laughed.

"No, thanks," she managed to say in a cool tone.

"Having trouble?" Tony asked, appearing between the racks of white terrycloth robes and the black teddies. He didn't look at Max but kept his gaze on Steve.

"About time you showed up," Steve said, giving Tony a grin that mixed friendliness with a warning Max couldn't read. Tony stepped closer and slid his arm around Max's shoulders. "How's anybody going to think you're her boyfriend if you let her walk around loose like this?"

"Oh, puh-lease," Max groaned.

"Not that it's any of your business," Tony began.

"We're not—" she said, turning to free herself from his grip.

"We should be."

"Tony!" She tried to jerk free, but he dug his fingers into her shoulder, holding her close against him. Either she submitted or she risked tearing her shirt in his tight grip.

And Steve just stood there, grinning at them like the big secret had turned into an even bigger joke. If the truth ever came out, she was going to give him two black eyes.

Forget that. She would take a page from Bekka Sanderson's strategy: put him in a book and then torture him for fifty pages.

"You know, there's something weird about a guy following a girl into the underwear department," Tony said.

"Pajamas, not underwear," Steve said.

"Nit-picker."

"Runs in the family." He met Max's eyes, then looked back to Tony. "You helping her pick out something? Looks kind of... dangerous to me, a guy helping his girlfriend pick out a nightgown."

That was all she could take. Max twisted free, ignoring Tony's tightening grip and the warning of bruises all along her shoulder.

"What I wear in bed isn't any of your business—either of you—so just leave me alone to do my shopping in peace," she growled.

She didn't wait for them to respond but turned and bulled her way out between the black lace and the red. Plastic hangars clicked and lace swished in her wake. Max felt Tony and Steve watching her through the shifting curtain of lingerie. She prayed they watched in utter silence. The way her day was shaping up, they would probably decide to team up against her.

Max grabbed a green silky shorts-and-top set, barely took the time to make sure it was in large, and stomped over to the register. She didn't wonder if it would really fit until after she had signed the credit card slip and took her package. There was no way she could go back now and try it on. Tony or Steve or both would probably waylay her en route to the dressing rooms.

~~~~~

"Look, I'm not a rival," Steve said, his voice soft as he and Tony watched Max stomp up to the register.

"Rival?" Tony concentrated on Max, knowing he might do or say something stupid if he looked at Steve and saw the other man smiled. Even the tiniest bit. He could use this later in a book. It definitely fit in with behavior Max labeled "thinking with your hormones."

Maybe later he could find this funny.

"You're lost on her. You were nearly spitting fire when you came over here." Steve rested a hand on Tony's shoulder, startling him so he jerked back and set the lingerie swinging again. "Look, my interest in Max is personal, but not like your interest is personal. Funny as it sounds, I'm glad she's got somebody so protective of her." A choked sound escaped him, and Tony realized it was laughter mixed with something he understood at the gut level, even if he couldn't put it into words. "I know what you are in her life, and her family's life. And I'm glad. You've been there for her ever since the accident."

"But I wasn't there for her when it happened," slipped out before Tony could think.

"Yeah, well, my family is pretty grateful. Don't ask," he hurried to add, when Tony opened his mouth. "Just keep looking after Max, okay?"

"Is that why you're here?" Pieces slid into place and he nearly crowed triumph when Steve flinched and looked guilty for half a second before that smug grin slid into place again. "I know your secret."
~~~~~

Chapter Seventeen

"Got no secrets," Steve said with a shrug.

"Did you know your family portrait is in Gabrielli Fellowship literature that all the finalists got?" He crossed his arms and fought a grin as different reactions cascaded across Steve's face. Confusion. Shock. Wry amusement.

"So Max knows... and she told you." Steve shook his head. "You two are so close, how come you're so stupidly oblivious?"

"Excuse me?"

"Now Max, I can understand. She's just about splitting herself in two, with everything she has to do. She can't see you, even though you're right in front of her... and everybody else in the world can see how you feel about her. Except Max."

"Everybody." Tony chewed on the idea for a moment. He thought Rose picked up on the whole mess between him and Max because she lived there at Homespun. The concept that his friends and people involved in the theater were laughing at how he and Max couldn't seem to connect... he didn't want to think about it too long. "How come, with all the romances we've written, we can't seem to find the right words?"

"Why don't you stop thumping your chest and just tell her?"

"You're the second person who's told me that."

"Then listen." Steve took a step back, making the hangers swing for a few seconds. "Look, I'm still getting used to the idea of having a sister. I like Max. If you make her happy, then I'm all for you taking care of her full-time."

"You know, that's something her father should say, not a big brother she won't even acknowledge."

"Which father?" His smile fell off his face.

"Ah. Yeah. That's another problem she's not ready to face yet." Tony sighed. He understand how Max got that bone-weary look on her face, and why she panicked and ran, instead of standing and arguing with Steve. "Look, there are more problems. Can we talk about them later? Max might just need a big brother before this is all cleared up."

"You got it."

Steve held out his hand and they shook, sealing a deal that Tony sensed went far deeper than their recent words.

~~~~~
~~~~~

Tony caught up with Max in the mall, just outside Kingsbury's. She had parked herself on a bench facing the entrance and mentally dared Steve to come out looking for her. Twenty minutes later, she vacillated between waiting for Tony or wandering down the mall and making him look for her. He appeared at last, arms loaded with those big, sturdy shopping bags with string carry handles. When she saw him, smiling and contented and clearly not hurrying, she had to fight a longing to kick him.

"You okay?" he asked. He had the decency to lose the smile when he saw her.

Max decided she wasn't quite mad enough to kick him. Yet.

Besides, after all the lifting and carrying she had done today, helping him move his books, she doubted she could lift her leg high enough to kick.

"I guess." She stood up and held out her empty hand. "Want me to carry something?"

"No, thanks. I have it balanced just right. If I try to hand something to you, I might drop it all." They headed for the door to the parking lot. Tony glanced at her small red paper bag. "So, what'd you get?"

"What does it matter?" She glanced up and saw him studying the bag, as if he could see through it to the contents. "You'll never see it anyway."

"I don't know..." He grinned at her.

"Tony!" She blushed hot but couldn't hold onto her sour mood. "You're just impossible, you know that?"

"Maybe not." He turned on his heel and backed up through the doors outside, pushing one open with his hip and holding it for her. "I think a lot of things are possible if we just try hard enough."

"Really?" She put all the scorn she could into her voice. Tony just grinned.

"Oh, yeah. For instance, what would it take to get you to buy one of those lacy red things?"

"Doesn't matter, because you'll never see it on me."

"Come on, Max. I'm your best friend. Your partner."

"Not *that* kind of partner."

"We could be, someday. You'd look really good in it, I betcha," he hurried on, while she scrambled for something to say that wouldn't sound utterly stupid—or worse, reveal how much she wanted him to be interested in her *that* way.

"How kind of you to notice," she managed to say.

~~~~~

"Miss Emily?" Steve stepped through the stage door into the living room. "I got your message."

"Thank you for coming." Emily looked up as Joel stepped in from the kitchen. She gestured at the sofa opposite her and put aside the lap desk
~~~~~

full of notes for the upcoming production of *Our Town*. "I want to thank you for being such a big help during our crisis."

"I'm just glad I could be here." Steve waited until Joel sat down next to Emily before he settled into the couch.

"I'm curious, Steven... did your father send you, or are you here on your own?" A tiny, gasping laugh escaped her when he froze, the widening of his eyes his only movement for ten long seconds. "Yes, I finally figured out who you were, when I remembered your mother's maiden name."

"Guess it runs in the family, huh? Max and me, both of us going by our mothers' maiden names." He shrugged and slouched back.

"Are you here because of your father?" Joel caught Emily's hand in his.

"Yes and no." Steve grinned. "I heard him talking with Mom the day he got the finalists list from the fellowship directors. I know Dad, how he works. His first and biggest concern was that anything he did could ruin Max's career. He didn't want to cause her trouble—of course, at the beginning, Dad was saying 'him.' I knew how much this was bothering him, and after what I put him through... well, I figured I should do a little scouting, figure out what was up. It was just luck that I'm friends with Buddy Sanker, and he had mentioned Tabor and Homespun and I made the connection." He shrugged. "Didn't tell Dad."

"So he doesn't know you're here?"

"Chuck Winters gave me a lecture when he was here. He said he'd keep my secret as long as I reported directly to him, everything going on here, and I looked out for all of you."

"Emily knew your name was familiar," Joel offered, "but she couldn't remember that day you first got here. If the accident hadn't happened, you would have been unmasked sooner."

"Maybe," Steve said, offering a cocky grin.

"You probably panicked when the media descended on us," Emily offered, her smile going crooked. "If any of them recognized you... well, quite a few people would have made the same connection you have."

"And that is?" Steve sat up again, tension radiating off him through a brittle shell of quiet watchfulness.

"That Max is indeed your father's daughter."

"So it's true?"

"What's surprised us in all this, all the reminiscing from Hollywood, is that more people haven't made the connection," Joel said.

"It helps that the people in this town are so protective of your whole family. They just closed up ranks against any new faces, as soon as that first camera showed up outside the hospital. Makes it hard for outsiders to get the information to make connections."

"Sorry about that." His grin made a lie of the apology.

"Remind me to kill Tony tomorrow, when I'm not so sore," Max said, coming into the room. She tossed a shopping bag down on her desk and reached for the power button for her computer. "And maybe get the youth group to teepee his house while I'm at it."

"Is that jealousy I hear?" Joel said. He winked at Steve and Emily.

"That's sore muscles, and utter frustration. First I had to help him move his books, then he insisted I had to help him buy all sorts of new junk." She sighed and dropped into her desk chair. "Yeah, some jealousy. All that space. All that privacy. And he wouldn't listen to me when I told him he shouldn't activate his phone."

"It sure looked like you were in misery when I ran into you at the mall," Steve offered.

"You didn't make things any better." She pointed her finger like a gun at him. "I swear, you're fitting in just a little too easily around here."

"Like a brother?" Joel offered. He grunted when Emily dug him in the ribs with her elbow. Steve turned his head to hide his grin from Max.

"Would someone please explain to me why Tony thinks it's so important that I have a say in everything that goes into his new place?"

"Maybe because you'll spend so much time there." Emily glared at both men.

"If you ask me—from a brotherly opinion, of course," Steve said, "it seems to me the guy wants you to move in with him."

"You know," Max said slowly, as the other three exchanged glances, "I am exhausted and sore and I have a headache ready to blow out the back of my head, and my whole world is falling apart because Tony is acting so weird—"

"How weird?" Joel asked. "Like he's finally noticed you're a girl, maybe?"

"Dad!" She leaped from her chair and stumbled backward a step.

"You're not making this any easier," Emily said, glaring at them both. She beckoned for Max to join them at the couches. "We need to talk."

"How come, just when I figure things are going to settle down and get better, because Mom is home and Tony is moving out of here and..." Max settled on the arm of the couch next to her mother. "How come things are just getting worse? Are we ever going to catch a break around here?"

"Always darkest before the dawn," Steve offered with an exaggerated grin. "How do you feel about having five brothers instead of two?"

"I already have—" Max jerked, leaping up from the arm of the couch, her face suddenly pale. Emily caught hold of her wrist. Even though it was a light, weak hold, Max couldn't fight it. She stayed standing there, held prisoner, trembling.

"Yeah, I know. And you know who I am. Tony told me after you left us together at the mall." He got up and stood in front of the three of them, shoulders hunched, hands jammed into the pockets of his jeans. "You look about as shell-shocked as you did that first day I walked in here. Like maybe you recognized me, and you didn't want to admit it."

"I never met you before in my life, until you walked in here and said Buddy sent you," Max said.

"That was kind of a lie. I came looking for you, because Dad was so churned up over seeing your name on the finalists list. I asked Buddy to vouch for me. Never made the connection until I started doing some research. And invaded Dad's office to read and copy a lot of his paperwork, like Jake was doing to you," Steve added, shrugging.

"Your father has nothing to do with me," Max said, her voice a rasp.

"He has everything to do with you."

"Hey, what's up?" Tony sauntered through the swinging door from the kitchen. "Did Max tell you all the great stuff she helped me... Umm, something wrong?" He slid to a stop, glancing from one somber or troubled face to another.

"Hey, Tony. The cat's out of the bag." Steve gave Max a teeth-bared grin when she just glared at him.

"Okay. That was fast." Tony stepped over to Max. "Are you okay?"

"No. I can't even breathe!" Max slid her wrist free of Emily's grip and dashed for the open door to the backstage area.

"That went better than I hoped, actually," Joel said, ending on a long, loud sigh.

"How long have you known?" Emily said, frowning thoughtfully at Tony.

"Max told me about her father the night of the accident. Then she had a picture of the whole family and..." Tony shrugged. He turned to Steve. "I think the ball's in your court."

"Yeah, I think so." Steve took a deep breath. "Wish me luck." He crossed the room to the stage door.

~~~~~

Max slid to a stop on the empty stage and kicked off her sandals. Her feet ached from all her walking today. A shiver ran up her back, that sense of being watched. She took a deep breath and turned to face Steve, framed in the light streaming through the backstage door.

"Why are you here?" she asked, trying to make her voice disinterested. She failed, miserably.

"What, you mean here, backstage? Or in Tabor?" He pulled the door closed behind him, leaving them in semi-darkness. She could only shrug her answer. "Dad wanted answers—"

"What have you two decided to do? Besides destroying my career before it gets started."
~~~~~

"That's not fair! Dad doesn't even know I'm here, for one thing. Your folks just figured it out, called me in to confront me."

"Hopefully to hand you your walking papers. You've got no right to be here."

"Now, see, that's the first thing you'll learn about Dad. Family means everything."

"I'm not your family."

"Look, you think it's easy for me, finding out I have a little sister all of a sudden?"

"Little?" Max choked.

"Yeah, five years between us. It's a long story." He waited, obviously expecting her to ask him to elaborate. He shook his head, a glint of amusement in his eyes when she kept her silence. "You aren't the only one Dad messed up, you know. I was mad at him for a long time, too, but at least I gave him a chance. That's all I want. Give our Dad a chance, okay?"

The door thudded open and Tony emerged from the darkness. "You okay, Max?"

"I'm fine." She didn't know if she should laugh or be angry with him, running to her "rescue" like he had.

"You know," Steve said, "you might be her boyfriend—"

"He's not my boyfriend!" Max shouted.

"Oh, yeah?" Her unwanted brother grinned.

Steve reminded Max too much of Carlo, in a movie scene with Emily when they had been arguing one moment and kissing passionately the next. Max shuddered. Steve was a figure from her most ardent dreams of romance and adventure. Just her luck—bad—he had to be her half-brother.

"You know what your problem is, little sister?"

"Besides you?"

"Max." Tony rested his hand on her shoulder. She shook him off and stalked away a few more steps. "This isn't solving anything."

"You don't know how to talk," Steve said. "Must run in the family. If our dad and your mom had just talked, we wouldn't be here right now."

"Yeah, I'd be stuck with you for a brother instead of Joe and Jeremy. Just more proof that God is merciful."

"Hey, you haven't gotten to know me yet," he said, his grin just getting wider. "Now, you and Tony here need to sit down and talk."

"All we do anymore is talk!" Max headed for the left wing, but Steve hurried around and stopped her. "Nothing but words. Making a joke about getting married. I wish you two would just put up or shut up!"

"Anybody tell you yet how hard he's been working to protect you? Me, him and Joe, we've been running interference with good old un-lamented Jake."

"Yeah. Tony said. Thanks." She grudgingly met Steve's gaze. His smug look had softened a little, like maybe he felt some sympathy for what she had been facing.

"See? It's not so bad having me for a big brother."

"Would you cut it out?" She clenched her fists. So much for feeling grateful for the big interfering jerk being there in the first place.

"Pass me the scissors." He snickered.

Tony muffled a snort of laughter. Max punched him in the shoulder. He yelped, but grinned.

"You're worse than Joe and Jeremy put together."

"Considering I've been around longer than them, that makes sense. Look, Max, we have to talk."

"Nothing to say."

"We've got lots to say. I want you to come to L.A. with me and meet Dad. Things have calmed down here some—"

"That just proves you don't know this place at all. It never calms down. We just go from crisis to crisis."

"Maybe you should leave her alone for a while," Tony said. "Let her think about it."

"Look, if I wanted to meet—your father," Max stammered, unable to force the name out, "I would be heading to Hollywood right now for the Gabrielli seminar tomorrow."

"Just proves you're a coward. And that makes me *soooooo* ashamed, having such a coward for a little sister."

"Don't," Tony said softly.

"Live with it," Max snapped, and turned again to move around him and get away.

"We're gonna talk, Maxine." Steve drawled her name as he scooted over to block her path. "I'll stay on you until you go talk to Dad. He's not such a bad old guy, once you get to know him."

"Maybe I don't *want* to get to know him." She headed for the steps to escape down the aisle. Steve grabbed her by the elbow.

"I know how you're feeling."

"No, you don't!" How could he, when she certainly didn't?

"Leave her alone." Tony grabbed hold of Steve's hand, freeing her from his grip.

"Look, this is between me and my little sister."

"Stop saying that," Max growled.

"I can say it." Steve wasn't teasing anymore. "It's the truth."

"Just get out of here." Tony put himself between Max and Steve. "Let me talk to her."

"You're not helping anything by—"

"Get out! Both of you!" Max tried to run again, but Steve grabbed her arm.

"You're staying here and listening to me, *little sister*, and that's final."

"Let go!" She dug her heels into the stage floor, but her bare feet skidded on the dusty wood.

Max punched him. She watched him go down, clamping a hand to his split lip. Then the impact ran up her arm. She jerked away, cradling her hand. The smear of blood across her cut knuckle startled her.

"Oh, Max," Tony moaned. He looked away. Max hoped she saw a grin warring with the disappointment on his face. "Are you all right?" He stepped over to offer Steve a hand to get to his feet. They both carefully avoided looking in Max's direction.

"Yeah. She's got a mean right hook, just like Nicky. That's our little brother." Steve dabbed at his bleeding lip with the ball of his thumb. He flicked a glance at her. "Guess that runs in the family, just like our lousy tempers."

"I suppose so." Tony had a breath of laughter in his voice.

"Don't let that send you running, okay? You two are good together."

"If I haven't let that bother me before, why should it now?"

"Stop it! Stop talking about me. I'm standing right here!" Max shrieked.

Then she realized she was indeed standing there, when she could have made her escape minutes ago. She snatched up her sandals and fled, down the steps, up the aisle, out into the lobby.

Chapter Eighteen

Max walked around town, stopping often when her legs ached. She had a few dollars of loose change in her pocket, not quite sure how it got there, and used it to buy a can of ginger ale and a donut at Heinke's. She couldn't have cared less about her diet right then. When sunset dimmed into evening, she headed home. Joel's vintage Mustang was missing from the parking lot behind the house, so that was a good sign. Her Cavalier was also gone, meaning Joe had borrowed it. Hopefully, he had asked out Karen Peterson.

She was tempted to go to Tony's house—he had given her a full set of keys for the house—but she was afraid he would be waiting for her, to make her sit down and talk.

Then she realized she was afraid he *wouldn't* be waiting for her, and he wouldn't force her to sit down and talk. That frightened her more than any impending lecture from her parents for punching Steve.

Her half-brother.

Ironic, that she had sometimes wished she had a big brother to look out for her and beat up people who made fun of her, teach her to drive, and let her borrow his car. The reality wasn't what she had seen in her daydreams by a long shot.

She stumbled going up the back steps, when it occurred to her that Joe was making progress on his love life, but she might just have put a bad dent into her friendship with Tony. If she lost him as her best friend over what she had done, how she had reacted today, she didn't know what she would do. She couldn't even pray, except for the small, almost wordless pleas for help that she had been sending up to heaven since Steve followed her out into the theater.

"Hungry?" Rose said, when Max crept into the kitchen. She sat at the kitchen table with a cup of tea, one of the scones she had baked yesterday, and a thick, battered book.

"No. Thanks." She could barely make herself meet the older woman's gaze. Max fought tears when she saw nothing but sympathy. "Where is everybody?"

"Your parents are out with Dr. Morgan and his lady friend. Joe took your car. I think Jeremy is across the street, pestering Tony." Rose sighed, echoing Max's sigh of relief. "I assume you want him to be kept busy?"

"Jeremy or Tony?" Max shook her head. "Thanks. How come you're here alone?"

"Like you, I need regular time alone so I can hear myself think." Rose gestured at the teapot sitting on the counter. "It's chamomile. Let me fix you a nice cup with honey and milk, then go upstairs and take a long, hot bath and go to bed. Everything will look a lot better in the morning."

"I don't think so." Max nodded her thanks and sank down into the chair opposite Rose. "Mom and Dad are going to give me one heck of a lecture in the morning."

"Knowing your parents, they'll expect you to chew over the whole situation all night, and they'll know that you'll be much harder on yourself than they ever would."

"Reverse psychology makes my head hurt." She managed a crooked grin when Rose chuckled and got up to fix the tea.

'What makes my head hurt is how stupidly oblivious you and Tony are. For two people who write wonderful romances, you can't seem to see what's between you."

"I wish Tony would get romantic," she sighed.

"Think, Max. Everything he's done for you and your family, isn't that what real love is? If I miss my guess, you wouldn't have been able to hold everything together like you have the last few weeks, if you hadn't been able to lean on Tony. He loves you. More than friendship." She set the teacup down on the table in front of her. "How do you feel about him?"

"Like I'd rather be dead than lose him." Max rested her head in her hands, pressing on her eyes with the heels of her palms. "I just wish I could *stop* wishing for the moonlight and roses and sweeping theme music and bells chiming, y'know?"

"Who says you won't have it someday? Morris and I had an arranged marriage, but our last few years..." Rose sighed. "Some things get better with time and practice. You and Tony have such a wonderful foundation. Don't throw it away."

Monday, May 12

Max woke up when she heard her brothers rattling around, rushing out the door for school. When she crept downstairs, she found only Rose in the kitchen. Her parents had gone out for breakfast at Stay-A-While. She knew she wouldn't be able to go back to bed for another hour, until she had to get ready for work, and she didn't want to face her computer when her brain was in such turmoil. Rather than sit around, waiting for her parents to get back and corner her, she decided to get ready for the day and leave. A ride might help settle her thoughts. Or maybe a walk in the park. Or just go to work early. Anything was better than sitting here, waiting for the boom to fall.

A quick shower and a quicker breakfast of cold spinach quiche got her on her way. Sandals and jeans, her new God's Gym T-shirt and her purse, and she was out the door. She didn't even mind that her car was down nearly a quarter tank of gas from when she parked it yesterday afternoon. In moments, engine gunning, she zipped down the driveway a little faster than was wise.

She ended up at the park behind City Hall. That suited her, so she got out and wandered past the skateboard arena—it looked wrong, empty of neon-colored boards and padded riders—to the gazebo looking out over Poe Lake. The former quarry made a nice, cool place to sit and think in peace and quiet. Her mother liked to come here, to enjoy the breezes and the thick shadows from the trees on almost every side, and the flocks of ducks and geese that made their home there.

The gazebo was empty for the first time in memory. Max leaned into the white railing and looked out over the water, envisioning how busy this place would be at lunchtime and when school let out. Thin, silvery-black shadows of fish moved under the surface of the brownish clear water. She couldn't keep track of them. Just like her own thoughts. If only the peace and calm of the lake could affect her mind like it soothed her body.

"Shakespeare!"

Max turned in time to see something white hurtling toward her. She nearly dodged aside, but something made her put up a hand and snatch the paper-wrapped lime fruit-sicle out of the air.

"Good catch. Maybe you should go out for football," Maggie called. She strutted up the gazebo steps and grinned. Her mouth was rimmed with purple from her own treat. Today she wore a battered Guardians cap facing backwards, a green plaid shirt over a purple muscle shirt meant for a man twice her size, black high-tops, and neon orange shorts.

"I don't think so."

"You have fast hands. I bet you hit whatever you aim at." The old woman winked.

Max grinned even as her face heated, remembering that punch yesterday, and the way Steve's eyes widened and he staggered a step before he went down. Her hand still hurt a little from punching him. She had cut her knuckle on his teeth.

"Think it's gonna rain?" the woman continued.

"No." She paused in peeling the wrapper. Sometimes, it was hard to figure out where Maggie was headed.

"You got the biggest black cloud hanging over your head. Gonna beat up on somebody? Maybe your book got turned down?"

Maggie settled down on a bench and crossed her legs. She stuck her grape ice in her mouth, freeing up her hands to re-tie her shoelaces. Grape syrup melt dripped down her chin. Fascinated, Max watched until Maggie finished with her shoes, took the ice out of her mouth and wiped the melt off her chin. Then she licked the back of her hand. She laughed at Max's expression.

"Hey, just because old Maggie is crazy doesn't mean she's stupid! Don't waste nothing, you hear me? Don't throw out nothing, not clothes or food or people. Especially people. Know what I mean?"

"Yeah, I think so," Max murmured.

"Melting." She pointed at the green drops slowly escaping through the tear in the wrapper.

"Thanks." Max finished peeling off the wrapper and licked at the melting ice. Cool slid down her throat, reminding her of the icy feeling that filled her last night.

Fear, mostly. Panic. She had dreamed of meeting up with Carlo Vincente, waking up a dozen times through the night. She couldn't decide how she felt about him in her dreams. Fear, regret, guilt. Now that she thought about it, Max realized she didn't feel the anger or hatred that she had half-feared every time she thought about confronting her natural father. She felt as if she had inhaled pure oxygen, when she realized she didn't hate Carlo Vincente. How could she hate somebody she didn't know, except as a face and voice in movies, and a memory that was so very precious to her mother, despite the tears and regrets?

"Maggie—" Max raised her head and saw she was alone again.

She grinned and took a big bite of the lime ice. Her teeth jarred on the stick. Cryptic words and vanishing like smoke seemed to be Maggie's stock in trade. Max knew she shouldn't be upset, but she did want to ask for some advice. It might not make sense, coming from Maggie, but she knew the crazy old woman cared.

She started walking, just because she had so many thoughts in her head she couldn't sit still. A jogging path led around the lake. Max wasn't up to jogging. It was too hot and she wore sandals.

At about the quarter point, she licked the last bit of syrup off the stick. A garbage can chained to a wooden post sat off the path ten yards ahead. Max bent and twisted the stick like her thoughts kept twisting inside her head, until the fragile wood snapped. Two more steps, she reached the can and tossed the stick in. She paused to lick the last few sticky drops off her fingers and the soft thumping of jogging feet broke through her disjointed thoughts. Max looked up and let her attention be caught by the perfect stride; muscled, tanned legs in bright blue shorts, black net shirt showing off sweating pecs and biceps, curly dark hair, square chin.

The sweet lime syrup turned sour in her stomach. That was her brother she had started to drool over. Correction: half-brother. That didn't make things any better.

Steve almost passed her. Max relaxed, believing he hadn't seen her, then his head turned and his gaze flicked over her. He broke stride and slowed to a stop.

"Hey, sis." His cocky grin made her hackles rise. Then she saw the swelling on his bottom lip and the bruise.

"I wish you wouldn't say that."

"What, you don't like being my sister?" Panting a little, he pressed against the post with both hands and did tendon stretches.

"I hardly know you."

"Well, get to know me." He flashed his cocky grin at her, wider, until he winced.

"How's your—" Max touched the corner of her mouth.

"It's been worse. Can't say I didn't deserve it. You should have heard some of the lectures Dad used to give me." Steve rolled his eyes and groaned. "How about your stepfather?"

"Dad never has to lecture me. He just gives me one of those looks."

"Yeah, Mom's that way. She can say in one little teary frown what it takes Dad an hour to get across." He wiped sweat off his forehead with the back of his hand. "You'll really like her. She fixed a lot of problems between me and Dad. When you come visit—"

"Slow down!" Max stepped backward, stumbling when her heel slid off the asphalt path.

"Come on, give Dad a chance, will you? He's a great guy, once you get to know him."

"You're biased."

"No, I'm not." He gestured down the path. "Can we walk a little, so I don't stiffen up?"

Max surprised herself by nodding. The smart move, she knew, would be to turn and run in the opposite direction. Then again, Steve was definitely in better shape than her, dressed for running and warmed up for a good long chase. She had an unpleasant image of him catching and tackling her and making up for the split lip she gave him the night before.

"I hated Dad for a long time, you know," Steve began. "My mother died when I was a baby, and her folks raised me. They told me Dad didn't want me." He shrugged. "They hated him. I didn't come live with Dad and Mom until after they had Nicky and Ray. I visited a lot. It wasn't fun for any of us for a while. Then Mom sat me down one day and told me Dad was afraid of me. She said he loved me and he wanted me to like him, but he didn't know what to do. You want to get a nasty kid's attention? Tell him his movie star father is scared of him."

"So you two get along now. That's nice." Max concentrated on the path just ahead of her feet. "What does that have to do with me?"

"He was scared when he realized you were his kid. He didn't know anything except that you were Emily Keeler's daughter and he owed you."

"He doesn't owe me anything!" Max flinched when her voice sent birds winging out of the trees over her head.

"Like I said, Dad's a great guy." He stroked his bruised lip with his thumb. "I got pushy last night because I know how much he'd like to meet you. If it wasn't for all the Gabrielli work, I bet he would have come to town already. It ticked me off, thinking about you not giving him a chance. Like I didn't give him a chance for a long time."

"Guess that runs in the—" She choked on the words that tried to spill out of her mouth. Had she actually started to agree with him? Maybe even tease him?

"You know, sis—" Steve grinned when she stiffened at the word. "Hey, I like having a sister. Even if she does beat up on me. How does it feel having an *older* brother?"

"Kind of strange," she admitted.

"The bottom line is, Dad still loved me, no matter how rotten I was, because I was *his kid.* When I got to know him, I loved him back. He loves you, just because you're his kid, without knowing anything about you. Why not take the chance that you could love him, too?"

"It's not that easy."

"I know." He rested a hand on her shoulder and squeezed a little, light and warm. Not oppressive at all. Max knew if she tensed, he would move back.

She looked around and realized they had come back around the lake to the gazebo.

"Nice little town you've got. I came here to get to know you, figure out what the story is with you and your mom... I'd really like to stay."

"What about those independent films you were talking about working on?"

"She actually listened to me!" He slapped a hand over his heart and staggered backward a few steps.

Max grinned, despite the jolting feeling she got when she saw Carlo Vincente in him, just for a moment, a scene from a romantic comedy he had done.

"I thought you were an okay guy." She sighed. "And I guess you still are, even if you are my... my half-brother."

"Keep practicing. You'll get used to saying it." He shrugged and gave her that part-sheepish, part-mischievous grin again. "I like this town. Especially jogging around here. You don't realize how good you have it here. Just compare it to some other places."

Max heard the unspoken words: *Like in L.A.*

He wasn't going to give up on the subject of taking her to meet their father. Funny, but she didn't feel her stomach tie into knots and lava erupt in her gut at the idea. She did feel a flicker of irritation, though, knowing he wasn't going to shut up any time soon. Things did look and feel better with the new day, like Rose had said. She didn't see Steve as an enemy any longer. A troublemaker, yes. Nosy and impatient. But not the enemy. Max thought that realization made her feel a little lighter, made it easier to breathe.

"It's good for thinking, isn't it?" She gestured back at the lake. "Mom loves coming here. She told me once it reminded her of a place where—where he—where our father used to take her for picnics," she finally managed to say.

Thanks to Steve, she had more to think about. She admitted she hadn't been fair toward Carlo. How could she be, when she didn't know his side of the story?

Emily had never told Carlo about her. Emily had avoided all contact with Carlo because she believed it was for the best. Max hadn't understood. For too long, she chose to believe he had abandoned them. In her teens, her mother had made her listen to the facts. Max supposed that despite Emily's explanations, she still harbored some resentment.

Steve's eyes sparkled. "How long is it going to take you to figure out what to call him?"

"We're just starting to get along. Don't push it," she growled, teasing. That startled Max—mostly because it felt so *natural* to tease him.

~~~~~

"Chuck." Carlo Vincente emerged through the press of people filling the ballroom of the Hollywood Roosevelt.

The welcoming reception for the Gabrielli Fellowship awards and seminar had been last night, an informal event where people came and went as they chose. This morning had started with a continental breakfast and opening remarks by the various speakers. The members of the board were not required to attend, but this evening they would speak at the evening dessert social, where they would formally introduce the finalists.

"Have you seen him?" Winters said, saluting his friend with a tall glass of ice and cranberry juice. "He actually had the guts to show up?"

"More like gall, from what Steven has told me..." Carlo glanced at several young men and women wearing nametags—painfully young, in Winters' estimation—who approached the two of them through the dispersing crowd. He shook his head slightly, met Winters' gaze, and turned to the newcomers with all the charm that had made him a sought-after spokesman.

Winters waited until Carlo was done welcoming and encouraging the seminar attendees, then the two of them moved out of the flow of traffic. Hopefully to give them uninterrupted time to talk.
~~~~~

"So you talked to Steve, huh? What prompted him to call? Or did you call him?" Winters murmured as they moved around the perimeter of the room. They both watched the attendees as they dispersed to their first workshop of the morning. It was obvious to him that Carlo was looking for someone.

"He called me." A mirthless chuckle escaped Carlo. "Emily confronted him, and it turns out that Max and her partner, Tony, both figured out who he was some time ago."

"I can't see Max welcoming her newfound brother with open arms."

"He says she gave him a fat lip." Carlo stopped and gestured at a cluster of people standing by the coffee and juice table. "He says it was a well deserved fat lip, too."

"I don't think I want to know the story behind that." Winters grinned, as his imagination filled in the pieces. He knew Steve and Max very well, having watched them both grow up. They were too much alike in many ways.

"Is that him? That young man in the dark blue shirt, with his jacket sleeves rolled up to his elbows?"

Winters studied the man in question, only a dozen yards away, talking and laughing with a group of brightly dressed people who all seemed to be hanging on his every word. Right now, he had his back to the two men, but his blond head and wide shoulders looked familiar enough to have Winters nodding. Then he turned and put his arm around a tiny, dark-haired girl with the face of a Madonna and big eyes that clearly spoke her adoration. One glimpse of his face confirmed it.

"Jake Holt. Just like we suspected. You didn't actually meet him face-to-face, did you?"

"Oh, yes. I made a point of watching for the finalists and greeting them last night. Your Mr. Holt made a point, in his turn, of telling me how often his mother talks about the movies she made with me."

"It amazes me, sometimes, how someone with so much talent on stage... doesn't have the brains to think his way out of a wet paper bag. Does he think he can actually get away with pretending to be Max Keeler? The first time someone asks him to write a script, his scam is blown." Winters quelled the urge to stomp over to that laughing, chatting group, and see that arrogant assurance fall off Jake's face the moment he recognized him.

"Maybe all he wants now is Max's prize money, and then he'll fade into the woodwork."

Winters shuddered. "No. If he only wanted the money, he would have stuck with having his agent accept the check for him. He's here for a reason, wearing Max's name." A dozen acts of petty nastiness he had witnessed Jake committing in the past two years flared before his eyes.

What could that arrogant snot do to damage Max's reputation?

They both watched Jake, who continued holding court with the knot of admirers. In the falling volume of the ballroom, his laughter came through clear and loud and rather coarse.

"I've been told that he has already attended two single-day writing conferences as Max Keeler," Carlo offered. "And the press office has found me three newspaper and online interviews, with pictures, where he has passed himself off as Max Keeler."

"It's gone too far already. We definitely can't handle the problem quietly." Winters turned his back on Jake and his knot of admirers and led Carlo out of the ballroom. "You'll straighten out the committee?"

"Immediately. I assume you'll send for Max?"

"If I have to fly to Ohio and drag her onto the plane kicking and screaming."

"I'm sure Steven will tell you to watch out for her right hook."

They separated at the ballroom doors and went in opposite directions. Winters headed for the parking garage and pulled out his cell phone. First, contact a travel agent friend who could work miracles. Next, call Max when her tickets were an accomplished fact. Or better yet, get her parents to gang up on her.

~~~~~

"Something wrong, Aunt Rose?" Max asked, pausing in the doorway of the kitchen when she came home from work at lunchtime. The next moment, she darted forward and caught the phone as it slipped from Rose's fingers. The good mood she had gained from avoiding a lecture before work vanished in concern. She hung the phone on the wall and guided Rose to her usual chair at the table. "Should I call for Dad?"

"No. I'm fine." She pressed her hands to her pale face, and a moment later blushed bright red. "Silly old fool... I'm sorry, Max."

"What happened? Who was that on the phone?"

"An old... well, I can't call him an old boyfriend. My father wouldn't allow me to date. I swear that made me even more sought after than if I had been available." Rose sighed and pressed her hands to her cheeks again, then rested them on her open book on the table. "Mischa... I have no idea how he found me, but he called and said he wanted to come call on me."

"He's in town?" Max settled into a chair, a little confused when Rose burst out laughing.

"No, I'm all right. It's just... I never thought to ask where he was. The silly old man is probably still in Boston. If he's the same ridiculous, extravagant boy I knew, he probably would hop on a plane tomorrow to come visit." She sighed again, the sound ending in laughter. "You probably think I'm an old fool, but you have no idea how good it feels to
~~~~~

have someone—even silly old Mischa—chasing me!"

"No." She tried to smile, but she felt something she suspected was bitter envy turn into a cold, nauseating ball in the pit of her stomach. "I really don't know."

"Oh, Max, for pity's sake!" Rose sighed and jammed her fists into her hips. "Don't make me slap you. Tony is the most wonderful young man. You love him, and I'm sure he loves you."

"Best friends. Family love." Max's face warmed.

"Give him some encouragement. I've heard him talk about you two getting married—"

"He was joking!"

"What if he isn't? What if he's trying to figure out how you feel before he takes a chance?"

"What's it like to be in love?" she whispered.

"I don't know, really. But I do know what it's like to love someone so deeply, you want to die when you lose him. It's rather nice to feel a little giddy and silly, and I plan on enjoying it while it lasts." She sighed again and reached for her teacup. Her hands no longer trembled. "And that's something to remember, Max. The fancy feelings of *being in love* don't last, but love lasts forever. Understand?"

She got up and went to the teapot on the counter to fill her cup, her feet taking strangely light, delicate steps, almost dancing.

Max watched her, a slow smile growing across her face. She found she liked the idea of Rose enjoying the attentions of a suitor who hadn't given up even after forty years.

What about her and Tony? That, she decided, needed a lot of thought.

The phone rang, startling them both. Rose set the teacup down on the counter with a thump.

"If that's Mischa, tell him I'm busy, but I can pencil him in next week." She tipped her nose up in the air and swept out of the kitchen, while the phone rang a second time.

"That's the spirit, Aunt Rose. Play hard to get." Max snatched the phone off the wall. "Randolphs," she said, barely remembering not to say Homespun Theater. Sometimes it was hard keeping track of which phone she was using.

Chapter Nineteen

"Max. Great. How come you aren't answering your cell phone?" Winters demanded.

"Because it's at my desk and I left it there when I went to work. Never mind," she hurried on. "What's up? Why couldn't you leave a message?"

"Your folks should have you packed by now. You're taking the next plane to L.A."

"Why?" Anger coiled immediately through her gut. If her parents had resorted to bringing her agent into the whole mess, and he was going to harass her to come meet Carlo, Max seriously considered firing him. Family friend or not.

"Jake Holt is here at the Gabrielli doings, passing himself off as Max Keeler."

"What?" Max winced, hearing her shriek echoing off the ceiling.

The next moment, she was sitting on the floor, her back against the cupboard doors, not quite sure how she ended up there. Footsteps hurried to the kitchen from throughout the house. The way her family surrounded her in silence told her they had all the details already. Just her luck—the one day she didn't take her cell phone to work with her, and she needed to be on top of things. She closed her eyes and concentrated on what her agent had to tell her. When the call ended and she opened her eyes, she saw Emily and Joel standing over her, holding onto each other and looking concerned, with Rose visible in the open doorway of the kitchen.

Tony was nowhere to be seen, and that hurt more than she had thought possible. For a moment, she flashed onto what Rose had just said about Tony, and wished she could launch herself into his arms and hold onto him and let him make things right. Just like all the fantastic heroes he wrote. She needed him. Maybe even more than her parents. How could she fly off to Hollywood without Tony to hold her hand and make jokes to calm her nerves, and maybe even be a little bit of a caveman when she had to face down Jake?

"Chuck is meeting with the Gabrielli board for dinner tonight." She fought another surge of angry, terrified nausea. "I have to be there, with my birth certificate and copies of my script, correspondence with the fellowship judges and my original entry form. I have to prove I'm me, and that I wrote my own screenplay, and Jake's name is Jake Holt and not Max Keeler."

"Already put together. Photos from our last few plays, programs, videos." Joel thumped the table. "All my office paperwork, with his photo and legal paperwork for his paychecks. If he denies his picture and signature and W9, then he's admitting to forgery. He's a forger and a fraud, one way or another."

Max braced her hands on the table and shoved herself to her feet. If she didn't get moving now, she never would. "Chuck has plane tickets, waiting for me at Hopkins."

"We started your packing," Emily said. "Joe is getting you to the airport. Go wash up and change and get going."

Fifteen minutes later, she was in fresh linen pants, a sleeveless top and matching overshirt, a set in dusty blue Emily had bought her two months ago. She tugged her suitcase down the stairs. Her mother had packed her notebook computer and a thick envelope folder stuck out of the side pocket, sitting on top of Joel's desk. Joe came tearing down the stairs, nearly running into Max at the bottom when she paused, just now realizing that her parents must have called him to come home early from school to drive her. This was even more of an emergency than she had thought. That realization frightened her, too.

Then a deep ache throbbed through her when she looked around, and Tony was still nowhere to be seen. She should have called him when she headed upstairs. Too late now. She would have to go to L.A. without him. What had happened to his famous radar that always brought him running in when she needed him most?

"You're all set," Joel said, standing on front of the fax that spewed papers. "Chuck just called back with your flight info and we're getting copies of the paperwork right now. You'll have a chauffeur waiting at the airport."

"And a chauffeur here to get you there," Joe added, nudging Max to get her off the bottom step. He wrapped his arm around her for a brief hug. "Give Jake a couple of black eyes from me, would you?"

"Joseph." Emily shook her head, but laughter sparkled in her eyes. A little more color touched her cheeks, and Max felt almost sick from a stab of guilt. Her mother still had a long way to go to be fully recovered from the accident. All this stress couldn't be good for her.

"Mom, it'll be okay. Don't worry about me." Max hurried to hug her, almost forgetting to let go of the suitcase. "Just... I don't know, call the church, get Pastor in on it. Tell Jeannette, would you? And yell across the street to Tony when I'm gone."

"Tony knows," Joel said, shoving the fax papers into the side pocket of her computer bag. "Did you really think anything could happen to you without him knowing?"

"Dad—" She choked and hurried to hug him before taking the

computer bag from his outstretched hand. "I'm scared to death."

"Means you're smart." He yanked on a handful of her hair. "Just remember to let God sort things out, hear me?"

"I hear you." She took a deep breath. "Well, come on, chauffeur. What are you waiting for?"

A horn honked out in the parking area behind the house.

"Him." Joe snatched up the handle of Max's suitcase. "Come on." He hurried through the kitchen door.

When Max stumbled outside a few moments later, Tony's car waited there, and Joe finished putting her suitcase into the trunk. Then he climbed into the back seat. Tony was driving.

"Come on," Tony called, leaning across the seat to shove the passenger door open. "By the time we get there, we'll only have an hour until our flight takes off, and you know how security is at this time of the day."

"Actually, no, I don't." Max managed to get in and close the door without dropping her computer bag or her purse. She swallowed hard. "Our flight?" It was hard to talk with a big, relieved, shaking grin stretching her face, but she managed.

"You don't think I'm gonna let you go running off to Hollywood without me, do you? Chuck managed to swing two seats for us." He stopped short, eyes wide enough to pop out of his skull, when Max leaned over and landed a kiss just on the corner of his mouth.

"Will you two save the gush for later?" Joe yelped, almost in her ear. "We got a deadline to meet."

"Yeah. Yeah." Tony swallowed hard and put the car into reverse before he looked in the rearview mirror. "You and me, we got a lot of talking to do, Maximilian."

"Lots of time to talk on the plane." She thought she could pop corn with the heat coming off her face. Max turned in the seat to face straight ahead, then she resorted to digging through the envelope of documents Joel had given her, just to avoid looking at Tony or Joe.

"Got enough there to do the job?" Tony asked, breaking the long silence when they were at the light, waiting to turn off Snow Road onto Route 237 to get to Cleveland Hopkins Airport.

"Chuck said we have to strike hard and fast and get Jake to slit his own throat." Max was relieved to hear her voice was calm and steady. She wasn't about to risk looking at Tony just yet. "We'll make plans with the committee tonight over dinner. The fellowship has to protect its reputation in all this."

"I think you need a big splash," Joe offered from the back seat. "So Jake can't go anywhere ever again, and nobody will ever trust him."

"It's a good human interest story," Tony offered. "People will remember your name because there's more than the Gabrielli tied in with it now."

"Free publicity. Great." Max closed her eyes and slouched a little, trying to relax and release the tension that threatened to turn her muscles into rocks.

"Look at it this way — all those author photos the different publishers are asking for — you won't have to pay for them. You'll have your pick of about a million different shots to choose from."

"Very funny." She opened one eye in time to see Tony glance over at her and grin. He patted her hand and turned back to driving.

Actually, it was funny, in a warped kind of way. And she did feel a little better. What would she ever do without Tony? He always knew what to say to turn something on its side and help her see it differently, or at least with a little bit of humor. He always knew when to make her talk and when to let her stay quiet and think.

I really do love him, she concluded in those quiet minutes as they drove down the highway. *Not that gushy, heart-pounding stuff we write. Real love. Forever stuff. Like what Mom and Dad have. Tony would do anything to help me. And I'd do anything for him,* she added, feeling a smile finally touch her face. *Please, God, don't ever let anything come between us?*

"Feeling better?"

"Just doing something about the problem, knowing it'll be over soon, that helps."

"Wish we had done more to Jake when he was getting everything he needed to pretend to be you," Joe grumbled from the back seat.

"I wish you guys had told me earlier what you were doing."

"We were trying to protect you. You've had a lot on your mind lately," Tony said, shrugging.

"Anything else you've been keeping quiet about, that you should tell me, now that we're handling all our crises at once?"

"Well..." He grinned at her as the red light ahead turned to green and he took his foot off the brake. "If I tell you I'm madly in love with you and you have to marry me, you probably won't say yes, will you?"

"I ought to say yes, just to pay you back." Max forced a grin, despite the dropping sensation his teasing created inside her. It had to be teasing. Her brother was in the back seat, after all. Something like that, if it was real, Tony would keep for private. Wouldn't he?

"That'll make a great story. Marry for revenge. Think it'll sell?"

"With our luck, it will, and our crazy editor will want a dozen more in a series."

They were still chuckling about the idea when they pulled up in front of the drop-off area and luggage check-in. Max refused to look at Tony, though; terrified he would see the wistfulness that put an edge on her laughter. She was grateful for the fuss of unloading their luggage and turning the car over to Joe, and then hurrying into the terminal to claim their tickets.

They had no trouble getting their tickets, and that just made her tenser. For every hurdle they passed over easily enough, Max expected an obstacle of equal difficulty waiting for them at the worst possible moment for a delay. At the security checkpoint before they went down Concourse A, she was positive she would be pulled aside in one of those random full-body searches that showed up in an urban legends-come-true site on the internet.

They slid through without a pause. That frightened her. If she hadn't had to take her computer out of its travel bag and put it in a separate bin for the x-ray machine, she would have suspected someone of stealing it during the three seconds she had to take her eyes off it. The tickets had stayed in her hand the entire time she went through the metal detector archway. Was it possible they were going to pass through without a problem?

That meant their flight information had to be wrong, and the plane would leave without them. She shoved the tickets into her computer bag and picked up speed.

"Hey, Max." Tony grabbed her arm when she would have half-jogged down the concourse right past their gate. He wrapped an arm around her shoulders and herded her to the first available seat. For some reason, the waiting area at the gate was only half-full. "What are you doing?" he demanded, when she popped out of her seat and pulled her tickets out of her computer bag.

"This must be a mistake." She looked at the details of the tickets and compared them to the gate number and the information displayed there. "First class! We're going first class."

"Yeah?" He glanced around to make sure no one was staring at them and guided her back to their seat. "Do you have a problem with that?"

"I can't afford first class."

"Chuck's paying for it. And he's pretty sure the Gabrielli people are going to reimburse him, so don't get in a snit about it."

"Why would they pay him back?" Max took a few deep, slow breaths, positive she wasn't getting enough oxygen. Tony's words just didn't make sense.

"It's their reputation at stake. And it's good PR."

"And Carlo Vincente is probably making them do it." She looked around, half-expecting a paparazzi to pop out from behind a cardboard Rock and Roll Hall of Fame display. She figured after that revelation about Steve and now this problem with Jake, half of Hollywood knew about Emily Keeler's big youthful mistake with Carlo Vincente.

"So what if he is? He's your father. Steve says—"

"Please don't tell me you've been teaming up with that—that—" She flung her hands up in the air and collapsed against the hard waiting area seat.

"Your big brother?" Tony snorted, fighting hard not to grin ear to ear when she glared at him. "You have no idea how relieved I was to find out that's why he's been showing up everywhere you go."

"He has not." Max felt a little better and was grateful for Tony's exaggeration and teasing.

"I can't begin to tell you how glad I am." He took hold of her hand, weaving his fingers through hers. "Max, this probably isn't a good time, but if I keep waiting for the current catastrophe to calm down, I'll never get this said."

"You've been hanging around with my family how long? And you still haven't figured out that the crises and catastrophes never end?" She slouched a little more and rested her head against the back of the seat, feigning relaxation when she felt like jumping through the ceiling from the moment Tony took hold of her hand.

"Very funny. Back to what we were talking about in the car—"

"Running Jake out of town on a rail?" Max fought not to yank her hand free. She muffled a cry of relief when the flight attendant announced boarding for their flight, starting with first class. She leaped to her feet, nearly yanking Tony off balance. He glared at her and she inexplicably felt giddy.

For the next half hour, they were busy getting into their seats and then waiting for the other passengers boarding the plane to file past them. Max tried to ignore the gazes of people who probably wondered who they were and why they traveled first class. The few times she had taken a plane, she had wondered the same thing. At least, she assumed people flying coach wondered about the first class people. Maybe it was only because she was a writer?

"It looks like we have the whole section to ourselves," she said, when a flight attendant got a signal from one of the ground crew and pulled the hatch closed. "We could take our own seat—how about our own row?— and sack out in style on the way to L.A. What do you think?" She gestured past Tony at the three rows of two seats on each side of the aisle.

"You are not getting away from me." Tony stretched his legs out, blocking her into her seat next to the window.

"What are you talking about?"

"Just... just think about things, everything that's been happening the last few weeks. Ever since I came back from California."

"You didn't have to ditch your teaching gig for us. I mean, I'm glad you did. You can't imagine how glad I was to see you standing there." She snorted. "Facing down Aunt Rose with that baseball bat ready to clobber you."

"Oh, I don't know. I was pretty glad to see you. Felt like I'd been away for years, not just a few weeks. I promise, I am never going away. And I'm not letting you get away from me, either. You and me, together forever."

"Tony, you shouldn't make promises like that." Max flinched when he caught hold of her hand.

"Good afternoon, passengers of Flight Six Thirty-Seven, bound for LAX," a woman said over the intercom. "I'm Captain Janice Rutherford, head of your flight crew. The skies are clear all the way across the country, with one stop in Denver. We have no anticipated delays at this time, and should be touching down shortly after 4p.m., L.A. time."

Max tried to tug her hand free of Tony's grip when the flight attendants handled the usual pre-flight show-and-tell. He tightened his grip, weaving his fingers through hers again. She pulled harder and Tony leaned toward her, growling under his breath. She giggled. Tony leaned closer when she refused to look at him. Max closed her eyes and refused to open them again until the last instruction had been given and she felt the plane building up speed as it taxied down the runway.

"You're stuck with me, Maximilian," Tony whispered, leaning so close she felt his nose touch her ear and his breath on her cheek.

"Should I be afraid?" She squelched a yelp when Tony yanked up on the armrest between them, folding it into the seat back. Her breath caught in her throat when he wrapped his arm around her shoulders.

"That's better."

"Tony—" Max thought about what Rose had said to her, about love versus being in love, and what she and Tony had together. Was it only today?

"I'll always be here for you, and I know you'll always be here for me."

"Please." Her voice cracked. She swallowed hard and wondered how soon she could ask for something to drink. "This day has just been too horrid."

"I plan on making this the best day of your life." He adjusted his grip on her shoulder, rubbing it a little. "Sounds kind of arrogant, doesn't it?"

"Mom says writers need to have big egos, just like actors. It's the only way we'll get anywhere."

"Now, back to what I was starting to say earlier. About waiting for crises to end." He sighed. "I was talking to Steve today. His mouth looks a lot better."

"I know." A big lump of laughter choked her, but it wouldn't quite come out. "We ran into each other up at Poe."

"You know..." Tony's voice rumbled as he lowered his voice. "If you ever want to give up writing, you could become a boxer."

"Don't," she sputtered. The sound turned into a few weak giggles. "I can't believe I—" She shook her head. The laughter died again as she imagined the lecture she had managed to escape from her parents. It would still be waiting when she got home.

"You decked your brother?" Tony took a handful of her hair and shook her a little. "I can believe it. I've gotten to know the guy, and he deserved it. Anyway... what's done is done. Nothing we can do to change it now, is there?" He rocked her a little. "Gee, Max, I thought you were the smart one in this partnership."

"It's not that easy!" She winced, hating how her voice cracked and seemed to bounce off the plastic shield of the plane window, even with her ears partially blocked from gaining altitude.

"I know." He rubbed down her arm again. Tony smelled good, and she liked the warmth that soaked from him to her, easing away some of the aching tension that had been there since Winters' phone call.

Max hoped he would keep his arm around her all the way to the coast. Tony made her feel safe and warm and understood.

"What's that grin for?" he said.

"Hmm?" She shook her head, feeling her mouth ache as she tried to tone down her smile. "I was just thinking, how you make me feel right now, you're just a great... big... security blanket."

"Oh, you are going to pay for that." He slid his arm down her side, stopping just short of jabbing his fingers into her ribs when she tensed.

"We are going to eventually kill each other, you know that, don't you? It's a miracle we've lasted this long as partners."

"That's just a sign..." Tony stared into her eyes, and for a few seconds Max's entire world narrowed down to the warmth in his eyes and touch.

Tony swallowed and looked away. He re-adjusted his arm to lie across her shoulders again.

Another band of her aching tension seeped away. She would have to face Carlo Vincente at the end of this journey. There was no avoiding it now. Especially since it was inevitable that Steve would report to his father—no, she had to admit it—*their* father—*her* father. But everything was all right because Tony was here, holding her.

"It's going to be okay, Max," Tony said.

"Promise you'll hold my hand the whole time?" she asked, her voice nearly a whisper.

"Day and night. For the rest of our lives, if that's what you need."

"I wish."

"So do I. You know, I do love you, Max."

"I love you too, Tony. You're my best friend in the whole world," she hurried to add.

"No." Tony nudged her to turn to face him. "I mean I *love* you, Max."

She could only stare and wait for the scene to fade into another of her dreams.

"I mean forever," he said, lowering his voice. "Wake up together. Fight over the toilet paper roll and squeezing toothpaste. Having kids. Long, rainy mornings just curled up in bed, doing nothing."

"You're serious?" Her voice cracked.

"Completely." He licked his lips. Swallowed hard. "I never was joking, Max."

She had to believe him.

She wanted to scream.

Not a good idea when the plane had reached cruising altitude.

She punched him in the arm. Mostly because his arm blocked her from his ribs.

"Did I have to beat it out of you?" she whispered, when Tony just stared at her. "Why couldn't you have just said it, without all the joking around?"

"Yeah, and when would I have found the right time, in all the chaos we've gone through lately?"

She sputtered laughter and waved a fist in his face. Tony cowered back, earning more laughter from her. "We've had plenty of quiet spells when you could have said something. You're a coward. Admit it."

"Maybe. But I still love you." He rubbed his arm. "I guess I should be grateful you didn't punch me in the mouth, like Steve."

"I happen to like your mouth," slipped out before she could think.

"Yeah?" Tony leaned in closer. "Prove it."

"How—" Max muffled a squeak when he cupped her cheek and swooped in, kissing her square on the lips.

The books were right. She buzzed like a cool electric jolt shot through her from her lips to her toes.

Tony laughed, soft and low, the sound trickling from his mouth into hers, stealing her breath, tickling inside her head and then down into the aching tight spot inside.

One kiss turned into several. The fingers of his hand cupping the side of her face trembled. Max sighed as his lips left hers, and she let him guide her head down to rest on his shoulder. Through the rumbling of the plane streaking through the skies toward the meeting she had hoped to avoid, she felt another kind of vibration, coming up from deep inside her. A soft, gentle humming that soothed so many jagged, seeping places that she hadn't even known were inside her until they eased. She kept her eyes closed and tried to imagine how it would be twenty, thirty, forty years from now.

"I guess you liked it enough," Tony whispered. "You're smiling."

"I was just picturing us sitting here, exactly like this, on the front porch of your house—"

"Our house. Which is why I wanted you to help me pick out everything." He smirked when she slowly opened her eyes and raised her head and met his gaze. "Ah ha. You believe me now, don't you?"

"Sitting on the front porch of *our* house, just like this, when we're old and gray," she finished, as a dozen memories collided in her mind. All the little things Tony had said, about how good it would be to always be together, his jokes about being married, and yes, his insistence that she pick what she liked to go into his house.

Again, she wondered how she could presume to write mysteries, when she certainly hadn't seen that coming, either.

"Oh, now you did it. You definitely have to marry me."

"One kiss, and you turn into a caveman?"

"Maybe I should have tried the caveman routine a long time ago."

"Maybe." She sighed. "You'll always be my white knight."

"So is that a yes?"

"You're—" She leaned back from him, staring into his somber yet shining eyes. "You *are* serious. Isn't that kind of... fast?"

"Not fast enough. Marry me, Maxine Randolph."

She couldn't force the words onto her tongue, so she settled for catching hold of his collar and holding him still to kiss him. She snuggled as close to him as the seat would allow, and depended on their years of partnership, of writing and working together to help him understand what she couldn't say, or even fully understand yet.

The flight attendants came through with snack boxes and an assortment of beverages. Tony had to take his arm from around her, and she decided it might just be better that way. They needed some time to get used to this change. It was good that they were in a somewhat public place, yet in some ways they had quite a bit of privacy in their enforced proximity to each other. All they could do for the next five hours was talk.

And steal some kisses, when the flight attendants were busy at the other end of the plane.

Chapter Twenty

"Where's Max?" Steve burst through the swinging door from the kitchen.

Emily and Rose were seated on one couch, conferring on stitching patterns. Joe and Joel were putting together a cardboard model of the stage to prepare the minimal set for *Our Town*. Everyone turned to look at him.

"Probably taking off right now," Joe said, glancing at his watch.

"I assume you heard about Jake and the fellowship," Joel said.

"Yeah. I got hold of my pal, Esteban. He's got a private plane." Steve paused to catch his breath. "He's at Hopkins right now. I asked him to take Max..." He shrugged, looking defeated.

"Thanks, but she's all taken care of. I'm sorry you wasted..." Emily sat up, eyes widening.

"What, honey?" Joel moved over to her, stumbling over his cane for a moment.

"It's not a wasted effort. Joel, Max needs us there. Steve, would your friend mind?"

~~~~~

The driver who met Max and Tony at the airport had carried a picture of them with Winters at a writing conference last August. She identified them, and identified herself to them that way, without resorting to the usual big cardboard sign held up in the air at the security checkpoint.

Their hotel reservations ended up being two spare bedrooms at Chuck Winters' apartment. Max couldn't comprehend that an apartment would have so much room. Winters had four bedrooms and a balcony bigger than the balcony at Homespun Theater. She forgot to tease her agent about his lifestyle when the three of them sat down in his office for a quick conference, to finalize their schedule that evening.

The Gabrielli board members weren't expected to appear that evening until the dessert reception. That left the dinner hour free. Max, Winters and Tony would meet with them to discuss their approach, and plan how they would face down Jake to provide the maximum public confirmation that he was an imposter. The directors were still trying to figure out who had helped Jake sneak in at the last minute. It was more than a mix-up in paperwork, because Winters had already notified them that he would be representing Max at the closing ceremonies on Saturday.
~~~~~

There should have been no hotel room, no plane ticket, no transportation from the airport, and no nametag. Someone either knew Jake was a fake, and helped him cheat the real Max Keeler, or someone very gullible and stupid had more authority than he or she deserved. Either way, that person would be out of work by morning, and a black mark on his record.

By morning, Jake would be facing criminal charges of identity theft, no matter how the unmasking was carried out.

"All right, that's enough for now," Winters said. "You have an hour to rest, then wash up and get ready for dinner."

"No time for sightseeing?" Max mumbled as she struggled to her feet.

"Yeah, I want to walk up Hollywood Boulevard and get some really stupid souvenirs or something," Tony said.

"Tomorrow." Winters gestured down the hall. "Get moving. Don't make me call your parents and tattle on you."

Max barely mustered the energy to stick her tongue out at him. She managed a lopsided smile when Winters laughed. It widened when she realized that she walked lopsided, too.

"Please tell me the floor is crooked," she said, as she passed Tony's guest room.

"Nope. Hey, aren't you forgetting something?" He caught hold of her arm, nearly pulling her off her feet when she wanted to keep walking the last five steps to her own room.

"Forgetting?" Max's heart went into overdrive when he grasped her by her shoulders and pulled her up against him. "Oh, yeah, that," she whispered against his lips. One kiss turned into three. She liked how their lips buzzed against each other with Tony's soft laughter.

"Excuse me?" Winters turned on the hall light.

Max stumbled backward from Tony, pressing a hand over her mouth. The shock on her agent's face made her want to giggle, but she was afraid if she started, she wouldn't be able to stop.

"Is there something the two of you want to tell me?" he continued, jamming his fists into his hips.

"You're our agent, not her father," Tony said. He winked at Max, stepped into his room, and closed the door.

"Uh huh." Winters tipped his head to one side, looked at the closed door, then at Max, then back at the closed door, then at Max. "What'll you pay me not to tell your mother you've been necking under the bleachers?"

"My mother will know you're lying. I'm not worried."

Winters' laughter faded away as he went down the hall in the opposite direction, to his master suite. Before she could step into her room, Tony's door opened and he looked out.

"Want to find some bleachers tomorrow?" He waggled his eyebrows at her.

"Tony..." Max leaned against the doorframe before she fell off her feet.
"Yeah?"
"I really do love you."

~~~~~

Joel tightened his hand around his cane until his knuckles turned white. He loosened his grip to let the blood flow back in, bright red and tingling. He would have laughed if his whole chest and throat hadn't felt so tight, ready to crack.

For years, he had known this moment would come. He had known all during the flight to Los Angeles that this moment lay ahead of him this evening, but he still wasn't prepared. He supposed he would never really be prepared for this confrontation.

"It won't get any easier," Emily whispered as she emerged from the ladies restroom of the Hollywood Roosevelt, near the ballroom where she and Joel were to meet Carlo. She linked her arm through his. She tried to smile, but the tension in her face turned it into a pitiful twitch of her lips. She looked almost as pale as she had the day she came home from the hospital. She had opted for the scarf-under-the-floppy-hat look to cover her bandages, instead of trying to carry off a wig. He thought she looked elegant and rather mysterious. Or maybe that was heroic, triumphing over suffering and tragedy.

No, he refused to let this trip end in tragedy. They were here to support Max, because they were family. He was Max's father. What mattered was love and devotion, not biology.

"Okay, God. We're really depending on You," Joel whispered, his voice cracking a little. "Please help us figure out what's best for Max."

He shook his head, a shaky grin taking over his lips when he thought of his stepdaughter's possible reactions. There was no knowing how Max would feel when she found out her parents were here to participate in the coming, unavoidable confrontation with her natural father. He had no idea what Max felt about the man, other than that she avoided all mention of him. It occurred to him that Emily wasn't sure either.

"Curtain's up, players in place." He took a deep breath and headed for the ballroom doors with Emily on his arm.

The ballroom was empty but for one man, standing by the lectern. He was little more than a dark figure in the half-lit room, short-cropped dark hair misted with silver that glowed a little when the dim lights touched it. Shoulders still wide and straight in his long-sleeved gray shirt. Carriage upright and steady as he moved to meet them.

Joel compared his aching leg and stooping shoulders and thickening build against the man weaving among the round tables to meet them. He shook his head and silently scolded himself for feeling that moment of uncertainty. Emily had married *him*. Was he starting to fear she would
~~~~~

leave him now, after all these years?

He knew the answer to that, and his moments of doubt made him feel ashamed.

"Joel?" Carlo stepped into the pool of light where they had stopped, near a table. "Emily." He paused and sorrow wrinkled his face as his gaze slowly swept over her from head to foot. He hurried to pull out a chair for her. "Thank you for seeing me. I know how much trouble it was, coming here—"

"Don't worry about it." Joel waved away the apology. He felt stronger, suddenly, more assured. He nodded thanks when Carlo pulled out a chair for him. He held Emily's hand as she sat down, then settled next to her. "We did a lot of thinking and talking on the way out here. The wise course is to forget about the past, except for how it affects Max. We have to decide how to handle things so she doesn't get hurt."

"Succinctly put." Carlo relaxed visibly, though he couldn't seem to take his gaze off Emily. She smiled a little sadly, a little wearily, and her grip tightened on Joel's hand. "I'm glad you two are taking this so calmly. I'm still somewhat in shock."

"Carlo, it was my choice," Emily said. "Joel has suggested several times over the years that you had a right to know. I simply... didn't have the courage."

"Of course." He studied his hands clasped in his lap. "How does Max feel about all this?" he asked after a few moments' pause, when the faint sounds of voices out in the lobby drifted through the open door.

"I have no idea. She doesn't talk about it."

"How long has she known?" He took a deep breath. "About ... me?"

"Since before I met Joel."

Joel studied him and realized he felt sorry for the man. What would he be feeling if he were in Carlo Vincente's place, coming to meet a daughter he had never known existed?

"How long did it take to figure out—" Joel stopped, coughing a little. Why was this subject so hard to handle?

"That Emily had my daughter and never told me? A while." Carlo smiled a little. "By the time your accident made the news, I was already curious about this young screenwriter who was ready to burst on the scene, but I was... well, let's say I was a little overwhelmed with all my responsibilities when I took over the leadership of the fellowship. We're putting out several fires behind the scenes that we don't want the media to find out about. This identity theft problem could not have come at a worse time."

"Max would be grateful if there was no fuss whatsoever, if it was kept as quiet as possible," Emily offered.

"Sometimes keeping things quiet might be the most comfortable way to handle an uncomfortable situation," he said slowly, "but the question is whether it's the right way. I could keep silent about her paternity, and she could keep her fellowship prize, but I admit that I am selfish. I want to get to know my daughter. I want to introduce her to my friends and associates *as* my daughter. She has talent, and I want to use all my influence to make sure she has a chance to use it."

"The question is if Max will sit still long enough to let you do that," Joel offered.

"Ah, true." Carlo nodded, one corner of his mouth quirking up. "What is she like?"

"Like you." Emily chuckled. "You and Joel are so much alike, and he's been around her since she was five, so..."

"So she picked up a lot of her stubbornness from me," Joel said. "Em always smiles when she says it, so I think we should take it as a compliment."

"Yes, of course." The struggle for words was visible in the wrinkling of Carlo's forehead, the way his lips parted like he would speak, then gave up, then tried again. "Emily, why didn't you ever tell me? I've learned about your struggles, how hard you had to work when Max was a baby. Why didn't you come to me for help? I could never be so angry at you that I'd refuse."

"We were wrong," Emily whispered. "We both knew better. We'd both been raised in church. We both said we were Christians, but we were living together without being married. When I got sick, we had been arguing so much, and you weren't my knight in shining armor anymore. When I suspected I was pregnant, you were going to France without me and I realized..." She paused to catch her breath. Tears touched her eyes.

"But, Emily —" Carlo began.

"No. Let me finish this. I wrote a letter explaining it all, for you to get if anything ever happened to me. You almost got it. But... Carlo, I knew if I told you I was pregnant, you would have stayed. You would have given up France to be with me. You'd marry me and be a good father to our child. But it wasn't good enough. I realized that I had already cheated our baby, but no father at all was much better than a father who wasn't right with God. I had to leave you to get my own heart and life right with God. And in a hurry." She tried to laugh and choked a little.

Joel wrapped his arm tight around her, wishing all his strength into her.

"I've followed your career, your life. I've prayed for you. I made Max pray for you, even when she was angry that you weren't there. I have to ask you to forgive me."

"Me, forgive you?" Carlo smiled, but his forehead wrinkled even more. "For what?"

"For still loving you, but not enough to be honest. I kept your daughter from you. I was more concerned about my own soul than yours. I've been a coward."

"No. Never a coward." He stood and crossed the floor to kneel in front of her and take hold of her hand. "Jeannette feels exactly as you do. She's urged me for years to find you. I've gone back to the faith I was raised in. You had nothing to worry about."

Emily cried. Quietly. Sitting very still in the warmth of Joel's arm, clutching tightly to Carlo's hand. The quiet of the ballroom insulated them from the world outside. None of them moved until the tears stopped.

~~~~~

"It's okay." Tony caught hold of Max's hand, interweaving their fingers, as they walked down the short hallway to the private dining room at the Hollywood Roosevelt. "I'm here. Nobody's going to hurt you."

"Aren't they supposed to be *helping* me?" she retorted.

"If we work it right," Winters said from several steps behind them, "you'll be helping them. There's a reason Carlo became the head of the board so late in the process." He flashed them a smirk when they both stopped short and turned to look at him. "And that's all I'm going to say on that subject."

"Am I supposed to be happy that I'm about to lose my fellowship money?"

Tony ached for her. He knew it wasn't the money that really bothered her. The fellowship rules disqualified her. It wasn't fair to her. She had entered the competition in all honesty and integrity. Now she would have a black blot next to her name, shadowing her career in screenwriting before it had even gotten started.

"If nobody knows he's your father, then they have no legitimate reason to take your money away."

"You mean lie. Lie by silence, actually." She turned to head back down the hall again. "Which I've been doing an awful lot, lately."

"Do I get punched if I ask how hard you prayed this morning?" Tony said. He laughed when Max tried to yank her hand free. Then she slumped a little and leaned against his shoulder.

"At least you get a trip to Hollywood out of this," Winters said. He stepped past them and reached for the latch of the door to the private dining room. He handed the thick folder of documents to Tony and opened the door.

Tony wondered if he was better off not knowing who all these somberly dressed, powerful, behind-the-scenes Hollywood people were. Most of their names didn't mean anything to him when Winters made introductions, going around the table, simply because he concentrated on writing books. At least he didn't feel nervous or awed, and could
~~~~~

concentrate on Max.

And on Carlo Vincente.

The ten men and women waited for them at an oval table, set for dinner with more crystal and silver and flowers than Tony had seen since his mother's fancy dinner parties. Three empty spots waited directly opposite Carlo's seat.

"Ladies and gentlemen, this is Max Randolph, who writes as Max Keeler, and her writing partner, Tony Martin," Winters said. "Together they're romance novelist Antonia Maxwell."

A woman with nearly glowing white curls, black Mandarin dress and ruby earrings, smiled broadly and put an enormous black brocade bag on the table. She pulled out a dog-eared copy of *Just for Kicks*, their latest release. She waved it at them as Winters handed the envelope folder full of documentation to the man on his right and explained what it contained, the long list of evidence both of Max and Jake's identities. Max's death-grip on Tony's hand loosened a little.

"I know this is off the subject," a man with a straggly goatee said, when the folder made its way around the table, "but how is your mother?"

"Emily is on her feet," Carlo said, surprising everyone. Max flinched. "I met with her and her husband this afternoon. They decided it was necessary to fly in and support their daughter during this... unpleasantness."

"And you three shouldn't be on your feet," the woman with the copy of their book said, gesturing at the empty seats. "I don't know about the rest of you, but this whole day has been taxing enough to make me ravenous, and they won't serve dinner until everyone is seated."

Laughter rippled around the table. Tony tugged his hand free of Max's and pulled out her chair for her. He put her between him and Winters.

Almost the moment Tony reached for his napkin and pulled it out of the crystal napkin ring, a troop of waiters filed into the room, carrying salads, rolls, a relish tray full of olives, cheese, and artichoke hearts, and pitchers of iced tea. He watched the man who ended up with the folder of evidence, two seats to the right of Carlo. He slipped the elastic band off, flipped the flap open and looked through the paperwork for a few moments while everyone was served, then he sealed the envelope again and put it on the floor. Tony glanced at Winters, who nodded and seemed entirely too relaxed. He supposed that was a good sign. They were taking Winters' word that the real Max Keeler was in the room.

"Please tell us about this imposter," Carlo said, after the wait staff had filed out again.

"Chuck gave us the basic information, and I've been gathering reports from those unfortunate enough to encounter him," the goatee man said.

"He's charming, but he's told one too many anecdotes about how things are done 'back at Homespun.' The way he tells it, he single-handedly pulled the latest production out of the dustbin."

"He tried to put it in the dustbin," Max said, shaking her head. "He had a hissy fit and quit in the middle of our run of *Taming of the Shrew*. Fortunately, my brother Joe was ready to take over Jake's role."

"That's his name? Jake?"

"Jake Holt," Carlo said, picking at his salad. "Max, you need to be warned that besides trying to steal your option money and cancel your representation with Chuck, he has attended screenwriting workshops under your name. As a guest speaker. He probably has several more lined up, and we will need to do fast work to avoid damage to your reputation when you fail to show up to teach as promised."

"I knew I should have thrown out all those invitations. Especially when I caught him going through my desk, reading my paperwork. I thought it was just his usual arrogance..." Max shook her head. "A lot of those workshops paid. That's the bottom line for him."

"Jake, a writing teacher? He wouldn't know proper grammar if it gave him a black eye," Tony growled. Max gave him a sideways glance, her mouth twitching into a grin. Chuckles rippled around the table.

"Why don't you tell us about your cloak-and-dagger routine, and what documentation you think Jake got hold of, while we eat?" Winters said.

Chapter Twenty-One

Tony gladly took over, giving Max a chance to relax a little more. He emphasized the part Steve played in keeping an eye on Jake, and how Joe played pickpocket several times, taking back paperwork that Jake had photocopied. He didn't miss the look of gratitude Carlo shot him. Tony wondered just what kind of trouble Steve was in, now that Carlo had learned he had gone to Tabor Heights to spy on his sister.

They didn't discuss how to handle the false identity problem until the main course had been brought in. Tony paid more attention to how Max disintegrated her salmon, chopped her asparagus into tiny pieces, not eating much of anything. Fragmenting her food was an obvious excuse not to look at Carlo. Tony hoped nobody realized that was why she did it.

"We need to do this publicly, to make sure he can't deceive anyone in the future," the white-haired woman said. Tony could only remember her first name was Grace. "At the same time, the scandal of it won't do the fellowship much good."

They tossed ideas back and forth, different tactics for removing Jake from the seminar, getting Max's face into the public so that the movers and shakers in Hollywood would know the truth without attaching a negative connotation to her name. Max didn't say much, except to point out how one tactic or another would either let Jake slip away without punishment or give the fellowship yet another black eye.

"There's no getting around it, is there?" Winters muttered, after the wait staff returned to clear away their dishes and bring in bowls of nuts and an assortment of sorbets.

For a moment, Tony had no idea what he was talking about. Then Max sat up, looked at Carlo, took a deep breath, and rested both her hands on the table on either side of her dish. She looked pale, and the aching look she shot Tony told him exactly what went through her mind. He reached his arm around her to give her all the support he could. He hoped Max remembered that he loved her, and he had promised he would always be there for her.

"I need to apologize to the board," Max said. Her voice was clear and steady. "A lot of this mess could have been avoided if I had notified you the moment I realized... I realized I had been disqualified."

Muttered individual conversations stopped abruptly and every pair of eyes at the table focused on her. Except for Carlo. He bowed his head and slowly, carefully folded his linen napkin and put it on the table.

"Disqualified how?" Grace asked, when Tony counted to ten in the silence.

Winters rested his hand on Max's on the table.

"A relative joined the board back in April. I should have notified you the moment I found out about it. I was hoping that because the announcement was made after I had been named a finalist, that technicality would let me stay in. Of course, it was about the same time my parents were hurt, and I had other things to deal with, but..." Max shrugged, swallowed hard.

"I'm sorry, Max," Carlo said. "I wish there was some other way. Any other way."

"Mom and Dad both told me it would catch up with me someday." She pushed away from the table.

"I fully intend to make it up to you."

"Carlo? What's going on?" the goatee man said.

"Few know that Emily Keeler and I lived together. For two years. I have only found out recently that Maxine Randolph is my daughter," Carlo said, spacing out his words as if testing each one before releasing it.

Tony expected an explosion. The silence was somehow worse. He caught the shock turning to suspicion, just a lift of an eyebrow, a pursing of lips, as the people gathered around the table looked back and forth slowly between Carlo and Max.

"I can testify that Max was born six months after Carlo left for France and Emily left Hollywood," Winters said. "Emily left it up to Max if her father ever learned of her existence. And you know what? Max is right. A lot of this is her fault. I mean, what are you going to do with a kid who insists on doing things for herself, not playing the guilt card on her famous old man, manipulating him to pull strings and give her a big break?"

Tony breathed a little easier when a few of those frowns turned to relieved smiles and nodding heads.

"Whatever the board wants to do, whatever announcement they want to make, I'll cooperate," Max said. She stood, shaking off Winters' grip and Tony's arm. "Thanks for dinner. If you'll excuse me, I—" Her voice caught. She ducked her head, avoiding Carlo's pleading expression, and hurried to the door. She was out in the hall before Tony could untangle himself from his chair and hurry after her.

They crossed the grand lobby of the Roosevelt, with the balconies lined with film industry memorabilia, before Tony caught up with her. He was grateful that Winters stayed in the dining room with the board. He could handle the details. Let him earn his keep as their agent.

"Hey, wait up," Tony said, finally getting close enough to catch hold of her arm.

"Hold me?" Max didn't wait for him to respond, but flung herself against him, pressing her face into his shoulder.

"Always." Tony wrapped his arms tight around her. They were in the traffic flow, so he led her down a hallway. There were benches along one wall, and he scooped Max up and settled down with her on his lap while her fingers threatened to dig holes in his suit coat.

In the silence while he rubbed her back, Tony heard indistinguishable voices rise up, and laughter, somewhere beyond that row of double doors far down the hall. He supposed that was the famous ballroom where the first Academy Awards had been held.

"That went really well, didn't it?" Max muttered, her voice muffled against his shoulder.

"Yeah, I think it was just right. I got you to sit on my lap without you freaking out and going all spastic on me."

"You—" She lifted her head. Her eyes looked reddened, but she hadn't cried. She took a deep breath, shuddered, and the left corner of her mouth quirked up. "I really do love you."

"Gee, I never get tired of hearing that."

Laughing voices echoed off the walls just when Tony bent his head to steal a kiss. A crowd of men and women in various levels of formal dress came around the corner, headed straight for their stopping place. Max rolled her eyes, her grin widened a little more, and she slid off his lap. She stood up and leaned into him as he wrapped his arm around her and they turned to watch the oncoming, laughing crowd. Then she stiffened.

"That scuzzbucket," Max growled.

"Huh?" Tony looked at her, then followed the direction where she looked. He didn't recognize Jake until Max escaped his arm and was five steps away.

"Max!" he shouted.

"Jake Holt." Max didn't yell, but she knew how to pitch her voice to be heard over the chatter and laughter. "You're an arrogant jerk, a thief, and a liar. And you just destroyed your acting career. When my father gets finished with you, no theater or film studio in this country will want anything to do with you."

"Max? What are you doing here?" Jake blurted.

Tony almost laughed. The worst thing Jake could have done was call her by name. Especially when he was pretending to be Max Keeler. He should have ignored her and kept walking with that pretty little girl with the long dark hair hanging on his arm. His reaction, and his bad choice of words, had already sealed his doom.

"I'm here to take back my identity. Which you tried to steal. Along with my prize money. It never occurred to you that my agent would be here for me, did it?"

"You're — *my* prize money," Jake insisted. "My new agent is supposed to get the check."

"You mean the agent who is scared he'll be blacklisted because he took on a client who presented falsified documents?" Max stepped up almost on top of Jake's toes.

Tony nearly cheered when Jake stepped back and his mouth worked for two seconds but no sound came out. Most of the people in Jake's crowd kept walking. A number of those people scowled at Jake, and several smirked at the sight of Max facing him down. He had done damage to the real Max Keeler's reputation that might be months or years in the mending.

Abruptly, Max turned to one man who stopped and paid attention to the confrontation instead of going around them. He was a redheaded behemoth, carrying his jacket over his shoulder, with a Navy emblem tattoo sticking out from under his sleeve rolled up past his biceps.

"Hi, I bet you're Skipper. We talked on the loop right after the finalists were announced. My screen name is Maximilian777." She held out her hand. "How's Scotty's Little League team doing?" She turned to Tony as he crossed the hall to join them. "His favorite nephew. The kid has an arm the Guardians would drool over."

"Great. I promised him a pizza party when I get..." Skipper looked at the hand he was shaking, then he looked at Jake. "You looked bored stiff when I told you about Scotty's batting record." His eyes narrowed and he turned back to Max. "Max?"

"She's lying," Jake yelped, his voice rising in panic. "She's a psycho bitch out to steal—"

Tony sensed it before he saw Max yank her hand free of Skipper's grip, pivot, and slug Jake right in the nose. He went down, eyes wide.

"That's two for two," Tony said. "Why don't you pull out your driver's license, Max, and prove to all these nice people who you are?" He nudged Jake in his hip, where his too-tight pants revealed a bulge where his wallet belonged. "Better yet, why don't you pull out your driver's license too, Jake, and show these nice people who you *aren't*?"

A single pair of hands clapping broke the whispers and bits of laughter from the people who stayed to watch the confrontation. Tony turned to see Steve standing a dozen yards down the hall.

"And that, ladies and gentlemen, is my favorite little sister. If she didn't have a brilliant career as a screenwriter, she'd be a welterweight champ." He sauntered down the hall, smirking at Jake. "What? No smart remarks, hotshot? Oh, by the way." He gestured as if he would put an arm around Max's shoulders. She glared at him and he stopped, slipping his fingers into his back pockets. "Before you threaten me again with how you have great connections, and I'm nothing but a stagehand, I should make a confession. My real name is Vincente. As in Carlo." He shook his head when Jake just stared at him. "You know? Carlo Vincente, the head of the Gabrielli board? My father."

Tony muffled a chuckle. Max didn't even try.

"There's been a big mistake," Jake said, holding his hand over his nose. The pretty brunette who had been attached to his side fled down the hall, with a couple other girls.

"Your mistake was trying to steal the identity of someone working in a very public business." Steve beckoned, and two men in the dark blue blazers and tan slacks of the hotel security stepped up on either side of Jake. Tony was impressed. He hadn't seen them approach. "Guys, could you make sure he doesn't go anywhere? The Gabrielli board is meeting right now, so they might as well handle him now than later."

"Steve?" A harried-looking, graying Asian man carrying a clipboard stepped out of the ballroom and looked between Jake and Steve and the security guards. "What's going on?"

"Hey, Bryce." Steve held out his hand to shake the man's. "I don't know if Dad told you about the problem with an intruder." He gestured at Jake.

Tony guessed from the flattening of Bryce's mouth, Jake hadn't made any friends among the fellowship's staff.

"Anyway, let me introduce you to the real Max Keeler." Steve caught hold of Max's hand and tugged her forward. "Who just happens to be my little sister. Half-sister," he corrected, when Max glared at him.

"You're never going to get tired of that, are you?" she muttered.

"Nope. Now, how about you two let me do my big brother thing and get you out of here before the fireworks start?"

"That would be great," Tony said. He wrapped his arm around Max to keep her from running or maybe taking a punch at someone else.

~~~~~

Max had turned off her cell phone when they arrived, and she kept it turned off while Steve whisked them out of the hotel. She couldn't handle getting a call from her parents right then. She gladly sat in the back seat of Steve's car and let her brain shift into numb half-awareness. Tony insisted on calling Winters when they reached Steve's car and let him know her brother was getting them away from everything and everyone for a while. Max prayed that her parents wouldn't think of calling Tony on his phone when they couldn't reach her.

Steve took them to a friend's house in the hills overlooking the city. No one was home, but the security guard at the gated community waved, leaning out the door of the gatehouse, and let him drive through. That told Max that he was a good enough friend to have full access.
~~~~~

Steve settled them on the massive, cantilevered balcony with a spectacular view of the city blanketed in lights, and told them stories about the owner of the house. He came from very old money and spent three-quarters of the year traveling the country, doing youth rallies with BMX and skateboard stunts. Max was grateful that Steve avoided the topic of their father. His cell phone rang four times during that hour they sat there. Each time, the conversation was little more than monosyllabic responses, with a few muttered questions that she made no effort to overhear. After the fourth call, Steve chuckled as he closed his phone.

"The trash has been officially taken out," he announced, and shoved it into his back pocket.

"Meaning?"

"Jake tried to skip town after the board got done with him. Guess who blew the whistle? The troublemaker who got him inside, in the first place. Turns out this guy had plans to bring down Dad with a big scandal, had the paparazzi and gossip rag reporters lined up. He couldn't get Jake out of the hotel fast enough to save both their necks." Steve snorted, clearly enjoying the story he had to tell. "I'm supposed to warn you that there's going to be some rearranging of the timeline, and letting people make assumptions, but the spin doctors are going to focus on this whole mess being used to catch some moles left over from the last chairman's regime."

"So they're clearing up a lot of problems all at once?" Tony said.

"Pretty much." Steve shrugged and his smirk got wider. "I have a friend who works the desk at the Roosevelt, and he was keeping an eye on the slimebag for me. Fortunately, Jake was stupid enough to use his own credit card for security. The Gabrielli people already switched the bill over to Jake, when they were notified he was an imposter. He's sitting in a cell right now, trying to find somebody to pay his bail. And get this—he's still trying to claim he's the real Max Keeler."

"He just never learns, does he?" Tony growled.

"I don't feel so bad about popping him one anymore," Max offered. Her throat and her jaw hurt from the tension and enforced silence of the last few hours.

"The mummy speaks." Steve leaned back in the chair and held up his hands as if to block a punch. "Tell me something, little sister."

"Would you stop that?" She was relieved to realize she didn't feel like bursting into tears. Maybe she was resurrecting.

"Eventually. Just ask Dad. He'll tell you I'm a smart-alec and I deserved that fat lip you gave me."

Max sighed and met Tony's gaze. He visibly fought not to laugh.

"What do you want to know?" she said.

"When you were threatening that bozo's career, which dad were you referring to?"

Max opened her mouth to say "Joel," but the word caught in her throat when she realized she could say "both." She shrugged, swallowed hard, and settled for, "I'm not sure."

After that, some of the pressure seemed to lift. Enough that she almost fell asleep when Steve drove them back to Winters' apartment complex. It was nearly midnight in L.A. time. Max marveled that she was still upright, because her body should have still been on Ohio time, making it nearly 3a.m.

"Breakfast, seven?" Steve said, when they climbed out of the car in front of Winters' building.

"It depends on if Max lives through the night," Tony said, as he slid an arm around her waist. "Chuck didn't say, but I can't think of where else Max's folks would stay in town."

"Knowing Mom, your folks might have been invited out to my folks' place."

"That's just too weird," Max muttered.

"No, what's weird is how much Ray and Nicky are like Joe and Jeremy." He flashed them a grin. "I really want to see their faces when you tell them I'm your brother."

"One thing at a time!" She flinched when her voice rose a little too high for that time of the night. Then again, how was she supposed to know what was considered too late to make noise, here in the suburbs of Los Angeles?

The apartment was just a little too quiet when Tony unlocked the door. Max saw a light streaming under the closed door of her agent's home office, but heard no voices. She looked around. No one was set up to sleep in the TV room.

"You go to bed, I'll face down the dragons," Tony said, gesturing at the office.

"My hero." Max tried to smile when he gave her a quick kiss and shoved her gently toward the bedroom hallway. She wondered how soon she could get into her pajamas and dive into bed and at least pretend to be asleep before someone came looking for her.

Emily was waiting in the guest room.

Max hesitated in the doorway as all the details of that day passed through her mind. She decided she was relieved the confrontation would be over soon. Sometimes the best punishment her parents had ever devised was to delay talking about her latest trespass and let her think about it for a day or two.

"I'm only going to demand one thing, Max," Emily said, sitting very still on the bed with her hands folded in her lap. Her shoulders slumped, but a flush of excitement touched her cheeks.

"I know, Mom."

"You will talk with your father—"

"He's not my father."

"—before we leave Los Angeles."

"Joel Randolph is my father." Max blinked hard against the pressure of hot tears. She refused to cry. Not with the feel of Tony's arms around her and his kisses still fresh on her lips.

"No, Max. Joel is your dad—Carlo Vincente is your father."

"Everybody's arguing semantics all of a sudden." She dropped down on the end of her bed. Emily sighed and put an arm around her shoulders.

"I know it's hard. I should have brought you two together years ago. Forgive me?"

"Forgive you?" Max sputtered. "I'm the one who lied to the board and kept secrets and decked Jake in front of half of Hollywood."

"You should have done more than give him a bloody nose."

"Mom!" She stared at her mother for a few seconds, then they both laughed softly, clinging to each other.

"I thought I was protecting you—and Joel and your brothers, by refusing to face my mistakes. Now, I think I'm hurting you even more."

"But what will people think, what will they say about you when they find out?"

Chapter Twenty-Two

"Max..." Emily sighed and shook her a little. "Max, how many of our friends have celebrated our wedding anniversary over the years with us? It doesn't take a calculator or a calendar to figure out you were born long before Joel and I married. And how many of your friends have we helped, by sharing the story of our struggle, our past?"

"Yeah, but—"

"Carlo is a Christian. When he was dating Jeannette, his wife, she wouldn't even go for coffee with him until he had gone to church with her, first. She made sure he had turned his face back to Christ before she even let him kiss her goodnight."

"Wow. That's pretty..." She shrugged, stumbling over words.

"Dedicated?"

"Old fashioned."

"I wish I had been that old fashioned when I knew your father. But then you wouldn't be here, would you? God brought good out of sin, once I turned my life back over to Him."

"But, Mom—"

"Carlo wants people to know you're his daughter. It's very important to him that he confess his mistakes, no matter what it might do to his reputation as a very ethical, spiritual man. He does have that reputation, you know, and he's respected for it even in the middle of Hollywood."

"But why? Won't it hurt him?"

"He's more concerned about making it up to you for losing your fellowship."

"He doesn't have to." Max squirmed, deep down inside. How many times had she daydreamed about her movie star father swooping down from Hollywood and carrying her away to instant stardom? At first her dreams had been about being an actress, but since high school they had changed to fame as a writer and director. How possible were those dreams now, with doors opening to her *because* she was Carlo Vincente's daughter?

Was she wrong to want it—or wrong to push it away?

"I met Jeannette and your brothers. They're very nice, warm people. The boys are thrilled to have a sister who can write scripts. Your father wants to help your career—well, I'm all for nepotism when it comes to my children." She chuckled. Max tried to smile. "Carlo insists that he has a responsibility toward you. He knows he can't make up for the last twenty-five years, but he wants to do what he can now."

"I don't want him to."

"Max, hating him only hurts you."

"I don't hate him!" She gasped a little at the shock of her volume, the ache the effort left in her chest. "I just wish things had stayed like they were. That's all."

"So do I. But if we stay where we are, we stagnate and die." Emily stood, resting a hand on Max's shoulder to help her gain her balance. "Talk to him?"

"I will." She glanced up at her mother's pleading face. It sent a twisting sensation through her heart. "I promise."

Emily nodded and went to the door, then paused with her hand on the doorknob, and turned back to her. "One other thing, young lady."

Max caught her breath. Her mother hadn't given her that stern, disappointed look in years.

"What's this about you necking under the bleachers with Tony?"

"Mom!" Max slapped both hands over her mouth, then flopped backward on the bed when Emily burst out in delighted peals of laughter. She covered her scorching face with her hands and wished this whole day could just turn into a bad dream.

But would that mean she still had the meeting with the Gabrielli board ahead of her? And Tony had never said he loved her?

"I'm delighted," Emily said, when she caught her breath. "Your father and I both think it's about time."

"I'm going to need a new agent. Chuck Winters is a dead man."

Emily chuckled and pulled the door open. Then she stood back. "Now, Max."

"Now?" Max sat up slowly. "As in…?"

Carlo waited alone in the kitchen when Max stumbled into the room, helped by a little shove from her mother. He looked a little more at ease than he had at dinner, dressed now in a polo shirt and jeans. He also looked tired. Max knew how he felt.

"I'd like to talk with you, Max, if you'll let me," Carlo said.

"Okay." She glanced down the hall to Winters' office. The door was closed. She put her money on Tony waiting in there, ready to run to her rescue.

Max couldn't make herself meet Carlo's eyes after that first searching, wistful look he gave her. She settled at the table at the far end.

"I imagine you've been very angry at me. I don't blame you at all," Carlo began.

"What's to be angry about?" Max's voice broke.

"I'm sure there are many things you missed as a child that I could have given you."

"Not a thing." Max choked on a bit of laughter, as she realized the words were the truth, not an attempt at being polite.

"Do you resent my showing up now, ruining the start of your career?"

"We're not sure of that, are we? See, Tony and I talked about it. And Steve offered some ideas. We figure, so I don't get the money now, but I can still say I was a finalist. The connections and the prestige are more important than the money." She finally turned to look at Carlo. His bemused look prompted a crooked smile from her.

"I will make it up to you, Max. For all the damage I've done you. All your life, not just now."

"Mom said if you knew, you would have taken care of us."

"Of course. That's why I'm here."

"No, not that. But I have to know something. You told my Mom you loved her. Did you say it because you were lonely, or to get sex, or did you really mean it?" The words burned a little as they passed her lips.

"As I understood love back then..." Carlo nodded and looked into her eyes a long moment. "Yes, I truly loved her and I meant it."

"Then what happened?"

"We were selfish children, playing selfish games and lying to ourselves about the harm we did to each other."

"That's one way of putting it," Emily said from the shadows of the hallway beyond the kitchen. She crossed the threshold into the kitchen. "I think, for this to work, I should be here, too." She beckoned for Max to move over, closer to Carlo.

Max hesitated, but then she saw the hopeful look in Carlo's eyes. Maybe she had hurt him, putting so much space between them? She moved over and let her mother have her seat.

"I was right," Emily said. "When I said you and Joel were so much alike, and Max took after both of you. You should know about Joel, to understand the decisions I've made. Max was our matchmaker. I met Joel at a summer theater project. Joel was the set designer. Max was four. She fell in love with Joel, right from the beginning. I think he fell in love with her before he realized I was around."

Max remembered that old theater, the basement rooms and the treasures of the scene shop. Helping her mother and Joel make dinners. Toting buckets of nails and paintbrushes for Joel. Cold mornings when she got up before her mother and Great-Aunt Maxine and struggled to make breakfast for herself in the communal kitchen because she was "a big girl." Joel always managed to show up and help her before she made a big mess. She remembered him taking them to the county fair; riding between her parents on the double Ferris Wheel and laughing when they squished her between them the first time they kissed. Max swallowed hard, fighting the happy tears from those memories. She hadn't thought about that summer theater in years.

"I think that wonderful summer prompted us to put Homespun together," Emily added. "We had a dream, and believed we could do good theater without big budgets and big names."

"You proved it," Carlo said. "Steve has told me all about your theater, and I've done some research. I wish I'd known. I would have liked to have helped. But you probably don't believe that."

"No. I mean, yes, I do believe you." Emily laughed. "You would have had the time of your life."

"And you still prayed for me? No resentment? No anger? No desire for revenge?"

"Oh, sometimes," she admitted. "When money was tight and you had a new movie coming out and I would wake up in the night wondering where we were going to go when the current job was over. And if we had to live in a hotel, how long my money would last. I knew it would only take one phone call to get help from you. Even if it was a threat of scandal. That was wrong."

"You never would have had to threaten me, Emily."

"I know." She slid an arm around Max's shoulders and squeezed. "I tried to convince Max I still loved you and she would love you if she ever met you. I don't know if I succeeded..."

"It's happening too fast," Max blurted. "I mean, I've known all my life, but I never thought we'd be here. Together." She hated the pressure she felt, from Carlo and her mother watching her, expecting her to say something, feel something. "I did pray for you, even when I was angry. Mom made me."

"I can believe that," Carlo said. He looked away. "We might have married and raised you to know God. But 'might have' isn't good enough. Is it?"

He reached out and gently lifted off a few tears from her left cheek with his thumb. Max didn't flinch from the touch, though she was surprised to realize she had been crying.

"No." She held still, waiting, finding it didn't hurt so much or make her feel trapped when she met his gaze. She had his eyes, just as blurry with pending tears and bloodshot and shadowed from lack of sleep.

"I never wanted to hurt either of you."

"I know," Max answered for both of them.

"We were both so proud and young and ... afraid, I suppose, deep inside where we didn't even let ourselves know." Carlo leaned back in the chair. His shoulders slumped, and he visibly relaxed a little more. "Your mother was everything I had been missing in life. So small, delicate, yet so strong. And pure. I wasn't pure anymore." He sighed. "Steven's mother died when he was only a few months old. Her family blamed me. They took him away from me and what could I do? I wasn't making enough money to keep myself alive, let alone pay for nurses and proper food and clothes for him. When I could take care of him, they wouldn't let me have him or even see him. They were strict, upright people. Very concerned about being right, about following the law to the letter. But not the spirit."

"If I had been a better Christian…" Emily shook her head. "Like Aslan said, don't ask about what 'might have been.'"

"We might never have had our two years together, and Max would never have been born. But you *might* have reformed me."

"And 'might have' isn't good enough," Max murmured. She managed to mirror his thin smile. They had the same mouths, too, she decided.

"I turned away from God because of Steven's grandparents. Your mother rebelled, too, in her own way. Then when she started going back to church and questioning the way we lived, I felt betrayed. We argued. I didn't want to take her with me when I found work in France. Maybe I was punishing her. It's so long ago, I can't remember."

"But I moved away and didn't leave a forwarding address," Emily said.

"And all your letters came back. You did write, didn't you?" Max added, feeling a worry she hadn't expected.

"Many letters. Many expensive phone calls." His smile didn't look so forced now. "I was furious. No woman was going to abandon me without a word of farewell."

"What did you do?"

"My wallet ruled my anger. Since I couldn't hunt her down, I chose to forget about her." He shook his head. "Men usually try to forget women by finding other women."

Max squirmed a little. It was nice, she supposed, that her father confessed to help her understand. Did he have to go into the gory details? Then Carlo laughed. He shook his head and rubbed at his eyes.

"Thank God I decided to chase Jeanette. Your stepmother," he added, his voice softening. His gaze flickered over her, as if gauging her reaction to that word. "Thanks to your prayers, I think now. Jeanette was a secretary at the production company and acted as translator and guide for those who couldn't speak French. She wouldn't go out with me unless I went to church with her, first. If I wanted her to drink coffee with me in a cafe, I had to go to morning prayers. If we went to dinner, I had to pay with a full-length service." He laughed again and Max smiled with him. "You see where this is headed?"

"Reformed," she said.

"It took several years of arguments and breaking up and coming back together. Your stepmother is a godly woman. She wouldn't budge an inch when it came to her soul. She wouldn't agree to marry me until after she knew I was right with God, as your mother puts it." He knuckled one eye like a little boy. "Now I know you two were praying for me. It's the only answer."

Max felt her face warm. She remembered temper tantrums before Emily let her stop praying for her unseen father.

"What about Steve?" she asked, casting about for something to focus on.

"It's taken me years to break the walls between us. He knows how you're feeling."

"I don't hate you."

"Thank you," Carlo whispered. "I feared that, though I feared indifference more. At least hate is a feeling."

"I just—I don't want things to change. We were so happy—and then that drunk driver—and all those vultures from the newspapers—and I just *knew* you'd start putting things together." She laughed, a ragged sound she preferred over sobs, and wiped a few stray tears from her cheeks. Emily hugged her harder.

"Steven taught me it's more important at this stage to be friends, than father and child. I want to make up for the lost time, Max."

"You don't have to."

"Yes, I do."

"I don't want—I mean, I don't need anything."

"Not even an older brother, to watch out for you for a change? A stepmother who wants very much to finally have a daughter?" He chuckled, and Max grinned. "Two younger brothers who want to be writers too, and already want to be just like you?"

"Stop!" she said, holding up her hands in surrender and laughing. Max had never thought she could laugh in Carlo Vincente's presence.

A tingling up her back made her turn, to see Tony peering into the kitchen. He looked so concerned, wide-eyed and solemn, Max sputtered more laughter.

Okay? he mouthed, ignoring Emily and Carlo.

Tony had always been there, and he would always be there. Maybe they wouldn't have the fun of falling in love, none of the fireworks and arguments and roller coaster feelings they put their characters through in the books they wrote. Max felt something settle inside as she realized this friendship that had turned into love between her and Tony was far more precious—and solid.

"You better get in here," she said, holding out a hand to him. Tony stepped into the room, shoulders hunched, looking like a little boy who had been caught doing something very good and wasn't sure if he was in trouble or not.

"Carlo," Emily said, "you did you meet Tony?"

"Yes," he said, "Max's writing partner."

"My best friend," Max said. She took a deep breath, bracing herself, knowing this wasn't how she wanted to tell the rest of the world — but as she had just learned, it was better to get something difficult over and done with as soon as possible. "And... the guy who's crazy enough to admit he loves me," she added, looking everywhere in the room but at her mother and father. "And marry me."

Tony burst out laughing and wrapped his arms tight around her, nearly lifting her out of the chair.

That was the way it was going to be from now on, Max decided. Something knocking her off balance, and Tony holding her upright. That wasn't so bad an idea, was it?

THE END

BOOK DISCUSSION GUIDE

Here's a fun and engaging set of discussion questions for your book club's chat about *Behind the Scenes*:

General Discussion:
1. *First impressions: What did you think of Max's writing process and her struggles with her characters? Have you ever felt like a character in a book (or your own writing) just wouldn't behave?*
2. *Aunt Rose's critique: Rose says Max's characters are "too rational." Do you agree? Do you prefer heroes/heroines who act impulsively (slapping, crying, running) or those who think things through?*
3. *Tony's romance idea: He describes a guy realizing his best friend is "a girl" in that way. Have you read (or experienced) a friends-to-lovers story that felt authentic? What makes this trope work — or fall flat?*

Character & Relationships:
1. Max & Tony's dynamic: Their banter feels easy and natural. What makes their friendship (or potential romance?) compelling? Do you think they'd make a good couple?
2. Family secrets: Have you read other books where hidden identities drove the plot?
3. Side characters: Brenda, Steve, and Jake all seem to have their own stories. Which side character would you want to follow in a spin-off?

Themes & Writing Style:
1. Art vs. criticism: Max writes romance novels but faces doubts. How do you think criticism (from others or yourself) affects creativity? Ever had a project you loved that others didn't "get"?
2. Humor & tension: The book balances funny moments with heavier themes. Did the tone work for you, or did you want more drama or lightness?
3. "Behind the scenes" title: How does the meta aspect of Max being a writer — while we read her story — affect your reading experience?

Creative & Personal Reflection:
1. Casting call: If this were adapted, who would you cast as Max, Tony, or Rose?
2. Rewrite a scene: Pick a moment where a character acts "too rationally." How would you make them messier — a slap, a scream, a

dramatic exit?

Wild Card Fun:
1. Title guessing game: If *Behind the Scenes* had a sequel, what would you name it? (*Front Page Drama? Secrets in the Script?*)
2. Pitch your own story: Inspired by Tony's idea, brainstorm a trope you'd love to see Max write next!

Bonus: For virtual meetings, have members share a GIF that sums up Max's mood during her writing struggles!

These questions keep things light but deep, with room for laughs, debates, and personal stories. Happy discussing!

THANK YOU!

Thank you for reading this book from Mt. Zion Ridge Press.

If you enjoyed the experience, learned something, gained a new perspective, or made new friends through story, could you do us a favor and write a review on Goodreads or wherever you bought the book?

Thanks! We and our authors appreciate it.

We invite you to visit our website, MtZionRidgePress.com, and explore other titles in fiction and non-fiction. We always have something coming up that's new and off the beaten path.

And please check out our podcast, Books on the Ridge, where we chat with our authors and give them a chance to share what was in their hearts while they wrote their book, as well as fun anecdotes and glimpses into their lives and experiences and the writing process. And we always discuss a very important topic: *Tea!*

You can listen to the podcast on our website or find it at most of the usual places where podcasts are available online. Please subscribe so you don't miss a single episode!

Thanks for reading. We hope you come back soon!

About the Author

On the road to publication, Michelle fell into fandom in college and has 40+ stories in various SF and fantasy universes. She has a bunch of useless degrees in theater, English, film/communication, and writing. Even worse, she has over 100 books and novellas with multiple small presses, in science fiction and fantasy, YA, suspense, women's fiction, and sub-genres of romance.

Her official launch into publishing came with winning first place in the Writers of the Future contest in 1990. She was a finalist in the EPIC Awards competition multiple times, winning with *Lorien* in 2006 and *The Meruk Episodes, I-V*, in 2010, and was a finalist in the Realm Awards competition, in conjunction with the Realm Makers convention.

Her training includes the Institute for Children's Literature; proofreading at an advertising agency; and working at a community newspaper. She is a tea snob and freelance edits for a living (MichelleLevigne@gmail.com for info/rates), but only enough to give her time to write. Her newest crime against the literary world is to be co-managing editor at Mt. Zion Ridge Press and launching the publishing co-op, Ye Olde Dragon Books. Be afraid … be very afraid.

And please check out her newest venture: Ye Olde Dragon's Library, the storytelling podcast. Interspersed between the chapters will be interviews with authors of fantastical fiction. Listen to the podcast on your favorite podcast app or listen on the website: www.YeOldeDragonBooks.com, and click on the Ye Olde Dragon's Library link.

www.Mlevigne.com
www.MichelleLevigne.blogspot.com
www.YeOldeDragonBooks.com
www.MtZionRidgePress.com

NEWSLETTER:
Want to learn about upcoming books, book launch parties, inside information, and cover reveals?
Go to Michelle's website or blog to sign up.

Thanks for reading!

If you enjoyed this book, would you help Michelle by posting a review on Goodreads?

Are you a member of Book Bub? If so, please follow Michelle on Book Bub, and you'll get alerts when new books are coming out.

As a way of saying thanks, Michelle invites you to the Goodies page on her website. It will change regularly, offering you a free short story, a sample audiobook chapter, sneak peeks at new cover art, inside information on discounts and new release dates, etc.
Please go to: Mlevigne.com/good-stuff.html

Also by Michelle L. Levigne:
Guardians of the Time Stream: 4-book Steampunk series
The Match Girls: Humorous inspirational romance series starting with A Match (Not) Made in Heaven
Sarai's Journey: A 2-book biblical fiction series
Tabor Heights: 18-book inspirational small town romance series.
Quarry Hall: 11-book women's fiction/suspense series
For Sale: Wedding Dress. Never Used: inspirational romance
Crooked Creek: Fun Fables About Critters and Kids: Children's short stories.
Do Yourself a Favor: Tips and Quips on the Writing Life. A book of writing advice.
To Eternity (and beyond): Writing Spec Fic Good for Your Soul. A book defending speculative fiction.
Killing His Alter-Ego: contemporary romance/suspense, taking place in fandom.
The Commonwealth Universe: SF series, 25 books and growing
The Hunt: 5-book YA fantasy series
Faxinor: Fantasy series, 4 books and growing
Wildvine: Fantasy series, 14 books when all released
Neighborlee: Humorous fantasy series
Zygradon: 5-book Arthurian fantasy series
AFV Defender: SF adventure series
Young Defenders: Middle Grade SF series, spin-off of *AFV Defender*
Magic to Spare: Fantasy series
Book & Mug Mysteries: cozy mystery series
Quest for the Crescent Moon: fantasy series
Steward's World: fantasy series reboot and expansion
The Enchanted Castle Archives: fantasy series